gilded PRINCESS

A FIVE FAMILIES NOVEL

special edition

D1677691

PENELOPE BLACK

GILDED PRINCESS

A DARK MAFIA ROMANCE

A FIVE FAMILIES NOVEL
BOOK 1

PENELOPE BLACK

A NOTE FROM PEN

Please note that Gilded Princess is a dark reverse harem romance, and it has darker themes that some readers may find triggering.
happy reading!
—pen

for my grandma + grandpa
who were unfazed by the spice and read every single book—several times.
this one is for you.

PLAYLIST

"Goodbye" by Apparat, Soap&Skin
"False God" by Taylor Swift
"Drunk In Love" by Beyonce
"Feel So Close" by Calvin Harris
"Don't Let Me Down" by The Chainsmokers and Daya
"Space Ghost Coast to Coast" by Glass Animals
"Hallelujah" by Jeff Buckley
"No Light, No Light" Florence + The Machine
"Shake it Off" by Taylor Swift
"Wasting My Young Years" by London Grammar
"Top to Toe" by Fenne Lily
"Don't Forget About Me" by CLOVES
"Cradles" by Sub Urban
"Smother" by Daughter

PROLOGUE
MATTEO

SWEAT CLINGS to the back of my neck and underneath my arms, but I don't move to wipe it off. I'd rather suffer the persistent itch than incur the wrath of my father.

He's on a warpath tonight.

Earlier at dinner, he told me to lay out my Sunday best and be ready at midnight. It was time for me to step into my role as a member of our family. Ma started crying, and then Dad got mad, and they started arguing—per usual.

I don't understand why she's so upset. I'm old enough to help out the family now, and it'll be good for me to learn how to do more stuff and make Ma's life easier.

Plus, the more focus I keep on me, the less time my father has to terrorize anyone else.

So here I am, baking in my black suit I wear to church on Sundays in my father's office. The air feels heavy this time of year, but my father's office doesn't have any windows to open. It's all dark wood and dark rugs. Intimidating and lightless, just like him.

My uncle Abram and my cousin Nico sit in the chairs across from my dad, who's reclined behind his massive oak desk. He's smoking a cigar and staring at the two men in front of him, his posture deceptively calm. His shoulders are loose, and he's casually puffing on his cigar.

It's a demeanor I've seen all too often.

Tension simmers in the air, so thick I can almost see it. Dad asked me to stand behind him to the right and stay against the wall, no matter what. I'm not entirely sure what will happen tonight, but I can't imagine it's anything good.

Uncle Abram adjusts his tie and cranes his neck to the side to release the tension as the silence continues.

Without a word, Dad slides open his top desk drawer and pulls out a gun.

"Half-assed murder plots are for boys. In this family, you act like a man. So, let this be a lesson to you, son. If you want to be the king, you have to kill the king."

My eyes widen as I glance between the gun my father placed on the desk and my cousin. He's eight years older than me, so we didn't exactly grow up together, but I always looked up to him. My palms feel clammy, and I stifle the urge to wipe them off on my pants. I know he hates it when I fidget.

"Do you understand why this is necessary?" Dad looks over his shoulder at me, waiting for my answer.

I nod, even though I don't understand. The memory of Dad making me watch *The Godfather* years ago flashes before my eyes. He told me this is what I should expect from our family, and at the time, I thought he was being sarcastic.

I was wrong.

He turns toward Uncle Abram. "The choice is yours, brother. Either you or him."

If he's surprised, Uncle Abram doesn't show it. He stares back at Dad, unflinching. "You know my choice, Angelo." He turns toward Nico. "I love you, son. No matter what."

Dad nods twice before he picks up the gun and points it at Uncle Abram. He fires two shots. Uncle Abram's body jerks violently, tipping over the chair.

I jump with each crack of the gun, unable to stifle my shock.

He shifts his hold to point it at Nico. His eyes look like saucers, bloodshot and wide.

"Uncle Angelo, please. D-d-don't do this. My dad—"

A gunshot splits the air.

Nico's eyes shine with tears, disbelief slackening his jaw. He pushes a hand to his chest, and bright red blood oozes out between his fingers.

Another shot lands in between his eyes, Nico's head jerking back in a swift, violent motion.

"I don't give second chances." His words are slow and contemplative like he's wondering if there's rain in the forecast today.

I bite my lip hard enough to draw blood, desperate to keep my fear inside. Anything to keep my dad's focus off of me.

It's selfish. A coward's move. But at twelve, I know I can't win against him.

Not yet.

CHAPTER ONE

MADDIE

"I CAN'T BELIEVE you're ditching me again, Mary. You agreed to go with me."

I shouldn't be surprised that my sister, who prefers books to humans, is abandoning me during event season, but I am.

She sighs, the noise loud in my ear as I squeeze the phone in my hand and press it against my face to hear her over the busy streets of New York City. "Don't be so dramatic, Maddie. You'll be fine. I don't even know why you asked me. You know I hate those things. Besides, they only ever invite me because of you anyway."

Now it's my turn to sigh. I shove my irritation down to the bottom of my stomach and exhale a calming breath. "You know that's not true. Clara Vanderbilt and Isobel Chambers specifically invited you to the masquerade ball."

"Yeah, well, I'm not going. Why don't you ask Lainey like you usually do?"

The scorn in her voice has me fumbling over my thoughts for a moment. I shove the concerning reason behind my cousin Lainey's impromptu cabin visit down deep and bury it alongside all the other things Mom said are wrinkle-inducing. It's easier for me to ignore it now that we don't have honest-to-god bodyguards following us around anymore. It only lasted for a few days, and I know it was more for Lainey's peace of mind than anything else, but it was strange.

My cousin Lainey is more like a sister than an extended family member. Sometimes she's closer to me than my actual sister. I like to think of her as the perfect balance between me and my twin, Mary.

Lainey's mom, Lana, and my mom are twins too—apparently it runs in the family. But outside of their looks, they're not that similar. It's kind of how I feel about Mary and me. Even though we're fraternal twins, when we were younger, we'd dress alike and it was hard to tell us apart.

These days, Mary and I couldn't be more different.

Where I wear my dark-red hair long and in waves, she cut hers short into a long bob and religiously straightens it. Mascara and lip gloss are about all she wears—*not* that she needs makeup. She's gorgeous, and sometimes, I think she's the only one who doesn't realize it.

You're more likely to find her in cardigans and sneakers than dressed up in a gown fit for a ball. I don't know why I'm surprised that she's backing out of this event.

I clear my throat to get myself back into the conversation, looking both ways before I cross the street. "You know why. Lainey's recovering—"

"Yeah, yeah, yeah. Tucked away at some cabin with a bunch of dudes, I know. I guess she should think about the company she keeps, huh? Maybe she won't end up in those shitty situations then."

I stop in the middle of the busy sidewalk, the flow of people swerving to move around me. "What the hell, Mary! I cannot believe you said that."

My sister scoffs. "What? It's true. Anyway, I'm not going to your stupid gala. So I guess you should find some other friends." She mock-gasps. "Think of what they'll say if you go solo?"

My jaw drops at her cruelty, and I clear my throat, swallowing down the emotion. "Wow. Are you going for a record of below-the-belt hits today, sister? Because I gotta say, you're hitting your marks."

She knows damn well how I feel about stuff like that. I don't have a problem with being alone, but who wants to go solo to those kinds of events? It's like daring someone to jump into shark-infested waters wearing Lady Gaga's 2010 award show dress—you know, the one made up of raw meat.

You need a buffer to these sorts of things—a plus one.

With a mother who offered to buy me a boob job, a nose job, and lip fillers for my twelfth birthday, is it any wonder why I have these sorts of thoughts?

If you're told most of your life that your only value is your appearance, after so long, you start to accept it as gospel.

She sighs, the exhale long and somehow sounding irritated. "Whatever. Sorry. I have plans, okay?"

My ears prick at the change in her tone. "What kind of plans?"

"None of your business."

I can just picture her folding her arms tight across her chest and shifting her weight. It's her tell when she's hiding something.

I gather my hair and twist it over my shoulder to let the hot summer breeze roll over my neck as the proverbial lightbulb goes off. "Oh my god. You have plans with a guy! You sneaky little—"

"Just drop it, Maddie. It's probably nothing, okay? And anyway, I don't want to talk about it."

I pause, sorting through my initial hurt. Her unwillingness to share picks at my decades-old insecurities and wounds. I know it's more to do with her than with me, but it still takes me a moment to wrap my mind around it.

"You used to tell me everything, Mary," I murmur.

Mary huffs. "Yeah, when we were like eight. You tell Lainey everything now, so don't act like it's *me* who has changed."

Shock stills my tongue. I'm not sure what's going on, but I have a feeling my sister is going through something. My heart pangs at the hurt in her voice. "I'm sorry if you've felt left out. You're my sister."

"Yeah, okay. Look, I've gotta go. I'll see you later."

As soon as the last word leaves her lips, she ends the call. I pull the phone away from my ear and feel my eyebrows reach my hairline. She didn't even give me a chance to reply before she hung up.

The summer sun feels heavy as it beats down on my back. I love summertime. It's the season of possibility and spontaneity. And this was supposed to be our summer. The one we'd been dreaming about for years.

We survived high school at one of the most prestigious all-girl academies in the country, and we had three months to revel in our accomplishments until we had to buckle back down and get to work on our degrees.

St. Rita's All-Girl Academy is a tradition in my family. All the girls attended, and for the most part, I didn't mind. I lived in a luxury dorm suite with my cousin and sister for years. And since we're all attending St. Rita's University, we're staying in the same suite. A perk of being a legacy member, I guess.

I tap my phone against my lips as I walk toward my favorite coffee shop. It's not too far from our dorm suite, and they have a new iced tea flavor every week from May to September. If I wasn't busy teaching adorable little girls ballet three days a week, I'd work here just for the free coffee perks.

I know I can't ask Lainey to go with me. Not only is she out of town, but she just went through some seriously scary stuff, and she needs time to rest and recharge. And honestly, I'm proverbially eating popcorn and watching her romantic entanglements play out.

And Mary's out, obviously.

I guess I could go alone. Despite the masks required to enter the event, I have a good idea of who will be there. It's generally the same group of people my age who attend every year. One of those legacy things. Lots of girls from St. Rita's—high school and college. Plus, the school has a lot of affiliations with other private schools around the country.

Every year, the private school board council throws a masquerade ball to raise money for a different charity. This year they're focusing on saving the rainforests, which is something I can get behind. The music's usually good and the food is always excellent. I could do without the monotonous small talk from random adults who don't actually care about the answers to the questions they ask.

Plus, there are only so many times I can binge-watch shows on Netflix.

I roll my eyes, annoyed with myself. It's not like I don't have other friends, just none as close as Lainey and Mary. I suppose now is as good a time as any to strengthen new friendship bonds, though.

With my mind made up, I quickly tap out a text to Blaire Hawthorne. If anyone knows the theme, it's her. That girl is like a real-life *Gossip Girl*, but without all the secrecy—she lives for drama.

I slide my phone into the pocket of my cream and light green linen skirt. The breathable fabric swishes against my thighs as I walk the last few feet to the cafe.

A blast of air-conditioning greets me as I walk inside and get in line. I wave to Amanda, the barista at the counter, just as I feel my phone vibrate with an incoming text.

Blaire: Madison, babe! I hope I see you at the Enchanted Forest masquerade tomorrow.

Enchanted Forest. Okay, I can swing that. A flicker of excitement blooms. I do love a good theme.

Madison: See you then!

I pocket my phone again as the line moves forward, my mind already spinning. I'm going to have to call my favorite designer and seamstress and see what she has in stock. Dolores is in her mid-sixties, but her eye for fashion is incomparable. And luckily for me, she took a liking to me when she volunteered for our middle school theatre production. She did the costuming, and we bonded over our shared love of high fashion and French truffles.

"Hey, girl. Surprised to see you here. I thought you'd be in Europe still," Amanda says, pulling me from my thoughts.

My answering smile feels tight. "Ah, yeah. Change of plans. Turns out, I'll be in the city all summer."

"I guess you'll get to try all the flavors this summer then, huh." Amanda smiles. "What'll it be today?"

That gets a wide smile from me. I've been coming to this coffee shop for a long time, and just about every time I'm here, Amanda is working. We've gotten to know one another over the years. "Too true. Busy today?"

Amanda nods and adjusts her daisy-printed apron. "Yep. Just getting over a little rush. And we have blueberry green tea today. I know that's a favorite of yours."

I chuckle and adjust the strap of my crossbody purse, peeling it off my sticky skin. "You know me so well, Amanda. Okay, I'll take one of those, large, please."

"You got it." Amanda turns around and pours my drink from the carafe on the counter behind the register. A few seconds later, she spins to face me and slides the to-go cup and straw on the counter. "That'll be four seventy-four," she says with a smile.

I shove my hand into my purse to grab my wallet, but I come up empty-handed. I open it wider and peer inside, moving a few things around as if my pink wallet will magically appear behind my lip gloss.

My heart settles in my throat and a flush that has nothing to do with the heat rolls over me and settles in my cheeks. My shoulders hitch toward my ears, and I flick my gaze back to Amanda. "I, uh, seem to have misplaced my wallet. Probably left it on my kitchen table or something." I force a laugh that sounds strained even to my ears. "Let me go grab—"

"Here." The deep, smooth voice comes from behind me at the same time a hand extends past me and places a black Amex card on the counter. "On me."

A shiver of awareness skates down my spine, and the small hair on the back of my neck stands on end. Amanda stares over my shoulder without reaching for the card.

Okay, so it's not only me then.

The man behind me chuckles, the noise soft and rich like melted dark chocolate. He steps forward again, his arm just barely grazes mine as he pushes his card further toward Amanda with his index finger. My gaze zeroes in on his veins like a homing beacon. What is it about those veins on a man's forearm?

"And an Americano, please."

The movement snaps Amanda out of her daze and she licks her lips before taking his card and ringing his drink up. "You got it. Seven eighty-four."

I snag my iced tea off the counter and take a step to the side so I can get a better view of the kind stranger. He tilts his head to meet my gaze, never shying away from my blatant stare. Taking a sip of my drink, I let the taste of crisp blueberries and tart lemongrass quench my thirst as I give him a proper once-over.

The corner of his pouty lips tips up on the side as he holds himself still, almost like he's encouraging my perusal.

He's tall—I'd say six-two or six-three with broad shoulders and a tapered waist. Colorful ink peeks out from underneath one sleeve of his black polo shirt, swirling down his arm and stopping at his wrist. I spot a familiar logo on the pocket, and a pair of Ray-Bans hang on the open top two buttons.

Light-brown hair with what look like natural highlights from time spent in the sun. And with the way his biceps strain the sleeves of his shirt, I'd bet he spends a lot of time either on a field or at a gym.

Long sooty lashes frame big dark-green eyes that currently have mirth dancing in them. Something low in my belly clenches when he sinks his teeth into his plump bottom lip and stares at me with an intensity that wasn't there ten seconds ago. It should be illegal for a man to have lips so plump.

"Here's your Americano," Amanda says, breaking the connection. He reaches for it and murmurs his thanks, never taking his gaze from me.

"Thank you. For the drink," I say after I take another sip.

"It's my pleasure." He trails off, and I know he's subtly fishing for my name.

"What's life without a little mystery?" I let the mischievous smile I've been holding back spread across my face as I spin on my heel and walk toward the exit. I pause with one hand on the door and flash him my most flirtatious and inviting smile over my shoulder. "See you around, Americano."

I don't wait for a reply and push open the door and let the thick, humid air greet me.

I swear I hear him murmur, "Count on it."

Slipping my sunglasses on, I pull out my phone and see that Dolores is ready for me. With a renewed sense of excitement, I make my way across town to pick out a showstopping dress.

CHAPTER TWO

MATTEO

"NO."

"What do you mean *no*?" Dante, my second, asks. He's also my best friend, so he's not afraid to call me on my shit.

"I mean, I'm not going to some fucking ball like we're in Georgia in the nineteen hundreds." I pinch the bridge of my nose. "I don't have time for this, Dante."

I loosen the tie around my neck and unbutton the top button. The claustrophobia lessens, but I can't shake the oppressive feeling of expectation from the meeting earlier today.

A full wall of windows behind my desk displays the stunning views of New York City from thirty stories high. The sun warms a path inside my office, highlighting part of my desk and matching armchairs.

My father said I was crazy to want an office—a proper office—to work out of. He much prefers the old ways of sticking to the underbelly of the city. To his credit, it's served him well for most of his life.

But that was before the Feds swooped in and started picking us off one by one. The five families used to be gods among men with armies five-thousand deep across the globe, and now we're down to scraps.

I tried to tell 'em—fuck, I tried to tell all of them that this wasn't the right path for us. I sure as fuck don't want to get picked up on some bullshit RICO charge. And I haven't done half the shit they have. Unlike so many of them, I have my own rules.

Morality is a gray area that ebbs and flows, but I never cross over my lines.

No skin.

And no children.

Ever.

It's one of the reasons I sought out and sat down with the Brotherhood a couple of years ago. They're an Irish *family* that operates similarly to ours—but their limits align with mine—and not the rest of my family's.

Which is why having their support is pivotal in my plans for the future. They have interests in a lot of different areas of the city, but they're based out of Boston. Mainstream movies and TV gave the general population a skewed version of how connected families run. Sure, some shit is eerily on point, but other stuff couldn't be further from the truth.

We usually keep to our own families, but that doesn't mean we're warring with everyone. We're mostly cordial with each other. Until we're not. And then it's every man for himself—five families or not.

But for now, we're on good terms with the Brotherhood. Affiliated with the IRA—Irish Republican Army—the Brotherhood controls the ports along the coast. My father and uncles have taken issue with their ban on skin through their ports, and they've had more than one run-in.

But I've never had issues with them—and I've never participated in any of my father's hair-brained schemes to double-cross the fragile alliance we have with them.

The Brotherhood isn't larger than us, but they have a different kind of weight around here. One that I'm hoping to harness when my full plan is executed.

"Matteo?"

"What?" I snap. I'm a little surprised that I was off daydreaming about shit while I was still on the phone. Fuck, I need some sleep. I run my hand down my face and sigh. "Sorry, man. What is it?"

"It's fine. But that masquerade ball? Madison's going. I just got word an hour ago from my source and I confirmed it myself before I called."

I clench my fists without conscious thought. "A date?"

"Nah. No cousin or sister either."

My mind spins as I try to see all the different angles and possible outcomes. If she's without a date, then she's alone, which could go either way.

"Think about this, man," Dante murmurs.

"That's all I fucking do is think about this—about *her*!" I flatten my palms to my desk and lean over it, my head hanging low.

Dante's quiet on the line, letting me work through my shit like he knows I need to do. After a moment, he says, "You know I'll back you, but you also know I caution you because I care. I just want you to be sure about this. Once you go public, and when someone spots you together—which they will because there are about a million people attending tonight—there's no way to undo that. It doesn't matter how you spin it."

"Yeah, I know." I blow out a breath and then my mind snags on something. I lift my head and look at my phone. "Wait. How many people are confirmed yeses?"

I hear papers rustle for a moment. "St. Rita's and their alumni, their sister and brother schools and affiliations, politicians currently campaigning, some minor royalty, and various socialites. And our boy finally snagged an invitation this year."

"Fuck."

"That was my thought at first, too. But maybe we can use this to our advantage? There will be close to five hundred people there tonight, and mandatory masquerade masks, so the chances of you two being in the same vicinity are slim. This might be your chance to see how he's really doing, too. This is the longest he's gone without a proper check-in."

Guilt churns my gut, sour and acidic, and I exhale through my nose. "Last we spoke, he said he had more secrets than we could ever need, but he was close to uncovering something big. Something that could ease our transition period when it arrives. I don't want to fuck that up by showing up tonight."

"And Madison?"

I walk three steps to my left before spinning on my heel and walking three steps to my right. I repeat this pattern a few times as my fingers tangle in my dark brown hair. I'm sure it looks like a mess right now, but I can't seem to stop tugging on my hair when I'm thinking like this.

After a minute, I stop in my tracks. "Fuck it. I'm going. Get me a new suit and a mask. And don't forget to get one for yourself. If I have to suffer through one of these bullshit events, so do you."

I don't trust anyone on a good day, but stick a bunch of dirty politicians and entitled rich assholes together, and I'm two seconds away from pulling my favorite gun.

"I saw her the other day, you know. Ran into her at one of her favorite coffee shops. She." He trails off, and my patience wears thin.

"She, what?"

He huffs. "I don't know, seemed sad or some shit."

I wave a hand in the air to dismiss his words. "I'm sure she's fine. She always gets cranky before she's had enough caffeine."

"C'mon, man. How long are you gonna do this?"

I bristle at his tone. "Do what?"

He sighs, the noise loud and full of disappointment. But he doesn't need to sling that shit in my direction—I'm plenty frustrated with myself.

"You can't keep her on ice forever. At some point, you're going to have to let her go."

Rage courses through me, swift and potent. The urge to cause destruction rides me hard, and the only reason I don't act on it is because he's my best friend.

"She's not on ice. I have a few *trusted* people check-in on her every so often. She's free to do whatever she wants—see whomever she wants—"

Dante's sarcastic laugh interrupts me. "Do you hear yourself right now? Did you somehow forget about that guy in the spring you scared off?"

I scoff. "That guy was an asshole. And his dad is a dirty judge—and not one we can benefit from."

"Yeah, alright, I'll give you that one. But what about all the other guys since you two split?" When I don't answer, he sighs. "Listen, man. I get it. At first, you had to have eyes on her for her safety because you were climbing the ranks, but it's been years. And if you're not planning on locking her down, then I think you should cut her loose."

My breath gets trapped in my lungs as I envision a life without her. Something a lot like agony protests the very idea.

I can't let her go. But I can't keep her either.

I'm the worst kind of bastard for it, but even knowing that doesn't mean that I'll change. I don't bend for anyone. Not anymore.

I can't bring myself to condemn her to this life, but if I don't choose a fucking wife soon, I'll never be the boss. Not of my family and not of the five families.

It's a bullshit archaic rule that I wish I could demolish, but even when I'm boss, I'm not sure I could immediately kill it. There are too many old school guys in the five families that still cling to it.

I'm acting as underboss for Dad, but it's not in an official capacity until I get married. For a bunch of sexist motherfuckers, they love to make sure guys are locked down first before they promote them up. I'd like to say it had something to do with holding onto your humanity, but it couldn't be further from the truth.

They like guys to have wives for leverage. Skim off the top? We'll ostracize your wife from the families for a while.

Fuck up a run? We'll take your cut and fuck up your house, terrorize your wife and kids a little.

Kill the wrong guy? We'll pass around your wife as payback.

So, no, I'm not fucking eager to bring a woman—any woman—into this life until I've cleaned house a little.

The problem is that the only woman I ever wanted to call my wife fucking hates me and has for the last two years.

Indecision plagues me for a moment.

Fuck it. I'll figure it out as I go. I always do.

I stand up and adjust the sleeves underneath my black Tom Ford suit. "We're going. I don't put it past any of those slimy fuckers to snatch her up in some ill-fated attempt at blackmail."

I don't mention that I know it would work too, and Dante's kind enough not to call me out. I don't know how many people would still connect her to me, but if they did their homework like I always do, it's easy enough to find.

"And our sleeper? Should we tell him?"

"Nah. We'll keep our distance from him too, so he can work his magic. He'll be home soon enough. I want him to have his freedom just a little longer."

The words taste like ash on my tongue. There's nothing *free* about what he's doing. And it's exactly the reminder I need of our stakes—and they're fucking high.

The last thing I need is the complication of a woman. They fulfill a need, but I can't offer them more than a night. Not while I'm in the middle of a coup—one that's taking a surprising left turn.

"How was the meeting? They pulling the marriage angle again?"

It's a testament to our lifelong friendship that he can read me so well, even through the phone. I rake my hand through my hair and blow out a breath. "Yeah. They're persistent fuckers, that's for sure."

"I bet," he murmurs. "How long do you think you can hold them off for?"

"As long as I have to. Everyone knows I can't move up until I pick a wife."

"And our plan is contingent on the support from certain families," Dante interjects.

The reminder just irritates me, so I change the subject to something less . . . hostile. "Any word on Mama Rosa's?"

"Nah, the fire marshall maintains it was arson, not an accidental kitchen fire, but we'll get his official report in a few days."

"Who the fuck attempts to blow up a pizzeria joint in the middle of the day?" I grit out between clenched teeth. I fucking loved that restaurant. "Alright. Keep me posted. I'll see you tonight." I end the call and spin to look out into the city, letting my mind wander a bit.

I'm not sure if the explosion at Mama Rosa's was a message aimed at me or something tied up with my friend from the Brotherhood, Sully, and his bullshit.

He's one of the most genuine friends I've made in the last five years, but man, does he have some shit going on right now. He's always been there for me, so I'm down to return the favor.

Most of my friends are my cousins or the kids of made men I've grown up with. And I can't exactly talk shit about different family members—especially not with what I'm planning.

No, I've gotta put my mask on and perform for everyone in the family like a goddamn circus act.

But soon, I'll be able to rip off that fucking fake piece of shit persona I've been wearing like a fifty-pound weight around my neck. Then they'll all wish they took my ideas—and my threats—a little more seriously.

When I'm done cleaning house, this city will run red.

"Yeah," he says after four rings.

I tip my head back to stare at the ceiling, looking for patience. Despite popular belief, I'm not a master of cool and unaffected like so many people think. I'm just better at controlling my impulses and keeping my face blank.

I'm still in my office, sorting through all the administrative stuff for my legal businesses—and my less than legal ones. I started a semi-underground fighting circuit six months ago, and I'm working on rolling out our unofficial street racing circuit.

It takes a lot of greased pockets and even a favor or two, but the return on this is going to be killer. Not only just the betting, but it'll help wash cash from my less than pristine businesses.

"Just giving you a head's up that I'll be there tomorrow night."

Even though we're talking on burners, I still keep my words clipped and my meaning intentionally vague. No need to tip anyone off of our connection just yet. We're not quite ready for that bomb to drop.

"Okay. That it?" The derision in his voice rings clear across the empty space of my office.

I soundproofed my office—my entire floor—when I bought the place. It gives me the freedom to put calls on speakerphone and walk around. Pacing always gives me perspective, something about the action shakes ideas loose and helps me focus.

"What? Too busy to chat with me?" My lip quirks up when I hear a feminine giggle through the line. "Ah, I get it now."

"Nah, I don't think you do. Later." He ends the call before I can respond, and I stare at my phone on my desk for a moment.

Not for the millionth time, I wonder if I made the right decision in sending him into the lion's den all those years ago.

CHAPTER THREE

MADDIE

I ADJUST the silk bow attached to the black-plated gold filigree mask on my face. The detail work is absolutely stunning, and as soon as I saw it, I knew it'd be perfect for tonight.

My blue eyes stare back at me in the full-length mirror of the ladies' room, the color bright and icy against the dark mask. I ducked inside as soon as I got here to give myself another once-over to make sure I don't have lipstick on my teeth and my makeup didn't completely melt off in this heat. Going solo to one of these events is bad enough. I don't want to give Blaire or anyone else any more ammo.

I touch up my favorite deep-red lipstick, making sure the line is sharp and smudge-proof. I can't believe Dolores forgot she had this masterpiece, or so she claimed. That woman is sneaky. I didn't need a single alteration, so I really wouldn't be surprised if she made it especially for me.

I smooth my hands down the bodice, marveling at the way it hugs my frame like a second skin. It's crafted to look like iridescent feathers overlapping one another, providing just enough coverage where I'm not indecent but still showing a few peeks of skin.

Two thick swaths of fabric from my waist up over my breasts to attach to a thin satin strap around my neck. There's a purposeful cutout from my belly button to my neck, showing just the barest curve of my breasts. Black silk falls from my waist to pool around my feet in a small train.

The overall effect is just stunning. I feel sexy and powerful, like I could not only reach a goal but crush it without much effort. A dangerous feeling.

Turning to the side, I take in my profile, then peek over my shoulder to look from that angle. My hair reaches the bottom of my shoulder blades, and the black satin fabric clings to my ass in a way that boosts my confidence a few notches.

But my favorite part is the back of the dress—or the lack thereof. The entire back of the dress is open, so you only see a few feathers wrap around my ribs to stop at my lower back. My deep red hair looks like lava as it gently tickles my back. I curled it into soft glam waves tonight and pinned it back at the sides to give off that old Hollywood vibe.

No, there's no way that Dolores forgot about this dress. Off the top of my head, I know at least five girls who would've grabbed this dress in an instant.

Lainey would love this whole look. I snap a quick photo to send her later and exit the bathroom. I follow the slow trickle of people walking toward the ballroom, murmuring my hellos to familiar faces.

That's something that always struck me as odd. They require masquerade masks at this event every year, but it's usually the same group of people who attend, so the idea of anonymity always felt a little silly. I mean, sure, these masks conceal a portion of your face, but usually I can deduce who it is by who they're talking to or the sound of their voice.

When we first started attending this gala a few years ago, I let myself get swept up in the romanticism of it all. I thought for sure that I'd meet my very own white knight or Prince Charming underneath a mask. He'd whisk me off my feet, twirling me until our legs cramped from dancing and our cheeks ached from smiling.

But I was fourteen and most of the guys my age were entitled assholes who couldn't handle their champagne. A few even tossed their cookies all over the dance floor. That was enough to kill any stars in my eyes, at least temporarily.

It's still the same group of assholes, but at least they can handle their alcohol now.

A teeny, tiny part of me still secretly hopes someone will sweep off my feet one year. Mostly, I just use it as a good excuse to wear a stupidly expensive dress and dance the night away while sipping on expensive champagne and popping delicious hors d'oeuvres in my mouth.

Usually I have Lainey and Mary by my side, and we spend the evening together. This is the first year I've gone without them, and I have a feeling that this is just the tip of the iceberg.

I naively thought that we'd all room together forever—at least until we graduate college. But then Aunt Lana met some random guy in Boston, who's apparently *connected*, and now Lainey's all tangled up in a mess that I'm still trying to understand.

Lainey's being taken care of by her soon-to-be stepbrothers slash boyfriends, so I only have to worry about my sister. My sister, who snuck in late last night and hasn't left her room all day today.

I exhale, knowing that if she doesn't start talking to me soon, I'll have to whip out my last-ditch move and call Mom. And neither one of us wants that.

Pushing my worries to the back of my mind, I pick up my skirts and climb the small staircase that leads into the main room.

My heart skips a beat when I get my first uninterrupted view of the ballroom.

The committee outdid themselves this year. It's transformed into an enchanted rainforest at sunset with shades of golden yellow and bright peach infused in everything. Soft, gauzy fabric runs from one wrought-iron chandelier to another, creating a tent-like effect.

Topiary trees frame the walls alongside various big, leafy plants, giving the space a lovely pop of color contrast. Plump red berries weigh down branches of the trees next to me, and perfectly formed Cara Cara oranges hang from the tree across the room.

Two dozen peach and golden peonies make up the centerpieces

on every table, and plush overstuffed chairs and chaises in deep velvet fabrics add a rich element. Caterers dressed in all-black with black masks circulate the spacious room with trays of hors d'oeuvres and champagne. I snag a flute off a nearby tray and take a sip. Bubbles erupt on my tongue, quickly followed by the crisp, sweet taste of strawberries.

I take a moment to look around and get a feel for the room. A ten-piece string band plays in the corner, mixing radio hits with classical pieces, and I idly wonder if I can convince them to play a little Taylor Swift. My lips twitch at the idea of the mayor and his wife, who are currently snacking on prosciutto-wrapped asparagus, dancing to the instrumental version of "Shake It Off."

I spot Blaire and her posse of frenemies from school making their way toward me, and I flash them a polite smile. Blaire leads the pack in a knockout dress that I'd bet my life she had custom-made.

"Solo tonight, Madison?" Blaire asks with a raised brow as she stops next to me.

Sammi, Peggy, and Hilary, all classmates at St. Rita's, stand around us and sip champagne. One of the perks of being the youth of the wealthy, connected, and well-respected members of society, I suppose. No one cares if we sip on champagne at these types of events. Dressed in what I'm sure was a coordinated effort, all three girls look beautiful in their blue dresses, each shade complementary to one another.

I quirk my lips and cock my head to the side as I scan all four girls before coming back to Blaire. She's not an enemy, and while I consider her a friend, I don't trust her with my most-guarded secrets like I do with Lainey and Mary. "You know I like options, B."

Blaire stares over the rim of her champagne flute as she tips it back for a sip. The deep emerald color of her form-fitting mermaid-style dress sparkles under the color-diffused light.

"Some of us don't have that luxury," she muses.

I know she's referring to the fact that her parents signed a glorified marriage contract when she was still a toddler.

That's how it is for a lot of these people here tonight. Most of the married couples here were arranged, and because of some archaic rule about bloodlines and shareholders, most of these families continue the tradition of arranged marriage.

Blaire's family is old money, made their fortune in oil, and rumor on the street is that she won't inherit her family's company—and fortune—until she's married with an heir.

It's a crock of patriarchal bullshit if you ask me.

In a rare show of vulnerability last year, Blaire broke down in the women's locker room and told me the whole thing. I'd never betray her confidence and share what she told me, but sometimes I wonder if there's something I can do to help her.

I can't imagine being eighteen and knowing that your husband has already been chosen for you. A virtual stranger who's going to be your partner for life, regardless of your opinions on the matter. If you're lucky, you get matched with someone who's pleasant enough and who won't flash his mistresses around town for all to see on Page Six the next day.

And how sad is that? Your best-case scenario is a man who won't publicly shame your sham of a marriage. No, thank you.

The concept of love is laughable to most of the people in this room. Something reserved for fiction and adolescents.

My mom isn't a saint by any means, and most of the time, she does the bare minimum in the adulting department, but one thing I can say with confidence is that she'd never marry my sister or me off like that. And it's not because of some misplaced sense of love either.

I'm sure she loved my dad, and I know he loved her. But they didn't have that fairytale type of love, which is ironic considering the stories he used to tell me when I was young. It was all princesses and white knights and eternal love.

My parents met when they were young, and my dad enlisted soon after they got married, leaving a pregnant wife at home. He was gone more than he wasn't, and I think we all got used to that kind of life—one that didn't include him.

"Earth to Madison." Blaire waves a manicured hand in front of my face, snapping me out of my fog.

I flash her a smile, and some of the tightness around her eyes relaxes. "Sorry. I'm just tired."

"Babe. Just wait a few hours until it breaks up a little. I brought party favors," Sammi says as she waggles her eyebrows and shakes her palm-sized handbag for the evening.

I work hard not to clench my jaw and settle on a forced smile and a noncommittal hum.

"Knock it off, Sammi. You know Madison doesn't roll," Peggy says as she flashes an apologetic look in my direction.

Sammi recoils and looks at Peggy with a frown. "Like I'd bring molly here with all of this and have the worst trip ever? No thanks. I brought my perfectly legal prescription tonight. You know, in case I need to concentrate." She smirks at us with her chin tilted high.

"Thanks, Sammi. I'll let you know, okay?" The olive branch seems to pacify her and they move the conversation to who's wearing what. I have no intention of taking her up on that offer, but I don't need to voice that right now. She'll forget all about it in thirty minutes, anyway.

After ten minutes and another glass of champagne, it catches up to me, and I excuse myself to the ladies' room. It's not the same bathroom that I used earlier, but it's no less luxurious. They brought the enchanted forest theme in here with colors of deep reds and mellow oranges, and there's even a small garden's worth of greenery in the powder room next to the full-length mirror.

Once I finish and reapply my lipstick, I walk back into the ball-room. My steps are slow as I people-watch. The crowd is decidedly larger than an hour ago, and I'm a little surprised at the size.

The familiar notes of Beyoncé hit my ears, and I can't hold back the chuckle at the boldness of the band tonight. A smile spreads across my face, and I glance around the room to see if anyone else has noticed. I see a few smiles and giggles, but it's mostly going unnoticed. Shame.

I glance at the huge ornate iron clock on the wall and silently count down the minutes until a DJ replaces the strings and the dance floor opens up. Only thirty minutes. I can do that. I nod my head along with the beat, impressed with the violinist as she absolutely smashes this song.

I grab another glass of champagne from a passing waiter with a smile, content to watch them fill the atmosphere with a whimsical take on this sultry song. My nerves jump with the need to dance, but I don't leave my spot along the edge of the room.

One minute, I'm enjoying the instrumental sounds of "Drunk In Love" and the next minute, my focus is pulled away almost involuntarily. My heart skips a beat before it beats in double-time as my awareness picks up on something behind me. Or some*one*.

"You look gorgeous tonight, as always." My breath freezes at his familiar voice. Too many emotions barrage me at once, and I don't have time to sort through them or settle on just one. "This dress is exquisite on you." I feel the barest of touches as he drags the tip of his finger down my spine, and a trail of goosebumps follow his ghosted touch.

"Matteo." I say his name on an exhale, my heart clenching at the thought of him here, now, after so much time.

I don't even need to turn around to see his face. He's the only man I've ever met who's had this kind of effect on me. Lust sends a flare up through my body, but shame settles it back down. Sometimes I still think about that night, and I can't believe that I didn't see it coming.

I shift my weight, but his warm palm on my back stops me from turning around to face him. I beg my traitorous body to harden its resolve against this charming asshole. But she's a fickle bitch, and she still craves his touch after all this time.

"Shh, doll. Don't turn around. We're concealed in the shadows here—"

Indignation soars through my veins and my hands fist on my sides. "What? Don't want your girlfriend to see you with your hands on another woman?" I'm actually a little shocked at the scorn in my voice, but the deeply feminist part of me cheers me on, ready to kick his ass verbally.

He chuckles, this deep, masculine sound that has my toes curling inside my Jimmy Choos.

He slides his hand up my spine until it tunnels underneath my hair, settling at the base of my neck. His long, warm fingers flex and tangle in my wavy strands. He gives them a gentle tug, and a gasp leaves my mouth unbidden.

"I don't even have my hands where you *really* want them. Not yet."

His words have the desired effect on me and a flash of lust rolls through my traitorous body.

His hand leaves my hair, and he trails a single fingertip down my arm, linking it with my pinky finger for two seconds. "I'll be seeing you, Cherry."

The move is so reminiscent of how he was when we first met— from the nickname to the familiar pinky-holding that my heart squeezes painfully.

Matteo hooks a finger around my pinky as we walk down the path in Central Park. It's an unexpected move but not unwelcome. We haven't been dating long, and I like his version of holding hands.

I twist my lips to the side to stifle the ridiculous grin that's trying to break free.

Mom came to the city to take my sister and me out to lunch with her newest boyfriend a few days ago. She told me through her pained, perfect smile that my smile isn't as straight as Mary's. I never thought about it much before, but now that she's planted the seed of doubt, I can't shake it. She made an appointment for the orthodontist for me next week, so at least I'll get it taken care of soon.

"It's a nice day for a walk, yeah?" He looks at me with a grin, his posture relaxed and confident. In an all-black suit minus the jacket, he looks like a young celebrity strolling through the park on a Wednesday afternoon. Black Ray-Bans shield his eyes, and his hair is tousled in that effortlessly messy way that shouldn't be as good-looking as it is.

I quirk a brow, desperately trying to calm the few butterflies that slowly circle my insides. I like Matteo, like really like him. We've been seeing each other for just shy of six months now. But we don't get to see each other too often, since we're at different schools. Plus, he's a couple years older than me.

And somehow, I've managed to keep him a secret from my mom. Once she meets someone, she either gets her claws in them, or they leave. Either way, it's game over.

And I think I want to keep him.

"Aren't you going to get warm in that?" I ask. *It's September, but in New York City, it's still hot this time of year. We lucked out with a cool seventy-degrees today.*

He pinches the fabric of his shirt between two fingers and lifts it out a few times with a smile. "What? This? Nah, I'm perfect. I'm here with you, aren't I?"

I playfully roll my eyes and nudge his arm with my shoulder. "Flattery will get you everywhere, Matteo."

He tugs me closer with his grip on my pinky finger. "Good, because I'm going wherever you are, Cherry."

I slam my lids shut and count to ten in French. It's about all I can remember from French class. Madame Fontaine was hard to follow, and well, school has never been my strong suit.

It does the trick though, and when I open my eyes and spin around, the space behind me is empty.

I knew it would be though. Matteo never stays in one place too long. I exhale a shaky breath, my loose strands of hair billowing out in front of my face. My heart beats frantically, fluttering against my ribs like a bird trapped in a cage. I press a hand to my chest and close my eyes again, willing my heart to calm down.

"Hey, you okay?"

I snap my eyes open, surprised to see Blaire's honey-eyed gaze in front of mine. Her head tilts to the side and a crease she'd be horrified to know is there mars her brows.

I paste a smile on my face, and I'm thankful when she doesn't call me on it. We're both skilled enough to spot a fake smile a mile away—it's practically the language of the entitled.

I open my mouth to respond with some stretched truth, but the lights dim and the ten-piece string band stops playing and exits the stage. Someone whoops, drawing my attention to the corner where the guest DJ is setting up, saving me from answering Blaire.

"Who's that?" I tip my chin toward the corner.

She stares at me for a moment longer before slowly shifting so she's standing next to me and looking in the same direction. "Goes by Zebra."

I quirk a brow, but I don't reply as I watch him set up, grateful for the few moments to get myself under control. To remind myself that I'm not that same girl with hearts in her eyes.

I watch the tables empty as the older generations retreat to the edges of the room and small patios outside the French doors. They sit at the small tables inside shallow alcoves. No doubt the next round of marriage contracts and familiar mergers are being signed tonight. I can only imagine how many other deals will be agreed upon over handshakes and too many cocktails.

"I know, I wasn't sure about him either, but apparently he's the hottest thing in the underground in London right now."

I nod a few times. "Good. I'm ready to dance."

"Me too, girl. Me too."

The familiar sounds of The Chainsmokers and Daya pump through the speakers and Blaire hooks her elbow in mine with a sly smile, and we head for the dance floor.

CHAPTER FOUR

MADDIE

FLASHES of colorful fabrics pulse around me in tune with the strobe lighting, the brightness sharp in contrast to the dimmed lighting. The air is thick and humid as the steady beat thumps through the air, settling in my veins and infusing me with the familiar need to move to the music.

My hair sticks to the back of my neck and I raise my hands in the air, letting my body sway to the pulsing beat. I look beneath half-open lids at Blaire grinding on Wes Rockford a foot in front of me. A few guys have danced with me in the last hour, but thankfully nothing more than that. I'm not in the mood to deal with anyone who gets too handsy.

Sweat slides down the back of my neck, and I twirl my hair around my fist and hold it out to the side, willing the hot breeze from the open patio doors to cool me down, if only for a moment.

Blaire winks at me as she shimmies her hips, her arms wrapping around Wes's neck. The DJ spins Calvin Harris, and when the beat drops, the air shifts into something darker, deeper. The change is tangible, weighing heavy on my body and forcing my hips to roll from side to side slowly.

A fog of awareness swirls around my head a second before I feel a warm body behind mine, hands sliding to rest on my hips. My movements stutter for a moment as my heart thumps wildly in my chest.

He steps closer, but not quite touching, and I just barely feel the brush of his suit against my back. My lip curls up on one side when he doesn't step into me like I thought he would. I've never known Matteo to not take what he wants, and there's no doubt in my mind that he wouldn't be out here on the dance floor if he didn't want something from me.

I'm not sure if it's the champagne or the music or the dress or something else, but I'm feeling reckless tonight. Bold enough to let Matteo have what he wants—or better yet, take what *I* want from him.

Emboldened, I step back so I'm flush against his front and slide my fingers in between his, anchoring his hold on my hips. He doesn't miss a beat, and his hands tighten against me, the hot press of his fingertips branding themselves against my skin even through all the layers of satin.

I arch my back, my ass swiveling and rubbing against him. His fingers flex against my hips, and I imagine the marks they'd leave on my bare skin if this dress wasn't in the way.

I close my eyes, shutting off my senses and giving myself permission to let go just for a little while. To lessen the tight reins I hold myself to.

I shed my stale bitterness from how our relationship ended years ago, and allow myself to take what I want from him without guilt. What I've never been able to get from anyone else.

Smoke from the DJ's table curls through the bodies, highlighted in orange and yellow every time the strobe light flashes. One song bleeds into two, and two into three, and before long, I lose track. I never turn around, and he never spins me to face him. We stay locked in this dance, him and I, and somewhere along the way it feels like a whole lot more than just dancing. We feel in sync, connected on a level far more intimate than an evening on the dance floor.

Our steps never falter, our rhythm never falls out of sync. It's as if our bodies already know something we don't and our minds are left to play catch-up.

He pulls my hair to the side and replaces it with his face on my shoulder. His breath warms my neck, and I silently beg him to press his lips against my feverish skin. To glide them along that sensitive spot behind my ear.

I don't know if I should be embarrassed by how quickly it turns me on, but I'm not. Thoughts of him consume my mind.

I hold off for as long as I can, but I don't think I can go another second without the feel of his lips against mine. I'm panting, my skin flushed and coated in a light sheen of sweat. Lust courses through my veins, begging me to take what I need from him.

I can feel him against my ass, hard and long and thick. A small kernel of satisfaction warms my blood at the evidence that he wants me too.

I bite my lip and tip my head back against his shoulder while I have an internal debate. Part of me wants to go there with him—to fuck him in one of the abandoned rooms that we all know are here just for those types of situations. But the other part of me, the more sensible part, knows I've never had a one-night stand for a reason. And I don't know if choosing my ex-boyfriend to check that particular box off my bucket list is the right choice.

I'm catapulted out of my swirling thoughts when warm lips trail up the side of my neck, nipping my skin softly. His hands slide up my ribs, his touch hot. His fingers flex around my ribcage, his thumb slipping underneath the fabric that just barely touches my back.

I roll my hips in a slow, deliberate move and he surprises me by smoothing one hand down to rest on my lower stomach, holding me against him. He grazes his teeth against the bottom of my earlobe and grinds his hips against mine. It's the first move he's initiated, letting me lead the entire time.

Like a match to a flame, that small dominant move lights me up. Faster than he can stop me, I spin in his hold, grab onto the lapels of his suit jacket, and push up onto my toes. Intense dark-brown eyes flash, but it's the last thing I see before I close my eyes and crush my mouth to his.

Our masks hit with an audible crack, but I don't stop. He slides his hand into my hair as he opens his mouth against my kiss. His thumb slides along my jawbone to control the angle of my head, and I'm more than happy to follow his lead.

He kisses me like he's running out of air. Like tomorrow isn't guaranteed—like the next *minute* isn't guaranteed—and this is how he wants to spend it.

I run my hands up his chest and curl them around his neck, tugging on his hair. He groans into my mouth, the sound almost painful and like a light switch, something flips. If I thought he was intense earlier, that's nothing compared to the way he kisses me now.

He tastes like spearmint and whiskey. Like dark promises and unfulfilled fantasies.

With a hand on my lower back, he hauls my body against his and maneuvers us so we're at the edge of the dance floor, shrouded in darkness. My back hits one of the stone pillars, the coarse stone dragging across my sensitive skin. I slip my leg through the high slit and hitch it up around his hip. He takes it for the invitation it is and slides his palm up to wrap around my outer thigh and steps into me.

My head feels foggy and heavy with lust, and I know I need to slow this down before I do something foolish in such a public space.

But when I feel the hard length of him press right where I need him, something short-circuits in my brain. A whimpering noise I didn't even know I could make falls from my lips on a gasp.

"Not here," I breathe out, arching my head back.

"Anywhere you want, babe," he murmurs with his lips against my throat.

I blame my delayed reaction on the feel of his lips—soft and plump and gentle. A few moments later, the persistent thought finally takes center stage in my lust-fogged mind. *Babe?* Matteo's never, ever called me that before. Cherry or the occasional doll, but never babe.

Suspicion worms its way through me, extinguishing my daze.

Pulling my head back, I open my eyes and peer at him through the colored strobe lights and lingering smoke.

Tall with dark hair that looks lighter in the flashes of light worn short on the sides and messy on top in that effortless "I just woke up like this" look. He has the same air of superiority and radiates possessive asshole like it's his job.

He lifts his gaze to mine, finally catching on that I'm not lust-drunk anymore. "You okay, babe?" He cocks his head to the side, and then it hits me.

His *voice*.

It's deep and alluring, but it's not Matteo's voice.

Holy shit.

My jaw drops. I reach for his flat black half-mask, intent on revealing this mystery man I was five minutes from getting intimately acquainted with, but his long fingers encircle my wrist.

"I heard that's against the rules," he murmurs.

And in a move too smooth to be real, he shifts his hold and brings the back of my hand to his lips. He sweeps his kiss-swollen lips across my knuckles, and his dark-brown eyes hold me prisoner.

"I—I thought you were . . ." My head spins and I wet my lips. "Someone else." I was so sure it was Matteo behind me, but maybe that was a leap my mind took because I saw him tonight.

He stiffens in front of me and guides my hand down to my side. "I see. My apologies, Raven."

"Raven?" I tilt my head to the side and watch in fascination as his mouth curves into a sinful smirk.

He gives me an obvious once-over before meeting my gaze. "Your dress."

My gut clenches when he takes a step back, and a lightning bolt of clarity hits me square in the chest. I would've gone home with him tonight. A total stranger.

And would that be so bad? a little voice inside whispers.

All tall, dark, and handsome and dressed in black, he reminds me of a villain in a movie.

Easily six-two with broad shoulders and a tapered waist, his deep black suit and matching shirt reek of luxury. He looks exactly like someone I'd expect at one of these events—wealthy, privileged, and not my type.

But he doesn't feel like he's not my type.

Underneath that Armani suit he's wearing like it was made for him, he feels different.

Like maybe he could've been mine in another life.

He runs his thumb across his bottom lip, and my skin flushes at the visual reminder of how his lips and hands felt on my body.

Okay, maybe less of a villain and more an antihero from one of my favorite romance novels.

Between the shadows blanketing us, the flashes of light at his back, and his masquerade mask, I can't actually place the face of my mystery dance partner. And perhaps that's part of the thrill.

He misinterprets my silence and takes another step back.

I bite my lip and remind myself to be brave.

Life is short. Buy the shoes. It's a saying my mom practically lives by, and while I do love a fantastic pair of shoes, I think it's better applied to other situations.

Mary and I haven't talked about it, and Lainey's going through her own stuff right now, but what happened to her—to all of us—at O'Malley's Pub left a mark on me. One that has me more inclined to say yes to this, to him.

Lots of people have one-night stands and their world doesn't stop spinning. Maybe it's time I step outside my carefully crafted, self-imposed safety lines and do something spontaneous.

And then I make a decision that has my heart racing for a different reason. "Wait." I cut the distance between us in half and place a hand on his forearm. His dark eyebrow arches above his mask, and he stares at me expectantly.

The lights cut out, and we're plunged into darkness.

CHAPTER FIVE

MADDIE

"RAVEN?" I feel his hand on my shoulder, but it's hard to hear him over my pulse thundering in my ears.

Icy tendrils of fear wind up my limbs, squeezing me tighter and tighter with each passing second in the dark.

It's dark in this corner of the room—too dark. The French doors leading to outdoor balconies are kitty-corner to us—too far away to offer any moonlight.

Shouts of confusion and fear pierce the air, ramping up my anxiety. I blink rapidly, my desperation to see overriding the logical part of my brain that's shouting at me that we can't see anything.

My chest rises and falls faster than it should, and my already-dark view gets darker along the edges. I imagine all sorts of people creeping along the darkest parts of the room with sticky fingers, ready to snatch unsuspecting girls and toss them into a van.

Just like those psychopaths did with Lainey.

Oh fuck.

"Raven? Babe? You okay? Just breathe." His breath fans over my face, bringing me back to myself, even if only a bit.

I latch onto his shoulders, my fingers digging into his expensive fabric. "Don't leave me back here."

45

He skims his lips across my cheek as he wraps an arm around my shoulders. "You're alright. I've got you now, yeah?"

I let him lead me along the edges of the room and toward the growing crowd of people. They bottleneck at the only doorway that leads to the hallway and ultimately outside.

Cell phones light up, the flashlight app cutting beams of light across the space. My dress snags on one of the topiary gardens, pulling me to a stop.

"Here," he says, angling the flashlight from his phone in my direction.

It's then I notice the stiffness in his shoulders and the way he keeps looking around us. He's acting like he expects someone to sneak up behind us too.

My pulse increases and my fingers shake from adrenaline and fear as I untangle the twig from the faux feathers along my ribs. "Thank you."

A few people yell, and it only takes a moment before those yells turn to aggressive shouts and then shoves. I free my dress just as some guy throws a punch at the guy next to him about twenty feet in front of us.

I blink and one punch turns into an all-out brawl between a bunch of guys and even a few girls. Shock freezes me for a moment, and I stand there with my jaw proverbially dropped.

"What the hell is happening?" My words are quiet in the ruckus.

Blaire's wide eyes fill my vision, and I blink again, startled by her sudden appearance. "Oh good. I thought you were caught up in that male posturing bullshit over there." She hooks her thumb over her shoulder toward the crowd. "Follow me, I know a way out of here that doesn't involve getting stuck in that fishbowl."

Peggy, Sammi, and Hilary slide next to Blaire, and she links an arm with two of them before walking back toward the way we came.

My mystery man slides his palm into mine, lacing our fingers together, and tugs me along. We sidestep a few knocked-over chairs and follow the flashlight from Blaire's phone.

I look over my shoulder, trusting this guy to lead me. My eyes widen at the scene—it looks like something from a movie. Tables are turned over, broken glasses litter the floor, chairs lay on their sides, and even the floral arrangements are in pieces. Guys are throwing punches and kicks and tackling one another without inhibition. It's no longer contained to that one small area—like a virus, the violence spreads.

A screech next to me captures my attention—it's a small group of people I recognize from St. Rita's and a few from the neighboring schools.

"I know you fucked my boyfriend last year, you backstabbing bitch!" Chrissy Charms screams right before she dives toward Hannah Valentine, aiming for her face.

Chase Walker, the boyfriend in question, steps up and attempts to peel Chrissy off of Hannah. But then some guy I don't know steps in and wrenches Chase away by his shoulder. "You fucked Hannah? What the fuck, man?"

Shoves devolve into punches, and two guys turn into four. All I can do is stare, wide-eyed, as people I've known for years just totally lose their shit on one another.

Someone gets shoved into me from behind, and I lose my footing and fall into my mystery man in front of me. I absentmindedly realize I need to ask his name so I stop referring to him as "mystery man."

His hands come up to my shoulders, steadying me on my feet. I look at his face, wishing not for the first time that I could see his features clearly. His dark gaze is intense as he holds my stare. The hair on the back of my neck stands up, and I fight the urge to kiss him. It's most definitely not the time for kissing.

But later, I vow to myself. *Later, there will be plenty of time for kissing.*

He uses his hold on my shoulders to move me to the side, smoothly stepping in front of me.

In a move so quick if I would've blinked, I would've missed it, he takes a step forward and punches a guy who was advancing on us with a folding chair over his head. He falls like a sack of potatoes.

I feel my eyebrows in my hairline. A wave of warmth rolls through me, followed by a tendril of lust.

He turns around to face me, his hand finding mine again, and walks like he didn't just knockout some guy with one punch.

I forget for a moment that we're in the middle of chaos, a little mesmerized by him. I shake my head and quicken my steps to keep up with his pace as he maneuvers us around the room.

"Aries." The word flies from my mouth before I can stop it. All that passion on the dance floor and that take-charge attitude—I'd bet my favorite pair of shoes that he's an Aries.

I bite the inside of my cheek as I study his profile backlit by the flashlights moving around the room. He's at home in the darkness, moving us around obstacles with ease.

Maybe he's more my type than I realized.

Shifting his gaze to look at me across his shoulder, he flashes me a smirk. "What's that?"

I feel my lips curling up to mimic his smirk. "You're an Aries, aren't you?"

He doesn't answer me for a moment, just quickens our pace until we catch up to Blaire and the girls.

"Jesus, what the hell is happening in there?" Peggy asks with a glance over her shoulder. "And why the hell did the lights go out? Is it storming?"

We cross the threshold to another part of the venue I've never been in before. Emergency lights line the ornate carpet runner— they must have a generator for this very reason.

"Rolling blackouts, remember? C'mon, we're almost to the alleyway exit." Blaire tips her head toward the space in front of her. I squint when I see a glowing red exit sign.

They've been talking about these rolling blackouts all summer— something about easing the burden of electricity so all the overuse doesn't totally fry our systems.

Peggy nods, her curls bouncing with the movement. "Right. If I don't have air conditioning when I get back to my dorm, I'm going to call a car to take me home. Daddy said they'd have the air on in one wing of the house."

Aries snickers next to me, quiet enough that the girls don't hear him, but I do. I don't look at him, instead roll my lips under my teeth to stop myself from laughing. But really, her entire sentence is so ridiculous.

Blaire pushes against a metal door, and I brace myself for some kind of alarm or something, but the silence greets us. Even the chaotic sounds of fighting have faded.

Billows of humid smog greet us, instantly weighing heavy against my chest. Looking around, I notice the darkness surrounding us. "How many blocks go at a time? Does anyone know?"

Blaire shakes her head. "I don't remember. I honestly thought Mayor Chambers was going to pull some strings so this block didn't get hit tonight like the city planned. I'm not sure what happened there."

Rotten garbage wafts into the air, and I turn my face to bury my nose in Aries's suit. I feel more than hear his chuckle, and he throws an arm around my shoulders, pulling me further against his hard body.

Our footsteps are loud, echoing off the surrounding brick of the venue's building and the neighboring one. I think it's a deli if I remember right.

The general noise gets louder the closer we get to the street, and I sort of dread going out there. I kind of expect cops to be there to question people about the fighting—especially since a lot of those guys attend the elite boys' school where they have a strict policy about violence.

I slow my steps and watch Blaire wave down her town car. The driver maneuvers it through the throngs of people pouring into the street like a pro. She stands between the car and the door, looking over the door and wiggling her fingers in the air.

"C'mon, babe! I'll give you a lift."

"I'll be right there!" I flutter my fingers back at her, and she gets back in the car.

We step onto the sidewalk, and only his quick reflexes save me from getting plowed over by some guys from the masquerade event. Masks askew, bloody noses and lips, and wide smiles, they laugh and pat each other's backs. I sidestep them, stepping back into my mystery man.

As one, the four of them turn to face us. I think I recognize a few of their faces—and I'm pretty sure Blaire dated one of them last year, a senator's son.

Charles Pinkerton leers at me before switching his focus to the man behind me. His eyes light up in recognition and something low in my gut clenches. "Oh, man, we were wondering where you snuck off to. Listen, bro, don't even waste your time with that one—"

Dale Hardin, the senator's son, claps one hand on Charles's shoulder. "C'mon, man. You've had too much to drink. Let's go."

Charles shoves Dale off and turns to look at us fully. "Nah, man. He should know—that's what friends do, right? They look out for each other, and I'm lookin' out for him."

I shift my weight from one foot to the other as dread claws its way up my throat, entwining with the hot flush of embarrassment.

"Move on, man. I don't need your advice—friendly or otherwise." His voice is deep and rich, exactly how I'd imagine it.

Charles sneers at him as he leans to the side a little, unsteady on his feet. "Oh, really? All the sudden you're not about that easy pussy?" He laughs, this sharp noise that grates on my ears, and I clench my jaw at the urge to flinch. "Hey, you wanna waste your time trying to get her on her back, be my guest. She's a fucking princess, man. And her pussy is in a goddamn gilded cage designed to tease the fuck outta you—she'll never give you the key without a ring, and even if she did, some asshole wannabe thug'll come and—"

My mystery man, my savior of the evening, steps around me and cocks his fist back in one smooth move. He unleashes his fury, and Charles doesn't stand a chance. His head whips to the side and he falls into his friends standing silently behind him.

"I fucking warned you to move on," he says, pointing at him. But by the dazed look on Charles's face, he's seeing stars, so he doesn't offer much rebuttal.

Dale rests his hands on top of his head, shaking it a few times.

"Fuck, man, you just never know when to shut your mouth. I'm sorry about that."

My mystery man just looks at Dale before stepping back next to me and throwing his arm around my shoulders again. He steers us toward Blaire's town car, and I wonder if anyone has ever had a heart attack from too many feelings at once—shame and embarrassment, anger and indignation, gratitude and fear—and lust.

I know I shouldn't feel embarrassed about some drunk asshole running his mouth, but I kind of am. And that alone is enough to flare those shame flames.

He pulls us to a stop a few feet from the curb and lets his arm slide off my shoulders and down my back to rest against my lower back for a moment before he drops it to his side.

"Don't let those assholes get to you, yeah? They don't know what the fuck they're talking about."

I don't tell him that they're kind of right—I don't sleep around. I've only slept with one person, and he was my boyfriend at the time. And if you would've asked me last week if I thought I'd ever find someone who could really pique my interest, I would've said no. But after tonight, I think I'm ready to explore a little.

I trace my finger down the edge of his masquerade mask. I'm surprised it stayed on through everything. The only reason mine did is because the satin ribbon is bobby-pinned in. It's not moving until I take those out.

"What's your name?" I breathe the words out, taking an unconscious step toward him.

Instead of answering me, he eliminates the space between us and slides his palms along my neck, tangling his fingers in the hair at the nape of my neck. His thumbs rest against my jaw, and he uses it to his advantage and angles my face upward.

He crushes his mouth to mine in a kiss that shakes me to my core. I have a feeling that was exactly the point.

He pulls back and whispers against my lips, "I'm an Aries. And in another life, I would've made you my queen. I would've dragged you back to my place and worshipped you until you begged me to stop."

My lips part on an exhale, and he wastes no time swooping in for the kill. As if his words didn't paint a picture my imagination ran wild with, he's now assuring that I'll feel his kiss for days to come.

We end our kiss slowly, neither one of us stepping back at first. I open my eyes, not at all shocked to see intense brown eyes locked on mine. He takes a step back then, letting his gaze roam all over my body as if he's memorizing it.

"Until we meet again, Raven."

"Until we meet again, Aries," I murmur.

His mouth quirks to the side at my choice in name but he doesn't say anything as he spins on his heel and stalks down the sidewalk, away from me.

"C'mon, look back. Don't let me down now," I whisper to myself, willing him to look back at me. It's something I saw in a romantic comedy a long time ago, and I'm not even sure how much truth there is to it. Apparently, if he looks back, it means you're destined to be together.

My heart lurches, and a feeling of loss coats my skin, thick and heavy. I watch as the shadows claim more and more of Aries with each step. And just before I can't see him anymore, he turns around and looks at me, holding my gaze.

My breath leaves my chest in a whoosh as the feeling of his eyes on me intensifies. I watch in fascination as he walks backward down the sidewalk, the surrounding darkness swallowing him whole.

I bite my lip and glance around, half expecting him to jog back to me and hit me with another one of those toe-curling kisses.

I try not to let the disappointment weigh too heavy on my shoulders and just be grateful for the experience—and the fact that he helped me get out of there safely.

I slide into the town car and sit next to Blaire, mindful of my dress.

"Who was that?" she asks with a look over her shoulder.

I feel the smile spread across my face slowly and shrug a shoulder. "I have no idea."

CHAPTER SIX

MADDIE

"BABE. Come to The Grasshopper for a late lunch today." Blaire mastered the art of making a request sound like a command years ago.

I roll my eyes at her tone, not that she can see me through the phone. I know her as well as she'll let me, and I know she's not doing it to be a jerk. She's just sharpening her already honed skills of careful manipulation. I swear she's going to rule a small country one day, and it'll happen before anyone even realizes it.

"Good morning to you too. How are you today? Did you sleep well?" I laugh a little before I get all the words out.

She huffs in my ear, but I hear the smile in her voice. "Good morning. I'm great. Yes, and no, I didn't take that asshole home. He's such a fucking pig, I can't believe I ever dated him."

It takes me a moment to connect the dots. "Ah, you saw Dale then, I take it?"

"As if anyone could miss his drunken embarrassment. I'm sure he was one of the assholes fighting in the middle of the gala too. Ugh. If that idiot thought he could win me back by that pathetic attempt at making amends, he's mistaken. As if I'd ever take his lying, cheating ass back. It's been ages, and I've moved on." She huffs, the noise small but still filled with contempt. "Besides, my mom and I have already hatched our plan of revenge, and phase one doesn't begin for a few months. When his daddy starts campaigning for his re-election." She delivers her words with such a nonchalance. If you weren't listening carefully, you'd be inclined to think she was commenting on the weather and not ruining a man's career.

We both know that she took it hard when she found out Dale was slipping into the back rooms with girls from the Praying Mantis strip club. That kind of betrayal isn't something you just forget. And from the sounds of it, she's got it covered.

"Well, he's an idiot, and he doesn't deserve you." It's my honor and duty as her pseudo-friend to always remind her she deserves someone better. I leave the revenge plots though.

She clicks her tongue. "I know. That's why we're going to lunch today."

My brow quirks high on my forehead in realization. "You have your eye on someone else." It's not a question, because I already know the answer.

She pauses a moment, and the line is quiet—no background noise. "We'll see. Four o'clock today."

Hesitation holds me back from agreeing. "I don't know, Blaire. I'm kind of tired—"

"It's the same circles as the masquerade, so it stands to reason that your mystery man could show."

Smug satisfaction bleeds from every word, and if I wasn't so irritated, I'd be impressed. She hasn't brought him up since she asked me who he was when we left the masquerade, but I shouldn't be surprised. A few days' time is practically an eternity to a girl who's a hub of information and gossip.

A streak of possessiveness slithers inside my veins. I selfishly don't want Blaire to find my mystery guy. Which is ridiculous, because I don't have any claim on a guy I met *once*. And Blaire's a friend.

But I can't deny the urge to hide him from her—from everyone, really. Something dark and wicked twists around inside me when I think of seeing him again. I know myself well enough that I won't hesitate a second time.

"Damn, babe. Straight for the throat, huh? Who else will be there?" She's got me, and she knows it.

"Does it matter?"

Screw it. I want to see him again. And without a name or a number, I don't know how else I'd find him.

"Fine. I'll meet you there at four."

THE GRASSHOPPER IS a vintage lover's paradise. Built in the late eighteen hundreds, it was once some sort of bank or government building. Rumor has it that it was once a speakeasy during prohibition too. I've never been to the lower basement levels, but it's supposed to be well restored.

There are three floors, not including the rumored speakeasy basement. The first one has most of their tables and booths with an ornate bar along one wall. The second and third floors both cater to events, from weddings to a bunch of elite kids who want to eat lunch together.

I have no doubt that Blaire got us a small room on the second floor to dine in tonight. Hell, she probably already had one of their mixologists make us a signature cocktail for today only.

Like most places Blaire frequents, there's a dress code. I decided on one of my favorite summer dresses today. Spaghetti straps angle toward my neck and crisscross over my back, leaving my shoulders bare to the summer sun. It's a modest v-cut that falls to the tops of my sandaled toes. Gray and white flower peony blossoms break up the blue, giving the dress a summery vibe. It's lightweight and breezy while still falling within the restaurant's guidelines.

I open the heavy door to the restaurant and step inside. The air conditioning is going at full blast, the force enough to send an avalanche of goosebumps racing down my body.

Everything inside is decorated in rich golds and deep matte blacks. A wall of detailed glass extends up all three floors. It looks more like a piece or art than just a standard window. It's frosted, so minimal light shines in, furthering the ambiance of the space.

It's moody with rich fabrics covering the chairs and booths. Textured tapestries hang from the walls, serving as volume control and decor. Golden sconces light up the space with dim light every so often and gold chain-link chandeliers hang over the booths.

As I make my way to the hostess station, I can't help my wandering eye. I'm looking for him without even really giving myself permission.

But how will I recognize a man I only saw in the dark—and in a mask?

"Madison!" Blaire calls as I reach the hostess stand.

"It seems my party found me already." I flash the hostess a small smile as I wave a hand at Blaire. She's waiting on the second-floor landing with her purse in hand. Surprisingly, she's not surrounded by her usual posse. They either didn't arrive yet, or she's late. Considering Blaire thinks five minutes early is ten minutes late, I doubt that's the case.

I take in her appearance as I close the distance between us. She's dressed in a tight black pencil skirt with a subtle texture print and an off-the-shoulder teal shirt. Her favorite red-soled shoes pull the look together, but it's oddly casual for her. Usually, she uses every opportunity to dress to the nines when she's in public.

"Hey, babe. You okay?" I ask as I ascend the stairs.

"Fine, why? I'm just working on that friend thing." She looks over the first floor as she talks, but I don't miss the slight pink in her cheeks.

The other thing Blaire confessed to me last year? She doesn't have any real friends. The girl's been groomed to be a gossip monger her whole life, so it's not hard to understand why. And even though I don't trust her like I do Lainey or Mary, I think we're slowly building a friendship. A real one, not that fake stuff she has with those other girls where they secretly gossip and one-up each other all the time.

"Good," I tell her with a twist of my lips.

No sooner than I stand on the landing does she link her arm with mine. "Let's go. I'm famished."

It's been an hour, and still, I don't see him. I find myself staring at every new face milling around. Blaire said this was a lunch, and it's my fault for not pushing it further, but it feels more like some sort of function.

Small plates are placed around various two-top and four-top tables at random inside the small hall usually reserved for banquets or parties. It reminds me of a round robin, only you're encouraged to go from table to table to chat and eat.

I sip a peach Bellini as I scan the room again, looking for any familiar—or unfamiliar—faces. I've eaten a few things here and there, but most of the people here are backstabbing assholes who'd rather talk about one of three things: parties, gossip, money.

It's all just so predictable and . . . boring.

With a realization that feels like one of those lightbulb moments you see in cartoons, I come to terms with the fact that I'm bored here. And maybe with the majority of these people. I almost expect to see a hand drawn lightbulb above my head.

All the parties and petty gossip and comparing net worths. It's exhausting.

And total bullshit. It's so bland and fake that it makes my ears bleed. Where's the passion? The genuine interest?

Maybe it's just a phase—or the closing of one phase, perhaps. I'm in a transitionary period. My morning horoscope told me as much.

Or maybe I don't fit in with these people anymore. Maybe I never did.

An outlier.

With that thought heavy on my heart, I excuse myself to the restroom. Not that anyone in earshot cared too much—the girls kept on chatting about the newest teacher at St. Rita's and rumors of her hooking up with a teacher from another school.

The hallways of The Grasshopper are dimly lit and quiet in this part of the building. I guess this is mostly original architecture back here, and since it was built in a time of narrower specs, the hallways are tighter than I'm used to. It's a good thing I'm not particularly claustrophobic, or this ornate hallway might be an issue.

Large, gold thick-framed paintings line the wall, breaking up the salmon-and-cream thick-striped wallpaper. Renaissance-style depictions of people I've never heard of watch me walk toward the ladies' room at the end of the hallway. There are only two additional doors in this hallway apart from the restrooms, and they're both small conference-room-sized spaces used for private dinners.

I've attended dinners and functions at The Grasshopper before. I guess you could say it's a favorite amongst this crowd.

I'm halfway down the hallway, idly humming a song I've been practicing for our next open mic night at O'Malley's Pub, when I sense it. The unmistakable feeling of being watched.

My steps slow and I look from side to side, seeing if the eyes on the paintings follow me. The sconces along the wall cast strange shadows on the unfamiliar faces. And then my mind immediately jumps to a scary movie where some serial killer waits behind the walls, using the eyes of the portraits to stalk his victims and—

No. Stop. You've been here a dozen times—maybe more—and nothing bad has ever happened.

I take a deep breath and let it out slowly, picking up my pace again. A few steps later, I reach for the gold inlaid door handle, turning it and pushing the heavy door open.

Darkness greets me.

CHAPTER SEVEN

MADDIE

IT TAKES me a moment to remember that the few windows in this ladies' lounge are covered by thick velvet drapes, and not even the waning sunlight filters through them.

I blindly reach out for the light switch with my left hand.

Then I feel it.

A crackle of awareness shoots through my body, followed by a dash of fear.

Goosebumps light a path down my body all the way to my toes when I feel his heat at my back. In the span of a heartbeat, maybe two, he steps into me, his front flush against my back and wraps his hand around my outstretched one.

"I heard you were looking for me." His breath stirs the hair next to my ear as he talks.

"Who are you," I breathe out. Excitement thrums in my veins, chasing away the fear. My muscles tense against the urge to spin around and touch him. To flip the light switch on and see his face properly for the first time. To feel the softness of his lips against mine again.

"Who do you think I am?"

I wet my lips. "Aries. You're my Aries."

"Hmm." He makes a noise in the back of his throat, and I swear I feel his chest rumble against my back. "And have you been asking around for me?"

Despite the thundering of my heart, excitement pounds heavy in my limbs. I can't believe he's here—that I found him. Or he found me.

But now the real question is: What am I going to do about it?

"I didn't go around asking about you. But I—I did want to see you again."

He places his hand on my stomach, his fingers splaying wide. My body arches without conscious thought, and I hear my breath hitch. The noise is loud, cutting through the absolute darkness of this room.

I lick my lips as adrenaline and lust war with my common sense. This is crazy—I'm not the kind of girl who gets turned on by a stranger's hands on me in the dark.

Right?

That narrative has been forced down my throat for so long that I no longer know if it's how I really feel or if it's what I'm *supposed* to feel.

My eyes widen, as if that's going to help me see anything. Fear pricks me, fast and quick, at the all-encompassing darkness.

"Close your eyes, Raven."

It's like he knows I'm close to freaking out.

I'm at a crossroads now.

Ten minutes ago, I stood in the middle of a sea of people and bemoaned my outlier status, begging the fates to give me something to end my boredom. And here I am—here *he* is.

I'd be a fool to not take advantage of the gift fate is offering me.

I exhale and let my lids close, my lashes fluttering. I take a tiny step backward, pressing into him. His hand presses against my abdomen in response.

His nose skims the shell of my ear. "Have you thought of me, Raven? Did you go home and slide your hand into those lacy black panties and touch yourself?"

Warmth rolls down my body, settling in my core. His words paint a fantasy in my mind, one that I want to make reality.

His hand lowers ever so slowly, his fingertips sliding over the lace band of my thong and edging to the side. He continues his exploration down the front of my right thigh, his thumb brushing against the place where my leg and thigh meet. His other hand sweeps my hair away from my neck with soft movements, exposing my skin to his grazing lips.

"Did you push two fingers inside that tight pussy and fuck yourself with my name on your lips?"

My head tips back, and a breathy moan leaves my lips. "This is . . . this is crazy. I don't even know your name. Or what you look like. I—"

"There's something intoxicating about the dark, isn't there? You can drop your inhibitions with your sight and follow your body's needs." His lips brush against the sensitive skin on my neck with each word, pulling my attention away from his wandering fingers. They tiptoe down my thigh, inching up my dress with each movement. Cool air wraps around my calves, then my knees, and finally my thighs. He strokes his fingertips in small upward motions on my thighs, inching closer to my throbbing core.

I feel him harden against my ass, the physical proof that this isn't all in my head. It's real.

He's real.

And I'll be damned if I let a connection like this slip between my fingers like sand.

"When your legs tremble with pleasure and you're at the edge, I want to see my name falling from your lips. I want those rich pricks to hear the name of the man who finger-fucked you into ecstasy in the bathroom of their bullshit party."

"Yes." A moan slips from my mouth as the picture he paints takes over my imagination. My panties are soaked with my arousal, and I'm so turned on right now, I can barely see straight. I hold my breath as his fingers tease me through the fabric.

"Is that what you want? You want me to fuck this greedy pussy?"

With one hand, I reach around and grasp the back of his neck, holding his face to me. I slide my other hand over his, encouraging him to touch me where I want him—where I need him.

He pulls my thong to the side, and with one quick motion, the strap holding the small piece of lace to my body snaps. The sting against my skin is enough to make me gasp, but he quickly covers my pussy with his hand, the heel of his palm pressing against my clit.

I don't worry about where my thong lands. I'm too busy floating ten feet above the ground in pleasure.

He parts my folds with his index and middle finger, and I can't stop the moan at his teasing touch. "Stop teasing me," I beg him, my voice breathless.

He drags his teeth along the column of my neck. "Oh, Raven, I'll do more than tease you. I'm going to fucking ruin you for everyone else."

My lips part on a silent exhale, the promise of his words sinking deep underneath my skin. My toes curl when he slides a finger inside of me and I clench against him on instinct.

"Fuck," he curses low, sliding his finger out achingly slow. "Does this greedy pussy need more?"

I'm nodding before he even finishes talking. "Yes. Yes, I need more."

I grip his wrist as he speeds up a little, climbing that peak quicker than I thought possible. I'm acutely aware that I'm in the middle of a ladies' lounge room at a party with a hundred other people fifty feet away.

Like a bad summons, no sooner than that thought flits through my mind, does the sound of the door opening reach my ears.

"Madison? I know I saw you come back here. Damn, it's dark in here. Where's the stupid light switch?" Blaire's voice trails off as it gets louder.

Oh shit, she's going to find the switch and turn on the lights and catch us.

Why does that idea turn me on?

Part of me wants her to throw the lights on just so I can see him clearly. All of our interactions have been shrouded in darkness and wrapped up in sin.

But the realistic part of me realizes that if she catches me here, like this, then my reputation could tank in an instant.

Fuck it.

I'm so close to coming, I can practically taste it. My muscles go taut, and my fingernails dig into his wrist, holding him to me.

"Goddamnit." His words are hushed but full of frustration. I don't understand why until a moment later, when he slides his finger out of me. My dress falls back down around my legs, and a noise of protest escapes me without conscious thought. "To be continued, yeah?"

He sinks his teeth into my neck and bites down for a moment. Not hard enough to break the skin, but enough to trigger a responding pulse in my core. I clench my thighs together, a moan slipping past my lips.

"I'll find you again. I promise," he murmurs against my skin.

And in another instant, he's gone. The space behind me feels cool, his absence larger than just a body behind me. I press a hand to my chest to calm my breathing. I'm huffing like I just ran a marathon, and in some ways, that's exactly what it felt like.

A goddamn orgasm marathon.

And I was robbed of my finish line.

Light fills the space, and I blink rapidly, my vision blanking while my eyes adjust.

"Babe, didn't you hear me calling your name? And what are you doing in the dark?" Blaire asks as her eyes narrow.

I squint and turn around to face her. "Sorry, I didn't hear you. And I couldn't find the light switch."

I hope she attributes my flushed cheeks to my faux embarrassment and not from arousal.

She cocks her head to the side. Her eyes sparkle with her critical eye she's known for, and I school my face into careful faux embarrassment.

"You know me—always so forgetful." I let out a little fake self-depreciating laugh to really sell it, hating myself a little for playing up the stupid-debutante routine that's been thrust upon me.

While the awareness never leaves her eyes, she nods after a moment. She crosses the space to stand in front of the mirror, tilting her head from side to side and examining her face. I take it as my cue and walk into the stall, hyperaware that I'm without panties.

"Well, I'm glad I came along then. It's pitch-black in here, and you could break an ankle just trying to pee. Now hurry up, because Ryan Pope was looking for you, and I have it on good authority that he's going to ask you to be his plus one for the Hamptons this year. It's Gatsby-themed, you know."

I exhale a quiet breath and talk from the stall. "Yeah, I know. I'm not sure if I'll go with Ryan though."

"Oh? Did you already get asked?"

"No, but I might have someone in mind to take." I flush the toilet and cross the space to stand next to her. She meets my gaze in the mirror as I wash my hands.

"Ooh, how very *Sadie Hawkins* of you. If Mother wasn't making me go with my betrothed, I'd follow in your footsteps."

I follow her out of the bathroom, and I make a conscious effort not to look around for my mystery man. The lights are bright enough that I think I could see his pores from here, but either he's extremely good at hiding or he's not in here.

I let Blaire lead me back into the event room and to a group of people. Offering polite responses and fake smiles, I check out of the conversation almost immediately. I let my mind wander idly, never straying to the *events* in the bathroom too much, lest I broadcast my thoughts and flushed cheeks to the shark-infested waters around me.

Finally, after enough time has passed where I can safely leave without offending anyone, I make my exit. I find myself looking over my shoulder every five seconds, slowing my gait as I reach the outer doors.

With one last look around, I don't see my mystery man anywhere. I had hoped that he'd be waiting for me so we could finish what we started. Disappointment sits like sour milk in my stomach, but I grind it down until I don't feel the bitterness it left behind.

I paste on a smile and join the crowded sidewalk, my steps unhurried as I make my way home.

CHAPTER EIGHT

MADDIE

IT'S BEEN six days since the masquerade ball. Five since The Grasshopper. Five long days where I tried my best to get two different men out of my head.

Admittedly, a certain pair of dark brown eyes is a little harder to clear, but I'm doing my best. I live in a city the size of a small country—the likelihood of running into Aries *again* is slim. Even if our schools are affiliated, the masquerade ball is the kickoff to summer, so events for the next three months are more focused on the social side and less on school. Besides, I've never seen him at events before, so he probably was just a friend of a friend or something.

Outside of the bathroom, I never saw him at that luncheon. He'd said he'd find me again, and I'd naïvely thought that meant like right away.

But it's been five long days.

I almost asked Blaire to text her ex, Dale, about him since it seemed like they knew each other, but I thought better of it in the end. I like Blaire, but I swear she runs on gossip and coffee and her daddy's black card.

The last thing I need is someone to get the wrong idea. It's bad enough that douchebags like Charles go around spouting crap about me like I'm some ice queen. They don't even know me, and honestly, Blaire hardly knows the real me.

Sometimes I wonder if I even know the real me. I spend so much of my time being who everyone else wants or needs me to be, it's easy to get lost.

And those guys? They never even tried to get to know me—any iteration. My mom was right about one thing: some men are fragile creatures and always need their egos stroked. She always told me I was too high maintenance for most guys—but definitely that type of guy.

As if I'd want a man who smells like he bathes in cologne, gets trashed at every school event, and delivers the least imaginative pickup lines.

No, I want a man who commands a room with just his presence, who inspires lust with a single touch, who conjures a little fear from an intense look. Okay, so maybe that last one is a little inspired by my novel choice, but can you blame me?

Mostly, I just want someone who sees past the layers of chiffon and lace to *me*.

My sister tells me I read too much romance and I need to be realistic about my expectations of men. Often.

And maybe I do have a specific bar set in mind, but is it so wrong to have expectations?

My lips twist to the side as two very different pairs of eyes come to mind when I think of my expectations.

A month ago, I might've scoffed at the idea of dating two men. But then Lainey casually dropped the little fact that she's interested in three men—at the same time. I still have to get all the dirty details out of her, but I find myself wondering if I'll get a collection of boyfriends of my very own.

I let my mind wander as I walk down the street, skirting groups of kids giggling behind their phones and businesspeople power walking with a coffee in one hand and their phones glued to their ears.

What are the odds that the night I run into Matteo for the first time in years is the same night I finally find someone I'm interested in.

Maybe. I'm maybe interested in him.

I don't know anything about Aries besides our mutual attraction. I'm sure a lot of people can claim the same thing, but that doesn't make them a good couple.

Jesus. I roll my eyes at myself as I cross the street. *Couple? Get a grip, Maddie. You don't even know his name.*

Almost without conscious effort, my mind replays my interactions with him. *Again.*

A wave of warmth rolls over me every time I think about my mystery man in the dark bathroom of The Grasshopper.

I know with certainty that I would've let him fuck me in there. Bent over the small velvet couch or straddling him on the antique chaise, or even against the gaudy wallpapered wall.

I would've done all those things and more had we not been interrupted.

The only thing more surprising than that is that I don't feel bad about it. I don't feel any shame or guilt about wanting to let some guy whose face I wouldn't recognize ravish me at a luncheon party. I have to think that he would've found a way to contact me by now if he was interested in more. It's been nearly a week, and he obviously knows some of the same people as I do.

Unless he can't.

Maybe he's traveling or hurt or tied up in a—

I roll my eyes at my own thoughts—forever dramatic and a hopeless romantic, I guess.

I can't let go of the idea of something so . . . explosive with someone. I don't *want* to let go of that. If anything, I want more—so much more.

The last time I felt anything close to the way I did with Aries was when I was with my ex-boyfriend. And we were just kids then. I can only imagine how it'd be if we were together now—even if only for a night.

And *oh my god!* What am I even thinking about right now—

sleeping with my ex-boyfriend *and* my—I don't even know what to call him!?

I blow out a breath and run my hand over my face to center myself.

Okay.

I'm okay.

I mean, I'm thinking about having sex with two different men at the same time—well, not the *same time* same time, but like during—

Okay. Now I'm definitely picturing that particular fantasy of both of them at the same time. I feel my eyes glass over as I walk down the street. Thankfully, passersby are oblivious to the debauchery playing out in my mind.

Instead of feeling insecure and shameful about my little casual hookup with a stranger, I woke up today and decided to be grateful. I now know what I've been missing on all the dates over the last couple of years.

Spark, flame, passion. There was none of that with any of them.

I blow out a breath, lifting the loose strand of hair from my face. I wonder for the tenth time if I should call Lainey. I could use a good venting session, and since my sister has been MIA for most of the week, I'm running low on options.

I suppose a call to Lainey wouldn't hurt, and maybe she'll have some ideas about what to do to help Mary.

No one knows my sister like I do—our bond is unbreakable. I know she's going through something right now, but I don't know how to help her if she won't talk to me. She's barely home, and when she is, she spends most of her time in her room. I thought she might be stressed about summer classes or something, but she swears she's fine.

I casually people-watch as I walk the last block to my favorite coffee shop. I've always enjoyed observing. There's something so fascinating about watching the way people act when they think no one is looking. Occasionally, Lainey, Mary, and I will sit in Central Park and make up stories about the people we see. Mary's stories always ended in practicalities, Lainey's usually had a twist of forbidden, and mine? Well, they always had a happily ever after.

I credit my dad for that. When I was younger, he narrated the most elaborate fairy tales of knights rescuing princesses and slaying dragons. When I think about all those years I was convinced I was a princess, warm nostalgia covers my soul, and the ache of him lessens a little.

As much as I pretend otherwise, some part of me will always look for those happily-ever-afters, if only to make his absence less painful with happy memories.

A group of a few guys and one girl are a few feet in front of me, heading in the opposite direction. Something about them slows my steps and turns my head. I watch under the cover of my oversized sunglasses as one guy throws his arm around the girl's neck, pulling her to his face and stealing a kiss. They look like the poster children for young love.

What really catches my attention is her other hand—and the fact that a different guy is holding it. Their fingers are laced together, and a glance at his face shows no signs of jealousy or irritation as his friend kisses his girl.

Huh, I guess Lainey isn't the only one who's openly playing with more than one guy.

They round the corner, and I lose sight of them. Honestly, I could've watched them longer just to figure out the inner-workings of that little group. I bet I could come up with some fun stories about them, that's for sure. Hell, and maybe even get really creative with a few ideas and pass them along to Lainey.

I snicker, thinking about that conversation.

Hey, babe. So, I was just people-watching, and I got to thinking. How's it going with your threesome—foursome—fivesome? Because I had a few different ideas you could try out.

She'd kill me, but seeing the look on her face might be worth it.

I see the awning for my favorite coffee shop, and my thoughts trail back to my mystery man. I can't help but wonder if I'll ever see him again, despite his assurance that we aren't done.

Just like most things in my life, I decide to leave it up to fate. And also, I already tried searching for him online, but without a name and a clear picture of his face, it's like a needle in a haystack. I gave up after an hour of scrolling through photos on Dale's page.

But I'm going to pretend I didn't do that, because even thinking about it makes me feel like some sort of stalker.

I adjust my crossbody purse as I walk, ignoring the cabs whipping around the corners and hugging the curbs like they're in the grand prix. I let the soothing sounds of Jeff Buckley's "Hallelujah" fill my ears. I snagged one of Lainey's playlists a few weeks ago, and I can't stop listening to it.

Sweat slides down my neck, and my purse bumps against my hip with every step. Summers in New York can be brutal—it feels kind of like you're in a giant oven—just you and a million other people baking on the sidewalk under the scorching sun. I heard them say it's already shaping up to be a record-breaking heatwave this year—hence the rolling blackouts already.

Opening the door to the coffee shop, I sigh when the huge blast of air conditioning hits me in the face. Taking out my earpods, I beeline toward the counter.

"It's a hot one, huh?" Jerry asks from behind the register. He's not a barista I'm super familiar with, but I've seen him a time or two.

I paste a smile on my face. "Yep. It's already in the nineties. Can I have an iced tea, please?"

He whistles. "Nineties? Yikes. That's much too hot for me. I'm born and raised here, but it's just too hot in the summers."

I nod and keep the smile on my face. Small talk is awful, but small talk while it feels like your skin might be melting off and you're parched is the worst.

"Mm-hmm. So whatever iced tea you have today, I'll take a large, please."

"Ah. You got it. We have blueberry green tea today. Is that okay?" He spins around to get the drink ready.

"Yes. That's perfect, thank you." I reach into my purse and pull out my wallet. I double-checked before I left that it was in here.

It's only then I notice someone leaning against the bakery case with a smirk. My heart skips a beat, and my smile relaxes as it grows.

"Americano?"

CHAPTER NINE

MADDIE

I TILT my head to the side as I give the guy another obvious once-over. I wasn't sure if it was him at first, but now the surprise is wearing off, I recognize those muscles in that royal blue polo shirt.

A wide grin spreads across his too-handsome face. "Ah, so she does see me. I was getting worried that I went invisible somehow."

A flush warms my cheeks as I fight the smile trying to break free. "Does that happen to you a lot?"

He pushes off the bakery case and takes a step toward me. "Do gorgeous women ignore me? No. Not usually."

I bite the inside of my cheek to stop the unexpected laugh. He's too charming for his own good—I can already tell. "No, I mean, do you often go invisible? Are you the next Marvel neighborhood superhero hiding in plain sight and just waiting to fight crime?"

His eyes narrow for a moment, and it's gone before I can put a name to the expression on his face. He moves toward me, leaving his coffee on the counter. He takes a moment to scan my face, and I find myself holding my breath without making a conscious decision to do so.

He nods, the movement small and slow. "Do you ever feel like you're alone in a room full of people? Like you might as well be

79

made of glass for how often people look through you—dismiss you?"

My breath catches and I feel a flash of raw intensity, like he just peeled back my layers effortlessly and saw inside. The only thing that stops me from either snapping on him or dismissing him altogether is the look in his gaze. The vulnerability and pain that's so unexpected it takes me by surprise.

When I don't answer, he leans back and grabs his coffee. "Yeah, me neither," he says before taking a sip.

I feel like I'm on the precipice of something here—and I don't know what it is, or what it means, but I know that I'm at a crossroads. I can feel it in my bones.

My horoscope today said to take chances and push myself outside of my comfort zone. What if—what if *this* is the chance I'm supposed to take? Two dark and broody men flash before my eyes, but I dismiss them. The likelihood of seeing either of them again anytime soon is so slim it's laughable.

Out of the corner of my eye, I see Jerry set my iced tea on the counter without a word and turn around to wash down the espresso machine. So I decide to seize the moment.

I leave my drink on the counter and walk the few steps that puts me just inside his space. He quirks a brow but doesn't say anything. I thrust my hand out, my pink-tipped nails inches from his chest. "I'm Madison."

A slow smile spreads across his face, and I'm hit with his dimples. I swear to god something inside me clenches at the sight. A man shouldn't be so good-looking. It goes against the nature of things—and it makes perfectly reasonable girls do stupid things. I can only hope that won't be the case for me.

Either way, I have a feeling this changes everything.

He clasps my hand in his much larger one, his palm warm and slightly callused. "I'm Leo."

I half expect the door to burst open and small woodland animals to barge in, chirping like I'm in a live-action Disney movie or something. I swear I feel an electric current zip through my body from his touch. If he notices my weird reaction, he's polite enough not to mention it.

"It's nice to meet you, Leo."

We're still shaking hands, though it feels more like just holding hands by this point. Neither one of us pulls away, and I bite the inside of my cheek to hold in the cheesy grin that's trying to break free.

"Believe me, Madison, the pleasure's all mine." A smile spreads across his face, flashing those dimples again. Jesus, those things are lethal. "You busy now? Got someplace to be?"

"I'm free now." My words come out rushed and a little too eager. And I'm sure I'll be reliving this embarrassment for the next two weeks, but for now, I don't let it affect me.

"Perfect. Let's sit down and enjoy our coffee together."

We each snag our drinks off the counter, and with his hand still holding mine, he pulls me toward one of the small bistro-style tables at the front of the coffee shop. It's nestled in the corner of the seating area, next to a small collection of watercolor art on the wall.

He pulls out my chair and waits for me to sit down before he steps around the table and sits down across from me.

"Aren't you quite the gentleman?" I tease with a quirk of my brow.

He shrugs a shoulder and takes a sip of his coffee. "I have many hidden talents."

The words are said casually enough, but there must be something in the air, because all I can think about is what other *talents* he has. And if I'll get to experience them.

I sip my iced tea to give me something to do and to cool myself down a little bit.

Leo leans back in his chair, never taking his eyes off of me. "So, Madison, how long have you lived in the big apple?"

"Most of my life. What about you?"

"Well, I just finished school outside the city, so I'm back home now."

I eye him over my cup, scanning his features and his clothes. "Oh really? How old are you, anyway?"

He smirks and tips his chin back. "What do you think?"

I huff and playfully roll my eyes. "I'm terrible with ages. Everyone looks between fifteen and fifty to me."

He laughs, the sound warm and inviting. I notice the laugh lines around his eyes, and something warm unfurls inside my chest. He looks like a man who likes to laugh.

And I think that's exactly the type of man I need right now. Forget about those dark, mysterious men who've been plaguing my thoughts.

"I just graduated from St. Bartholomew's Academy," he says with a shrug.

"Wow. I thought St. Rita's was tough, then I heard about what your classes are like at St. Bart's, and it really put it into perspective."

"Ah, so you're a St. Rita's girl, yeah? That explains it." He snaps his fingers with a smile teasing the corners of his mouth.

I arch a brow. "Explains what?"

He shakes his head. "Nah, it's nothing. Just a rumor that the girls from St. Rita's are groomed to be ball-busting bitches."

I sputter a laugh, choking on the tea I just took a sip of. I wave off his look of concern. "I'm fine. You just took me by surprise is all. By that logic, you must be a playboy asshole like so many girls claim St. Bart's boys are?"

He presses a palm to his chest. "You wound me, Madison. I thought we were friends?"

"Friends? We just met," I say with a flutter of my lashes.

His smile slips off his face, but the warmth stays in his gaze. "Sometimes you just know these things, yeah? We're going to be fast friends, you and I. Can't you feel it?"

My breath stalls in my lungs for a moment. Because even though I'm sure he's just flirting and he probably uses this line on every girl, it's really working on me.

"I bet you use that line on all the girls." Despite my racing heart, I laugh it off. I'd be lying if I said I didn't feel a connection, but I also felt one with the guy at the masquerade ball. And let's not forget Matteo. I wonder if I'll ever stop feeling connected to my ex.

So maybe my instincts aren't that reliable.

Maybe I'm just lonely.

No, no that doesn't feel right either. I scan his face, looking for the hidden deception or a reason for the virtually instant connection.

His gaze remains steady on mine. "Nah. It's not a line, I can promise you that. You don't know me well enough to trust my word yet, but you will."

Like his words hold the power of premonition, thunder cracks through the air. I jump about a foot off my chair when a lightning bolt streaks across the sky.

"See? Even the gods agree with me." He flashes me a smile that's somehow sincere and teasing.

"The gods?"

"The gods, fate, the universe, whatever you want to call it."

I shake my head a little with a small smile. "I know not everyone believes in it, but I like to follow my horoscope. It's been right more often than not."

My cheeks warm with embarrassment, and I'm mentally face-palming. Here I am spouting off about the very same thing most people make fun of me for. Sure, maybe not to my face, but I see the girls at school roll their eyes anytime I bring it up. I'm not embarrassed that I like following the stars, but I don't usually blurt it out so quickly after meeting someone.

There's something sort of comfortable about Leo—almost as if I've known him for years, not hours.

"Hey, where'd you go?" His voice is low, the deep timbre warming me up from the inside.

I meet his gaze. "Hmm? Oh, nowhere. Just thinking that I should get going, so I don't get stuck in the rain."

I look out the window next to me and see the dark thunder-clouds eclipsing the sun, promising a good downpour soon. Because that's what we need—more humidity in this oven.

He nods and takes a drink of his coffee before setting it back on the table. "I want to see you again, Madison."

Without being overconfident, I've been asked out countless times before, and I turn down most of them. Hell, if he would've asked me a month ago, I might've said no.

But here and now?

I flick my gaze over him, letting my smile play at the corners of my mouth. "I'd like that, Leo."

A wide smile spreads across his face, his dimples winking at me. "Perfect. Tonight then."

A laugh bubbles up. I swear I have a mini Blaire and a mini Lainey on either shoulder, each telling me something different. Mini Blaire wants to make him work for it harder, and mini Lainey encourages me to just say yes and have fun. I settle for something in between the two.

"I can't tonight. But I'm free tomorrow."

He nods a few times, his eyes sparkling. "I'll pick you up at seven and take you to one of my favorite restaurants."

I bite the side of my lip in hesitation. The stories from Mary's favorite true crime documentaries flash in front of my face. "Which restaurant? I'll meet you there."

He doesn't skip a beat, and his smile stays firmly on his face. "Louisa's."

"I know where that is." I nod a few times and release the hold I had on my lip.

"Perfect. Here, let me give you my number just in case you need it." He slides his hand across the table, palm up, and wiggles his fingers.

I unlock my phone, open a new text message, and place it in his hand. He hands my phone back when he's finished, letting his fingers linger on my hand longer than necessary. I try to ignore the way that simple gesture sends sparks up my arm.

Pushing back from the table, I stand up and gather my things. He does the same and we leave the coffee shop next to one another, our arms barely brushing.

He pauses at the crosswalk. "Until tomorrow, Madison."

My chest feels light, excitement buzzing in my veins. He links our pinkies for a brief moment before turning and walking down the block backward.

"Tomorrow."

I watch him with a secret smile on my face until the crosswalk sign flashes, and I cross the street with a wiggle of my fingers in his direction.

I hum to myself the whole way home with a noticeable pep in my step.

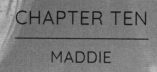

CHAPTER TEN

MADDIE

I RUN my palms down my hair, taking my time to apply the smoothing oil to keep my barrel waves intact and flyaway-free. My blue eyes look almost frosty lined in black, with a subtle wing extending past my eyelashes. I kept the rest of my makeup light and natural, but I can't resist a good eyeliner wing.

Florence + The Machine plays quietly from the portable speaker on my dresser across my room. I exhale a breath in a weak attempt to calm the stirring butterflies. I don't know why I'm so nervous to meet Leo, but I can't help the Monarchs that keep circling every time I think about it.

I thought if I gave myself plenty of time to get ready it would help, and I guess it has a little. I took a long shower with one of my favorite shower bombs—mint and lemon—and moisturized absolutely everything with my mom's favorite cream. She calls it *youth in a bottle*, and I'm sure it's crazy expensive. Most everything Mom loves is.

But I guess I started too early, because now I still have forty-five minutes before I have to leave, and I'm pretty much ready. I only need to slip on my favorite pair of wedge sandals, and then I'm ready to go.

I kind of thought I'd see Mary by now. I heard her creep out of our apartment early this morning. She left a note in the kitchen saying she was studying in the library all day and wouldn't be home until late tonight.

Apparently, she has some new study group. And while that's not usually cause for concern—Mary's the *smart one* after all—I know for a fact she's not taking any classes. The summer session doesn't start for another few weeks.

I don't know why she won't just tell me she's been hanging out with someone. I'm happy that she's dating. She deserves happiness and love and all those gooey feelings that go along with it.

I want her to be happy—I always have. She's been so busy making herself different from me that she doesn't realize the distance it puts between us.

I sigh, shoving the twinge of sadness down deep and apply another coat of mascara to my dark lashes. I guess I'll just leave Mary a note since that's what we've been reduced to lately. Six words on a Post-It note. I can't wait for Lainey to get back home. She's always been the glue that holds us together.

Satisfied with my lashes, I grab my phone to check the time and send a quick text to Mary. I'm not sure when she's coming home, and this way, she'll at least know where I'll be tonight in case she doesn't see the note on the counter. Who knows, maybe the news that I have a date will open her up a little.

I expel a breath.

Thirty minutes until I have to leave. My thumb hovers over Lainey's name in my text messages. I don't want to bug her, but I already miss her. It hasn't even been that long since I've seen her, and we just video chatted the other day.

With a shrug of my shoulder, I press on her smiling face and listen as ringing fills the air in my room. On the fifth ring, she picks up.

My cousin's beautiful face fills the screen. "Maddie!"

A smile spreads across my face as happiness simmers underneath my skin. I let my gaze trail her face just like I've done every time I've seen or spoken to her. She looks good for a girl who was just kidnapped and held in a random cabin in the woods. "Hey, Lainey. How are you? Still doing okay?"

She cocks her head to the side, a smile teasing the corner of her mouth. "You mean since yesterday when you called me?"

"I worry about you." My voice is quiet, but she hears the worry just fine.

Her face softens to a more serious expression. "I'm fine, Maddie —well. I will be. Promise."

I nod a couple times, the movement slow. It's the same thing she told me the other day and the time before that, but I can't stop the churning in my gut. It's a poisonous combination of guilt and worry —I should've been looking out for her. It's my role in our family to look out for everyone.

She brings the phone closer to her face, the screen filling with her dark-brown eyes. "Hey. I mean it. I'm okay. They're taking good care of me, and I even sweet-talked them into teaching me a few things."

I raise a brow. "Yeah? And just *how* good of care are they taking?" Her cheeks flush, and my grin grows. "That good, huh?"

She glances to the side before looking back at me with a shrug and a small smile. "You know I don't kiss and tell."

"Ah-ha! So there was some kissing. Thank god. Because honestly, I love you, girl, but if you weren't taking advantage of your situation at least a little bit, I was going to have to smack some sense into you."

She waves her hand in the air as if to shoo my words away. "Enough about me. Where are you headed? You're awfully fancy for dinner with your sister."

I play demure with a hand to my chest and flutter my eyelashes at her. "Oh, this ol' thing?"

We both know it's not old at all. It's one of the few things I picked up when my mom skirted Mary and me to Europe a few weeks ago with her newest boyfriend. A cream-colored minidress that hits about mid-thigh, it's form-fitting from the waist down, but the top is flowy. The neckline is a loose-laying deep vee with soft, big ruffles cascading from my shoulders to my belly button, creating a short-sleeve effect.

It's a bold-cut softened by the ruffles and the cream color, and with my bright-red hair in soft waves, it's an eye-stopping look.

Perfect for a date. And I know by the sparkle in Lainey's eye, she's thinking the same thing.

"I'll let you know if it goes anywhere, okay? But I'll text you my location in an hour or so, okay? Because you know—"

"Serial killers," we say at the same time before we both pause and then giggle.

"Oh! Before I forget, I'll be back in town soon. Wanna grab lunch at Blue Lotus? I'm dying for their lunch special."

"Of course! I miss you! I feel like I won't be able to stop worrying about you until I see you in person, ya know?"

"I know," she says with a nod. "I'll be there Friday. Tell Mary for me?"

The notification alert I set up to let me know what time I have to leave for my date goes off. I don't know why I even put it in my calendar like I'd forget or something, but something about the action just soothed my nerves. "Hey, I gotta go, babe. But I'll tell her. And I'll see you on Friday!"

"Yeah, me too! Have fun!"

I waggle my eyebrows at her. "You too. Talk soon!"

I end the call and slip my phone into my small white leather crossbody purse. I grab my lip gloss and swipe another coat on before tucking it into my purse. After slipping on my favorite pair of tan wedge sandals, I'm pulling up my car ride app and checking the status of the car I ordered. I don't mind taking public transportation, but I don't want to arrive looking like I just stepped out of hot yoga either. And walking all over the city in this heat practically guarantees I'll arrive no less than drenched.

I lock our door as I leave the suite, waving at a few friends in the hall who stay year-round like we do.

Throughout the years, we really got to know the girls whose parents shipped them off here year-round. Summers in the city are brutal, and no one stays here the whole time unless they have to.

There are even fewer girls here now though, since a lot of them opted to go to a different college—or no college at all if your parents already signed your marriage contract like Blaire's did.

My ride is two minutes away, so I leave the cool confines of the front foyer, push open the heavy door, and walk into the thick night air. Dusk turns the sky a hazy blue, and the humidity feels palpable, instantly sinking onto my skin and weighing me down.

With my gaze glued to my phone, I shuffle to the side of the door toward my favorite cherry blossom tree as I watch the dot move closer to my dorm building on the screen.

I sidestep the broken sidewalk square in front of my building, the neon green spray paint a bright beacon of caution. A dog barks, the sound deep and loud and nearby, startling me. I flinch and reflexively turn toward the noise. The toe of my wedge sandal catches on the jagged edge of broken concrete, and I lose my balance.

My arms windmill in that instinctual move everyone does, but I don't actually think helps, and I know I'm going down.

Right into Miss June's rosebushes.

I cringe, a curse falling from my lips as gravity takes over.

But something halts my downward motion—or should I say someone—and I collide with something hard. Before I even lift my head, an apology is on my lips. "Oh my god, I'm so sorry . . ." The word stalls as it leaves my mouth, floating in the air between us before it sinks to the dirty concrete sidewalk. "Matteo."

Surprise tightens my muscles, and it takes me a moment to realize that he's gripping my shoulders. His long, tattooed fingers curl underneath the few layers of chiffon to touch my skin.

My surprise fades as suspicion clouds over. Cocking my head to the side, I step back to right myself, but he doesn't release his hold on me, so it ends up being the smallest step ever.

"I went years without seeing you in a city this size, and all of a sudden, I run into you twice in as many weeks?"

I watch in fascination as his hazel eyes darken to a deep green. I haven't had the chance to look at him—really see him—in years.

Not since we broke up. And since he doesn't do social media, I never lurked on his profile like my friends do post-breakup.

He's still one of the most gorgeous men I've ever laid eyes on.

His lip twitches in the smallest motion, which might as well be a belly laugh for all the emotion he's showing. "I was in the neighborhood."

His voice is just as deep as I remember it. The tenor sends a shiver of arousal over me. And I'm not too proud to admit that I give in for a single second. I let myself revel in the feel of his touch against my skin. In another life, I might've been getting ready for him tonight.

But I'm not.

And the reminder of my waiting date at Louisa's is enough to break the spell. I slough the attraction off and work double-time to adopt an unaffected demeanor.

I raise a brow at his flimsy admission. "Really? Do you live around here now?"

He stares at me for a moment, his thumbs moving back and forth over the sensitive skin on my upper arms in small strokes. Who knew that area was so damn sensitive, anyway?

"Maybe I was visiting a friend."

It's not a question and it doesn't answer mine, but it causes me to pause nonetheless. His thumbs pause their movement, and I wonder if he's remembering the same moment in time as me. The one where he told me that he doesn't have a lot of friends—real friends. The kind that rescue you from a terrible date or pick you up when you've had too much to drink or offer their shoulder to cry on when some asshole breaks your heart.

I hold his gaze as sadness settles over me like a lightweight blanket. We could've been something, him and I, if only we met at a different time. Regret feels sluggish in my veins, and I can't believe I'm going to say this, but I hope he was visiting a friend here. It means he has someone in his life he can count on.

I nod a few times and look to the side. "Good. Friends are good."

I look back at him and see his gaze has shifted. Gone is the playful curiosity and in its place is an intensity I haven't seen in years.

Matteo stares at me, his expression uncharacteristically serious.

"Is everything alright?" I bite my lip to keep the rest of the words inside my mouth. My mother was on the warpath the other day and made me a to-do list of all the things she thinks I need improvement on. And even though I know it's ridiculous, I can't help the doubt creeping in.

Tall, handsome, and charming. A guy like Matteo has girls panting after him, and yet, here he is. With me.

He takes a step toward me and slides his hands along my neck and into my hair. With gentle pressure, he tilts my head back and brushes his lips across mine with excruciatingly soft and slow kisses. I swear it feels like my soul sighs with the contact.

My lashes flutter closed without conscious thought.

"I can't go another moment without telling you something," he murmurs against my lips.

My eyes pop open as a whooshing sound fills my ears as my heart speeds up. Oh no, this is it. He's going to end things, now, isn't he? I try to step back, pull away from him, but he doesn't let me get very far.

"I love you, Maddie. I love you, and I want to tell the whole world, but I thought I should tell you first before I start shouting it at random strangers."

His lips twist to the side and he flashes me that smirk that gets him in trouble. My fingers dig into his arm at his admission, and my heart hitches for another reason.

"I thought you were going to break up with me," I say around a smile. We're too close, so I can't see his entire expression, but I like the feeling of his lips on mine with each syllable too much to move.

He tilts his head to the side. "Did you not hear me tell you I love you?"

"I did. And I love you too."

And it's true. I do love him, more than I realized I could love someone. I push onto my toes and press our lips together. It's all the encouragement he needs, and he quickly takes control of the kiss.

We get lost in one another in the middle of the sidewalk, expressing our newly declared love for one another with each swipe of our tongues and brush of our lips. My heart soars with happiness, and we don't break for air until someone bumps into me.

"I have to go." I step back, and this time, he lets me go without a word. In three steps, I'm on the sidewalk, a healthy distance between us.

The fates must be smiling down on me today, because in the next second, my Uber pulls up. I open the rear passenger door, but before I slide inside, I look over my shoulder at the first man I ever loved. He radiates power from ten feet away, and if I'm not careful, he'll pull me into his orbit before I can blink. I don't have the guise of too much champagne like I did at the masquerade, either.

"Take care, Matteo."

He slides his hands in his pockets, his biceps bulging against the tight confines of his suit jacket, and nods at me with a small wrinkle in his brow.

CHAPTER ELEVEN

MATTEO

I DON'T HAVE to turn around to know Dante's standing next to me, watching her move further away. The man's a fucking ninja. I swear he could sneak into the most heavily guarded places undetected. He was a thief in another life, I'd bet my savings on it.

I'm not a fucking idiot, so I know he's staring at her with the same longing in his gaze. But he doesn't have the same amount of drive and determination as me, not when it comes to her.

And he's too fucking loyal ever to go for her. I'd bet my life on it.

He's hellbent on me letting her go—*really* letting her go. But no matter how many times I tell him no, he doesn't understand. I know he thinks I'm a selfish prick for still having her followed and looked after, and it's true, I am.

I make no apologies for that.

But more importantly, I fucking can't let her go. I'm aware of the driving force behind my actions.

See, Dante? He'd let her go under the guise of keeping her safe from our enemies—to put a smile on her face and quietly suffer while she goes out with these entitled rich dicks who have more money than sense.

But me? I'll douse every enemy in gasoline, light the match with a spring in my fucking step, and watch 'em burn with a smile on my face. Until the enemy is wiped off the face of the Earth.

Then she can come back to me. Where she fucking belongs.

I see him open his mouth out of the corner of my eye. Before he utters a single syllable, I slice a glare at him. "Don't even fucking say it."

His jaw hardens and he stares forward. "If I don't even have to say it for you to know what I'm talking about, then don't you think that's the right thing to do?"

I shake my head a few times. "You don't get it, man. But one day, one day you're going to find the woman who changes everything."

I used to think it was an advantage to have tasted her, but now I realize I was a fool. Dante's in a much better position because he doesn't know what he's missing. He doesn't realize that no matter how exquisite he thinks she is, she's a hundred times more—a *million* times more.

She's an uncut gem, raw and nestled into her cozy life in the big city, unaware of the dangers lurking around every corner. And being with me would triple—*quadruple*—the dangers around her.

She's priceless to me.

And you don't just let go of that.

He thinks I've been working all these years to recreate what the five families should be out of some altruistic idea, and maybe it started that way. But I knew the first time my dad threatened to give her to Gideon Warren. The self-proclaimed king of the East Coast pipeline.

That was the last straw for me.

Fuck him, and fuck all the other sick fucks who think it's okay to sell kids to pedophiles.

Just thinking about that fateful night has my blood boiling in my veins.

The sound of flesh hitting flesh cracks through the air, reverberating in my skull as my head rings. I wrench my neck back to look at the piece of shit who bears my last name with contempt screaming in my gaze and a cruel smile on my face.

Blood trickles down my nose, but I don't bother to wipe it away. The action only fuels his hate, and I'm just about fucking done with this shit.

My dad stands before me in a false pillar of patriarchal confidence. He knows the tides are starting to change. More soldiers and capos side with me every day, but he's clinging to the old ways by the skin of his teeth—him and a few of my uncles.

He couldn't make shit easy, no, not the proud Angelo Rossi, he'd detonate us from within before he'd ever give up control willingly.

And how fucking embarrassing it must be that his nineteen-year-old son won the favor of half the family so quickly. It's tradition to pass the title down to the first-born son, but it doesn't happen so soon. What the fuck did he expect when I became a made man at eighteen?

Blood trickles into my mouth, no doubt shading my teeth crimson, and a real smile stretches across my face. I stare my father in the face and take a single step forward. He's not fast enough—or he's too drunk—to hide the flinch, and I'm perversely satisfied.

"I've been waiting a long time for this, father." The word tastes like treachery in my mouth. A mockery of the foundation of a family and the role a father should take.

I watch in fascination as he attempts to bolster his courage. A single light bulb illuminates the space we're in, a circle of dim light in the dank basement of the Praying Mantis strip club he likes to frequent.

"You don't have the guts, boy. What happens between your mother and I is none of your business, so keep out of it. So I'll give you this one pass, but the next one's going to cost you." He sneers at me, attempting to regain control of the situation.

I laugh, the noise caustic and cruel. He thinks this is because he's been smacking Ma around for years? Cute. She's had several opportunities to leave— whole new lives already in place for her, and yet, she stays. And it sure as shit isn't for her kids.

Without another word, I take the three steps and cock my fist back, letting it fly across his face. My knuckles split on his jaw, and blood arcs across the room from his mouth. The joy that settles into my heart at seeing him bleed by my hand is a worry for another day.

Before he can react, I hit him again. And again. And again. He falls to the floor, and I stand over him with one fist gripping his shirt to hold him up. I exer-

cise my years of pent up rage on his face, and it's so goddamn cathartic that I know I've awoken something inside of me that I don't think I can shove back into its box.

I don't stop until I feel hands on my shoulders pulling me back. My brother's voice murmurs in my ear, and the familiar cadence snaps me out of my fury.

I uncurl my fingers, letting the material fall from my hand and my father's unconscious body thump to the floor. I hold my hands up and roll my shoulders back. "I'm done. I'm done, man."

"He's going to fucking kill you, man. You can't go after the boss like that. Uncle Paulie is going to drop you off the Whispering Eye in the middle of the Atlantic."

My brother sounds scared, but I don't share the sentiment. If anything, this was exactly the push I needed to realize that I've been going about it all wrong.

My whole life has been about family—and the families. And all I ever wanted was out.

As the oldest son to the boss of the Rossi family, my destiny was sealed long before I took my first breath. And for nineteen long years, I've done everything I could to get out. But that was never my fate.

"Nah. That was a father-son dispute. Had nothing to do with the families. Paulie'll see it my way." I turn and look at my brother, the whites of his wide eyes bright in the dank basement. "They're about to see a lot of things my way, brother."

It's time to stop fighting the tide. It's time to become the fucking tide. I'm going to bring down a tsunami unlike anything they've ever seen.

And it'll be the last thing they ever see.

"Matteo?" Dante's voice penetrates my memory, jolting me back to the present. My hands feel clammy, and I ignore the urge to wipe them off.

"What?" The word comes out harsher than I intended, but I just watched my girl jump into a car dressed to impress. And I'm the guy standing on the curb in the eighty-degree waning sunlight like an asshole.

"I said that Russel called. He's open to a meeting tonight."

I feel Dante's gaze on the side of my face, but I keep my focus on the direction Maddie's car drove off in.

"Good. Tell him I'll meet him in three hours," I say as I start walking down the block.

"Where?"

"Louisa's. I'll call my aunt ahead of time and make sure she saves us a table."

"Are you sure that's the best move? Remember what happened to Mama Rosa's?"

He's right to be worried. It's a risk to take another meeting at one of my family's places of business. But the problem is that I don't trust anyone or anywhere else. At least at my family's places, I know that the recording devices are for our benefit not our downfall.

He keeps pace with me, the two of us taking up a lot of space on the sidewalk. "Yeah. Set it up and meet me there. I have a few things I need to take care of first."

"Got it. I'll see you then." He turns at the corner, but I don't bother watching where he's headed. My mind is stuck on something else—one very alluring redhead.

CHAPTER TWELVE

MADDIE

IT TAKES some effort to banish the hazel eyes from my mind, but after thirty minutes or so, I feel myself finally relaxing. Seeing him again is messing with my mind, and I'll be damned if I let it completely ruin the first enjoyable date I've been on in years.

We're seated in the back corner booth at Louisa's. It's a cozy Italian restaurant with a new take on traditional dishes. I've never eaten here before, but I have a feeling it's going to become a favorite of mine before the night is through.

The plush leather cushions stick to my skin as I adjust my legs, crossing one over the other at my ankles. No matter how much air conditioning they pump through the vents, every time someone opens the door to enter or leave, a billow of humidity fills the room.

Ornate sconces set the mood with pools of soft yellow light against the exposed brick walls. Rows of wine racks cover the back wall of the restaurant, the rich mahogany of the wood creating a warmth in the restaurant.

Modern touches like mini fairy lights curl around a slimline wrought-iron chandelier over a few different tables, and cream-colored distressed tapestries hang on a few walls.

I like it here. It feels welcoming and inviting, like I'd spend an entire night here just drinking and eating and enjoying my company.

I sip my ice water, looking out at the different couples seated around the restaurant before bringing my gaze back to Leo.

"Ah, there she is," he murmurs with a smile playing around his lips.

I cock my head to the side as I set my water down. I thought I was doing a good job of covering up my preoccupation. A light flush warms my cheekbones at the idea that I wasn't as stealthy as I thought.

It's not fair to him, and I genuinely enjoyed his company at the coffee shop, enough that I said yes to this date—not that he realizes how rare that is.

I clear my throat. "I'm sorry I was a little distracted."

"Everything okay?" Concern lines his face and lowers his brows.

"Yes. It was nothing." The words feel like a lie on my tongue. I don't think Matteo could ever be nothing—not in this life or any other.

He nods a few times without pressing.

Our server stands at the end of the table to collect our dishes. "And how was everything?"

"Delicious, thank you." I slide my napkin off my lap and fold it, setting it on the table next to my glass. I ordered a grilled chicken salad. I thought about splurging and ordering the oven-fired margherita pizza, but then I heard my mother's voice in my head drilling archaic dating tips. No matter how much I tried to drown her out, in the end, I opted for a safe bet—her go-to, something light.

"Excellent. Any dessert tonight?" our server, Marcus, asks as he stacks our dishes along his forearm with practiced ease.

It's on the tip of my tongue to decline when Leo beats me to it. "We'll have the crème brûlée. Two spoons. Thanks."

"Of course, I'll bring that right out." Marcus leaves the table and I stare at Leo with a raised brow.

"Crème brûlée? How do you know I'm not vegan or allergic to berries or something?"

He sits back in the booth, a smug smile playing around the corners of his mouth. "You ordered a salad with strawberries and feta—you're not allergic or against either of those things."

He rubs the back of his neck, the movement straining the material of his shirt. The color blue is so pale, it's nearly white, and it does everything for his sun-kissed complexion and green eyes. It's hard to tell, but it almost looks like a light blush colors the tops of his cheekbones.

"I need to confess something."

Dread coils low in my gut and I sit back against the booth, the cool material sticking to my skin instantly. My heart pounds, and I surreptitiously glance around, looking for someone to clue me in. I knew this—*he*—was too good to be true. This was all just some prank or something.

"Okay."

"My aunt and uncle own Louisa's." He expels a breath when I don't react right away. I'm too busy letting the relief course through me.

"And?" Am I missing something?

He drops his hand to the table. "And that's it. My aunt and uncle own this place and a few others. And I didn't tell you at first because I didn't want you to think I was only bringing you here because of the free food."

I let my smile grow. "You had me scared for a moment. I thought you were about to confess you have a wife and kid at home or something. Your aunt and uncle owning this restaurant isn't that big of a deal."

"Me, married with a kid? Babe, how old do you think I am?" He smiles at me, and those dang dimples wound me they're so potent.

I reach for my glass with a chuckle. "I don't know. That's just where my mind went when you said you had to confess something."

"Don't phrase it that way again. Noted," he murmurs. He finishes his drink in one swallow and sets it down on the table. "Well, Louisa's makes some of the best crème brûlée in the city. Just don't tell my aunt Rosalie that." His eyes twinkle with mischief.

"You have another aunt who owns a restaurant too?" Though

we've chatted, we didn't really dive deep into any family stuff. It's been mostly basic get-to-know-you questions. Typical first date stuff. Or is this our second date? Does the coffee shop count? I make a mental note to ask Lainey when I see her next.

"She runs a bakery that sells to other businesses in the city. But not here."

"That sounds awesome. I bet your family holidays are full of food. And what about your parents? Are they restauranteurs or chefs too?"

The skin around his eyes tightens for a moment before he reaches for his glass, sipping his cocktail. I was surprised they didn't even blink when he ordered a whiskey, but knowing that his aunt and uncle own the place, it makes sense that they didn't object.

"Nah, my dad's a businessman, and my mom does a lot of charity work. What about you? What do your parents do?"

"My dad died when I was younger. Military. And my mom splits her time between the city and wherever her newest boyfriend wants to visit. Usually somewhere in Europe." The words come out quick, I don't offer him the chance for any comment. Embarrassment feels itchy along my skin, and my nerves creep up my throat, threatening to strangle any more words from spewing all over the table.

Either the fates are smiling down on me or he picks up on my social cues, because he doesn't ask me to elaborate. And I'm grateful for it.

"Siblings?"

"Yeah, I have a twin sister—and a cousin who's like a sister."

"What a coincidence. Twins run in my family too," he says with a smirk.

"We'd for sure have twins then—" I cut myself off as the words register in my brain and disbelief etches across my face. "Oh my god. I didn't mean it like that. I—uh—just genetically speaking, the probability of us having twins if we—" I snap my mouth closed, cutting off the rest of my embarrassing ramble. My face feels like it's on fire, and I curse my fair complexion for broadcasting my embarrassment to everyone within a twenty-foot radius.

His laugh pulls me from my spiraling thoughts. "It's fine. I know what you mean. And before you even think it, no, you didn't scare me off with your talk of genetic probabilities. I like it."

Some of my chagrin cools as a different kind of warmth fills me.

I'm saved further when our server places a saucer and ramekin of crème brûlée down between the two of us, two spoons resting on the saucer beneath. "Enjoy and please let me know if you need anything."

We murmur our thanks before we each pick up a spoon.

"You do the honors." His voice is low, the smooth tenor rolling over me.

I gently tap the rounded part of my spoon on the torched caramel top, cracking it perfectly to let the baked custard peek out and grabbing a spoonful.

A moan slips from my lips as the decadent taste hits my taste-buds. I let Leo take a bite before I dive in for my second spoonful.

"You're right. This is delicious." I groan around another bite of the rich dessert. My eyes flash open when I hear a grunt. My eyes widen when I realize I'd closed them. "Sorry. I can get carried away when it comes to desserts."

"Remind me to take you to my Aunt Carm's house. She's an amazing pastry chef."

"You must have a big family," I murmur around another bite.

"You have no idea." The words are delivered in an even tone, but I swear I see a cloud of something dark flash across his gaze for a moment. When I blink, it's gone, and he flashes those dangerous dimples at me.

We finish the rest of the dessert in a comfortable silence, and I can't deny the fluttering butterflies swirling around every time I meet his gaze.

He's charming and funny, and I can't wait to tell my sister and Lainey about him. Excitement thrums in my veins in anticipation of the end of the night. He looks like the type of guy who'll go in for the kill at the end of a date—not in a creepy way, but like back me up against a wall and kiss the daylights out of me way.

After we're done eating, he waves to a few employees as we make our way outside. Night has fallen, but the temperature stayed.

The hot air smothers my hair, instantly frizzing out some of my waves.

Adjusting the strap of my crossbody purse, I look at my date over my shoulder. "I had a lovely time tonight."

In a move too smooth and yet still charming, he slides his palm against mine, links our fingers together, and brings my hand up to his lips. His breath warms the back of my hand as he places a chaste kiss there.

"Let me walk you to your car."

My breath hitches like I'm in some historical romance, and that's the way to express desire. I never realized how erogenous the back of my hand could be.

"I ordered a car. It should be here in a few moments." My voice is thin, my heart thundering loud in my ears.

He smiles against my hand, flashing those lethal dimples at me. Suddenly, I understand why those women always carried around those paper fans. If I had one right now, I'd be fanning the thing at my face like I'm gunning for a gold medal.

He lowers my hand but doesn't let go, and I find myself following along with wherever he's tugging me. We walk a few feet away from the restaurant and over to a big weeping willow tree.

It's not uncommon to have trees on the sidewalk in this part of the city, but ones this size are. Weeping willows have always been my favorite. My father used to set up picnics underneath one at my grandparents' house and tell me the stories of the stars.

We duck under the long branches, the leaves a few feet off the ground, providing enough cover for the illusion of privacy.

"What are we doing in here?"

"I wanted to show you something," he says as he tugs me toward the trunk of the tree. "Here." He points to something carved in the bark.

Unlinking our fingers, I lean in closer to take a look and trace the letters with the pad of my finger. The indents feel smooth, aged against the rough bark.

Leonardo was here.

"I know, it's not the most original." His voice is close enough to stir the hair by my ear, causing a shiver to skate down my spine.

I tilt my head to look over my shoulder at him, bringing our lips closer than I anticipated. The air feels electric, as if static is charging the space between our mouths, gearing up for the moment they collide.

I flick my gaze between his eyes and his lips, involuntarily wetting mine.

"I didn't realize your name was Leonardo." My words are whispered into the cocooned space. It's a half-assed attempt at breaking the tension, and it backfires.

"I like the way my name rolls off your lips." He cocks his head to the side, and his lips graze mine ever so lightly with his words.

My breath hitches at the contact, and sharp needles of anticipation prick at my nerves. I bite my lip to stop myself from bridging the gap between us and ravaging his lips like some sort of kiss-starved wanton woman.

The truth is I had another man's hands down my pants a week ago, and here I am, literally panting after someone else.

Rancid tentacles of shame flex, their tips brushing against my lusty haze, threatening to douse it entirely.

But then Leo whispers against my lips, "Say it again."

And just like that, the uncertainty vanishes, leaving only Leo's hypnotic green eyes and his kissable lips.

Shifting my head, I breathe his name on an exhale, "Leonardo."

He seals his lips against mine on a groan, and my lashes flutter closed. One firm press before his tongue flicks against the seam of my lips. I answer his request with pleasure, opening my mouth and turning around in the same instant.

My back hits the tree trunk, the bark digging into my skin. But all I can focus on is the way Leo feels against me. He steps into me, placing his hands on either side of my head against the tree.

It's a dominant move, one that has my thighs clenching with anticipation. I fist my hands, my fingernails biting into my palms to stop myself from grabbing onto his shirt and pulling him against me.

I don't know what the hell is going on with me. It's like Mercury went into retrograde, and instead of messing up my communication skills, it heightens my lust.

Only our lips touch, fused together by passion. And yet, it feels like every nerve ending is alight with expectation, hope.

Vibrating and persistent beeping penetrates the moment, and I pull my head back. I'm slow to open my eyes, savoring the moment. His darkened green gaze holds mine, an intensity I haven't seen from him yet carved into his features.

"Your purse is ringing." His voice sounds like gravel and grit and all those delicious things that have my core tingling.

Reaching into my purse with one hand, never taking my eyes off him, I pull out my phone. I spare it a quick glance.

"My car is here."

"I want to see you again."

Mirth warms my chest at his directness. I do like a man who knows what he wants. My lips twist to the side. "I'd like that."

He scans my face for a moment. I'm not sure what he's looking for, but he must find it. He steps back, trailing his hand down my arm to link our hands again. With a gentle tug, he leads me out from underneath the tree and over to where a running car is double-parked.

We weave between the parked cars, and he gets to the car first. Opening the door with his hand still around mine, he steps to the side so I can get in.

Before I slide into the car, he brings our linked hands together and places another kiss against the back of my hand, right by my knuckles. If he keeps that up, I'm going to start associating kisses there with him.

"Until next time."

I push onto my tiptoes and brush my mouth across his. "Next time."

He lets me go, and I scoot into the car. We merge into traffic, but I can't take my eyes off of him. Not yet.

Bringing my fingertips to my mouth, I press against the swollen skin with a smile.

Now that's a memorable first kiss.

CHAPTER THIRTEEN

MADDIE

I SLIP my phone into the pocket of my light-wash jean shorts, a smile on my face as I let the warmth of Leo's text messages sink into my soul. We've been out twice more in the last week, and it's been amazing—he's amazing. I don't think I could keep the giddy smile off my face if I tried—and I haven't tried.

I haven't seen Aries—my mystery man—at all, and I take it as a sign from fate. Maybe my dreams of several boyfriends will remain a fantasy. The fact is that he probably could've found me by now with only a few phone calls, but he hasn't.

Maybe I'll see him again, maybe I won't.

But I'm too excited to see my girls today to worry too much about boys. I mean, I'm dying to tell them all the details, but not beyond recounting romantic kisses under a willow tree—and scandalous romps in the bathroom.

I'm thankful I dressed casual today instead of the off-the-shoulder black romper I laid out last night. It's so cute, and it's flattering on me, but it's a pain in the ass when I have to pee. And it always rides up if I have to walk too long. I can only imagine how bad it would stick to my skin on such a sweaty day.

I'm a couple blocks away from the Blue Lotus Café where I'm

meeting Lainey and Mary for lunch. Lainey came back to town—kind of. She's not actually staying in the city right now, but she's tagging along with one of her guys today, so we made plans to get together. Honestly, if I was shacked up with the likes of the guys she's around, I wouldn't be eager to leave them either.

I hope Mary will be more open with Lainey there. There's something calming about having her there—not that I think I need a mediator between my sister and I. But I know there's something going on with Mary, I just can't put my finger on it yet.

I made plans with Leo to visit my favorite frozen yogurt place and walk through Central Park tonight when it's closer to dusk. There's a fun a cappella group that gets together to perform at night, so I suggested we check it out when we texted this morning.

I twist my hair off my neck as I wait at the end of the block for the crosswalk sign to flash. The sun beats down on me, and I'm thankful that I tossed on a lightweight tee. Hot air blows across my neck, and I stretch it from left to right to work out some of the tension.

A horn blares to my right, triggering a chorus of horns and grabbing my attention. Panicked shouts pull my attention to the left, but before I can fully turn to look, hands curl over my shoulders and yank me backward into something hard. Yells and shrieks split the air, and I stare wide-eyed at the space I was standing five seconds ago.

An overeager cab driver barrels through the parking lane and swerves to avoid a parked car. He must have over-corrected the wheel, because somehow, he ended up on the curb of the sidewalk —exactly where I was standing.

My heart thunders in my ears, threatening to drown out all sound. Women yell and two men hammer their fists on the hood of the car, curses falling from their mouths faster than I can process.

The cab driver shouts something with his hands in the air, and then floors it. The tires squeal and burnt rubber marks the sidewalk a foot from where I was standing. He takes off, weaving in and out of traffic, and after a moment, he's lost in a sea of yellow-hooded cars.

"What the hell was that?" My whisper is lost in a chorus of curses and New Yorkers bemoaning the shitty cab drivers. I press a hand to my hammering heart.

I spin around to face my savior, intent on thanking him or her profusely, but the words die on my lips as my gaze connects with a familiar hazel one.

"Matteo," I breathe his name, expelling a shaky breath.

He brushes a lock of hair off my face, his gaze roaming me as if he's looking for injuries. "You alright?"

"I'm fine, thanks to you." On an impulse, I step forward and wrap my arms around his neck, hugging him close. "Thank you, Matteo. Jesus, I would've gotten hit by a car if you weren't there. You—you saved me."

My head feels light with the knowledge that fate was on my side today. If Matteo had been five seconds later, I wouldn't be standing here right now.

Fate's a tricky mistress on her best days. Why does it feel like she's purposely putting Matteo and I together? And why now?

Whatever the reason, I'm grateful for it today.

My nose presses against the soft fabric of his suit jacket, and I inhale the familiar smell of sandalwood, only it's darker, richer now. Nostalgia sprinkles into my psyche, and for the first time in a long time, something warm and thoughtful nestles inside of me when I think of Matteo.

His hands slide up my back, his arms holding me tight to his chest. "Timing is everything, Cherry."

I allow myself to bask in his warmth for another moment before I pull away, letting my hands slide down his arms. I'm not too proud to admit it's with some reluctance.

That thought alone has guilt slithering in my veins.

Leo.

In my peripheral vision, I see the light change to green and I take another step back, away from him. "Thanks again. I have to go." I flash him a small smile and hook my thumb over my shoulder.

He nods as he slides his hands into his pockets, the move stretching the fabric of his navy blue suit pants across his thighs. He's a man who wears a suit well, and he knows it. I swear I hear a few women sigh as they walk in the space between us, obscuring my view of him in flashes.

I allow myself one single moment where I imagine a life where I don't have to hold myself back, where he didn't break my heart and I didn't still harbor a small spark of *something* in my heart for him.

And when he tips his chin up and flashes me that ten-thousand-dollar smile, as my mom would say, I know with no uncertain clarity that he'd be lethal for me.

Because he did break my heart, and yet, here I am, ready to let him wrap his arms around me and trick me into believing everything is perfect. Right before he rips my heart out. *Again.*

I'm a different woman now, though. Hell, I bet I could have some fun with Matteo *without* letting him into my heart.

When a trio of giggling socialites passes between us, deliberately stopping in front of him to drop something, I take it as my cue. I spin on my heel, my lightly curled hair swinging out around me with the motion, and quicken my steps.

I wait until I'm safely on the other side of the crosswalk before I glance over my shoulder. Matteo's gone, only the giggling girls remain in the spot he was, and I can't decide if I'm relieved or disappointed.

Ten minutes later, Blue Lotus Café is in view. I'm already mentally ordering a cheeseburger and watermelon lemonade in my head when I feel another hand on my shoulder.

A split-second later, I feel something cold and metal prodding my lower back, and any warm feelings or thoughts of Matteo flee.

A tingle of fear ripples down my spine as everything around me zeros in on the unwanted touch.

"Keep walking and nobody gets hurt," an unfamiliar voice threatens in my ear.

My body flushes with terror, an overwhelming warmth that has me still longer than this attacker would like. He prods me with the cold metal against my back, and I've watched enough movies to let my imagination fill in the blanks.

It's a gun.

Some psycho is holding me at gunpoint outside the café, where I'm set to meet my sister and cousin in ten minutes.

Oh my god. Lainey and Mary are going to be here any minute! I don't know what to do. My mind spins too fast to latch onto any feasible ideas—not one where I don't get shot, at least.

"Let's go, bitch, or I'm going to paint the sidewalk with your brains," he spits the words out between clenched teeth. His sour breath overwhelms me, and I hold back a gag.

My fight or flight instinct kicks in, making the decision for me, and I will my body to move. I take a step forward, then two, and even though it feels like my body is made of rigid, wooden pieces, I walk.

"Turn right." His voice is low in my ear, terror pricking my nerve endings. Once we're around the corner from the cafe, I breathe a little easier. At least I got him away from Lainey and Mary. That's the important part.

They can't play the hero card, which is totally something Lainey would do. Okay, just focus. I need a plan to get away.

The relief is short-lived as panic unlike anything I've ever felt floods my body. A blacked-out utility van is double-parked in front of an alleyway, and I know in my gut that this is where he's herding me.

I know enough about kidnapping from movies and documentaries that if I get in that van with him, I'm as good as dead.

No. *No.*

This can't be how it ends for me. In the back of some dirty utility van in a forgotten alleyway that reeks of rotting garbage?

I don't fucking think so.

"Help! Hey, please help me!" I shout at the group of kids closest to me.

The guy tightens his grip on my arm and digs the gun into my back hard enough to break the skin. "Don't talk, or I kill them before I kill you."

My lips slam shut with a cry, and I'm begging everyone who looks my way with my eyes and my shuffled feet. But this is New

York City, and people are so far up in their own bullshit, they can't see past their face.

And my oversized sunglasses don't help anything either. I'd like to think that if the situation were reversed, I would stop and help—or find someone who could help.

Too many young women disappear off the streets each day, their bodies showing up days or weeks later, if at all.

I can't decide if I regret watching that docuseries on trafficking last month because I know how common it really is or if I'm grateful because now I have a better understanding of what could happen to me.

I will my racing heart to calm down enough to come up with an idea—to think of *something* to help.

"I don't have much money, but here, just take my purse." I hold my purse away from my body by the crossbody strap.

He jerks my shoulder toward him, the gun digging into my lower back at a new angle. "Shut up."

Adrenaline flies in my veins. "I'll give you my purse, and I won't report anything. I didn't even see your face, so—"

"I said, *shut up!*" He spins me around, and I realize with dread that this is it. My last stand between my unknown fate, so I do something I've only seen on a screen or read about, and I duck down low and charge him.

I don't waste time looking at his face or his clothes. My only goal is to distract him long enough for me to run away and get help.

But fate isn't on my side right now. She demands balance.

My attacker easily deflects my attempt at a takedown, grabbing a handful of my hair in the process. He rips strands out of my head, the pain only a small blip thanks to the adrenaline flooding my veins.

"Goddamn fucking bitch!" He raises the gun above my head and brings the butt of it down hard.

And then everything goes dark.

CHAPTER FOURTEEN

MATTEO

DANTE'S NUMBER flashes across my screen, and I pick it up on the second ring. Looking both ways for any rogue cabs, I jog across the street, forgoing the crosswalk. I don't have time to fuck around with them and the hordes of people waiting at every block.

Something's wrong, I can feel it in the air. There's a certain electrical charge, something that feels ominous and pressing. At first, I thought it was because I pulled Maddie from certain injury earlier, but it didn't dissipate.

Then I attributed it to the gigantic mess that the Irish are in right now. The Brotherhood and the five families are technically at peace, but I've grown close with their junior council. Friendly, even. I stepped in and helped out, got them sorted and safe*ish*, so that can't be it. If anything, it's gotten worse since then.

"I'm in the middle of something. Let me call you back," I say by way of greeting.

"It can't wait, boss."

The use of the title has me pausing. I continue walking down the street, but I focus my attention on him.

"What's wrong?"

"Gio's Pizzeria and two of our bodegas were targeted about

thirty minutes ago. I have our guys looking into it and checking-in with everyone in our territory as well as your aunts' and uncles' places."

I stop in the middle of the sidewalk and spin around, side-eyeing everyone. Raking a hand through my hair, I clench my jaw to keep the rage threatening to spill out onto the dirty concrete.

My gaze darts around me, pausing on everyone I can see. I'm searching for weapons, shifty movements, and most importantly, fucking exit strategies. I like options, and right now, there are only a few. These blocks are long, and only two of the four alleyways open up on the other side.

I've never walked away from a fight in my life, but I'm not an idiot. If twenty people cornered me here, I might not make it out unscathed. And these innocent bystanders don't stand a chance.

Satisfied that this isn't some elaborate set-up, I pick up my pace toward the shortcut alleyway.

"What the fuck is going on, Dante?" The words come out louder than I intended, and the woman next to me flinches.

"Dunno, Matteo. But I don't like it, and I don't think it's over."

I've long gotten used to his intuition, so I don't even bother asking him for more. If he doesn't think it's over, then it's probably not.

I clench my jaw as anger and paranoia infiltrate my bloodstream like a virus. "Motherfucker. I just left a member of the Brotherhood at O'Malley's with a hole the size of Georgia. You think someone knows the party we're planning?"

You think someone knows we're planning to take out the boss?

We've been talking in code over the phone ever since my cousin got pinched for grand theft. He was bragging about it to his girl-friend. Fucking idiot.

We were thirteen.

No matter how many sweeps we do for bugs or how many times we switch burner phones, I don't take those kinds of reckless chances. If we can't speak in person, then we use our code.

"Nah, I don't see how they could know about the surprise party."

"I fucking hope not. There's a very small party planning committee," I say through gritted teeth.

There's a small number of people who know about our plans.

I fucking knew siding with the Brotherhood could be risky, especially when they started making moves to step into their presidential roles earlier than planned. But we've been solid with them for years. There really shouldn't be any reason for any sort of retaliation.

"Gio doesn't know our Irish friends. Same with the bodegas. From the reports from our guys, it was sloppy. Some punk kids in black hoodies with their hoods pulled up were seen running away."

I glance behind me, looking for anyone out of place. Those dumb motherfuckers in black hoodies stand out on a hot day like this. Fucking amateurs.

"Okay. So coincidence."

"Could be. Or it could be something else."

I blow out a breath, purposely pausing before I voice what I know we're both thinking. "A declaration of war."

"That's my thought. Where you at? I'll meet you."

"I'm on my way to Blue Lotus Café. I promised I'd look for their girl. He wants eyes on her given his situation, and fuck, I don't know, man. Something doesn't feel right. It's in the air. It feels ominous and foreboding—and fuck, I've been watching your horror movies too much lately or something."

"No, I feel it too. And there's no such thing as *too many* horror movies."

"Good to see you haven't lost your sense of humor in the middle of war—"

"Possible war. We don't know for sure yet. Or who's behind it," he interrupts me.

"Yeah, I hear you. Did anyone claim Mama Rosa's yet? If not, I'd be willing to bet that it's the same person behind it all. And it's not whatever punks were at the scenes."

A cab honks in the background wherever he is, the noise shrill in my ear. "Nah. Not yet."

My mind spins with all the possibilities. It feels like the walls are closing in on me, forcing me into a position I didn't plan for.

Surprisingly, I didn't have a contingency plan for how to take over the family while we're at war. I see now that was a mistake.

"Okay. Who else knows about this?"

"Not sure. You were my first call after a few of our boys called me," Dante says.

I exhale a breath, preparing to put on my dutiful-son mask. "I'll check-in with him. And Dante? Watch your six."

We end the call without another word. After another scan of my surroundings, I dial my father.

"What," he answers, forgoing pleasantries.

"I just heard from a few of our soldiers. Gio's and a few bodegas are down. Not sure how widespread it is or if the other four families have been hit." I keep my tone even and my words clipped.

He's quiet for a moment, no doubt signaling for his consigliere, who's always nearby. "How bad?"

"Possible declaration, at the very least, a message."

"Do we know from whom yet?"

"No one has publicly stepped up yet, but I've got our boys in the streets searching for the people spotted at the scene," I tell him, staring at two guys wearing gray hoodies with the hoods thrown over their heads and obscuring their faces.

I slide my hand into the pocket of one of my favorite suits. It's dark enough to hide the blood I'm no doubt wearing, and the pockets conceal my favorite pair of brass knuckles perfectly. I leave the gun tucked in the back of my pants. That's a last resort.

Sliding my fingers through the holes and grasping the weapon, I casually look over my shoulder with my phone to my ear and see the two guys still behind me. My heart thumps loud in my ear, and my gaze darts around for a half-assed plan on the fly.

Dad makes a noise in the back of his throat. "Good. Let me know what you find. And, Matteo? Do I need to remind you how we treat our enemies?"

"No reminder needed," I say through my clenched jaw. I've been clenching it so much today, it's throbbing. I need a fucking aspirin.

While the reminder isn't new, his phrasing is. My father is many things, but subtle is not one of them. I chalk it up as a new phrase he picked up on and dismiss it.

He hangs up without saying anything else. I grip my phone tight as I pocket it.

I need to find out who's targeting us and fast. I won't be derailed from my ultimate goal, and whoever threw the gauntlet down is going to regret it.

I've had another taste of my girl, and the need to have her by my side only increases by the day.

If anyone thought I was dangerous before, they haven't seen anything yet. There's no way I'll back down from my ultimate goal.

I'm so close, I can practically taste it.

CHAPTER FIFTEEN

MADDIE

THE SMELL of sulfur and rotten garbage assaults my nose, wrenching me into consciousness. My body jerks, and panic douses me like a waterfall, overwhelming and oppressive.

My head throbs in time with my racing heartbeat, and something warm oozes down the side of my face. Fear freezes my lungs when I realize I can't move my arms or legs. I'm tied to a chair.

Instincts kick in and I can't hold back the yell. It's a cry of fear —and it does nothing to expel some of this terror blanketing my nerves.

I quickly realize my mistake. There's a piece of fabric in my mouth, acting as a gag of sorts. And for all my yelling, it only pushes more fabric into my mouth, causing me to heave.

I choke on the fabric and the panic, vomit climbing up my throat. I swallow reflexively, breathing through my nose and blinking my eyes to clear the tears that gather.

"If you choke to death on your own vomit before they arrive, you'll miss out on all the fun."

I flinch at the voice coming from behind me, my shoulders hunching toward my ears.

"It's been brought to my attention that you were not the intended target."

I wait for this mystery man to continue his statement, to follow it up with something, but he never does.

As my heart races, I try to breathe through my nose and assess the situation. I feel so ill-prepared and naïve.

A few minutes go by, and through the throbbing of my head and my darkening vision, I try to figure out where I am and how the hell I'm going to get out of here.

Think, Maddie. I wrack my brain, calling on all those hours spent watching crime documentaries and thrillers that Mary loves so much.

I'm definitely in a warehouse of some kind, but from the looks of the rundown room, it's an abandoned one. Which means I could be anywhere, really.

A pair of mourning doves coos somewhere nearby, and I can't stop the foreboding from tiptoeing down my spine.

Exposed metal and raw wooden beams run across the ceiling, giving me another detail. I'd guess this is an old warehouse, they don't use those materials anymore. And the only reason I even know that is because I overheard some big construction tycoons bemoaning the available materials on the market at an event a few months ago.

Straining my ears, I try to figure out where my kidnapper is behind me. Even though his voice is different from the man who forced me into the van, there's no doubt that he's the mastermind behind this little kidnapping—

And oh my god, how am I so calmly thinking about my fucking *kidnapping*?!

Lainey always did say that I'm absurdly organized and that I can compartmentalize things like no one she's ever seen before. Yeah, let's go with that.

I hear a shuffle to my right, and I crane my neck to get a glimpse of him. I war with myself on what to do next.

I have no idea who he is or what he wants. Every movie and TV show and news report tells us that your chance of survival goes down dramatically if you get moved to a secondary location—and exponentially if you see your attacker's face.

I can't stop the need coursing within me to see his face though. To put an image to the monster who will no doubt haunt my dreams for days, weeks, months to come.

With my mind made up, I start rocking my body from side to side. The metal legs scrape against the cement floor, this screeching noise that silences the mourning doves instantly.

"Ah, listen, it's not personal, alright? But it'd be so much easier if you weren't awake." In a move too swift for me to follow, he steps in front of me, arm raised up by his shoulder. I raise my gaze to meet his for a split second before he backhands me hard enough to send me crashing to the floor.

I don't know what surprised me more, the feeling of my face meeting concrete, or meeting the red-eyed gaze of the man who hit me.

As my vision fades dark around the edges, I find no peace in the quiet darkness of my mind. Flashes of images that sum up my life fly through my mind.

Regret tastes bitter on the back of my tongue as my lashes flutter closed.

SOMETHING JABS MY ARM, rousing me. Something cold and hard rubs against my wrist uncomfortably, and I hear voices, but they sound distorted, muffled like they're underwater.

Consciousness is an odd idea to wrap my mind around. It arrives both swiftly and slowly. It feels like my mind is wading through molasses, but my nerve endings are snapping and popping, sending messages to my brain to wake up, wake up, wake up.

I crack an eyelid open, groaning at the movement and dropping my head to the side. My neck feels weak, limp, and I don't understand what's going on or where I am.

The voices get louder, and I think I recognize one. My brows wrinkle in confusion. "Lainey? Is that you?" I ask, but my mouth isn't working properly.

A loud rumble cracks through the air, and it feels like the floor beneath my feet sways.

Wait. When did the chair get upright?

I lift my head up and squint at the two figures arguing in front of me.

"Am I dreaming?" My voice doesn't sound like my own, and it takes me a moment to realize my ears are ringing and I still have the gag in my mouth.

Something loud crashes somewhere, the noise reverberating through the whole building, shaking the floors and walls. Dust and debris fall from the ceiling and settle on my lap and the tops of my shoes.

I shake my head to the side in a desperate attempt to clear it and make sense of the scene in front of me. I open my mouth to voice one of my many questions when I feel the pressure around my wrists go slack.

My hands immediately go to the gag in my mouth. I wrench it out and take a large lungful of air. I realize my mistake when a cough wracks my body, the concrete dust and mold floating in the beam of sunshine in front of my face. The danger of what I just inhaled gets shoved to the back burner, more pressing matters at hand.

Another rumble cracks through the air, and either the building moves or I have a serious head injury because it feels like I'm on the damn teacups ride that I hate.

The shrill noise of windows breaking adds to the chaos unfolding. Guns pointed, dust billowing, frenzied conversation.

A loud boom adds a baseline to the destruction all around me, and the ground shifts again. I feel the pressure on my ankles release, and suddenly I'm not tied to the chair anymore.

Voices raise, yelling something I can't quite make out, but I don't have time to worry about that right now. I have to get out of here, but I'm not leaving without her.

My best friend looks at me, eyes wide and indecision on her

brow. She hauls me up from the chair and practically drags me out of the room. My legs are asleep, and I keep tipping toward the right side.

Lainey's grip is strong as she wraps her arm underneath my arms, holding me to her body as we navigate the building.

We dodge fallen beams and missing stairs as we make our way down a set of stairs. We're nearly to the landing when a large piece of the ceiling falls, crashing to the floor next to us with a deafening thud. We scream so loud I feel the fear etch into my bones.

Lainey doesn't move, she just stares at the busted piece of the roof, and even though I have less than zero idea what the hell is going on, I do what I always do, and take care of us.

I lace my fingers with my cousin's, and pull her down the remaining two sets of stairs. We skid to a stop at the bottom of the last staircase, both of us looking around at the destruction.

It looks like a battleground.

Metal pipes, wood beams, and concrete pieces are everywhere.

Piles of garbage, broken and molded palettes, and forgotten pieces of machinery litter the space.

I don't know how I got inside, and I have no idea which path to take to get the hell out. Something rattles nearby, and my pulse jumps to hummingbird level, threatening to beat right out of my chest.

The urge to move and move now pounds at my tender temples. As if she can read my mind, Lainey tugs on my hand.

"Follow me and stay close."

I think I respond, but there's a persistent ringing noise in my ears, and if she can hear me, she doesn't show it. She tugs our joined fingers again, and without looking at me, starts cutting a path through this destruction graveyard, dodging trash and debris with precision.

The next thing I know, I'm standing in the street in front of the warehouse. Alone.

The sun beats down on me, making the thick layer of dirt and dust stick to my sweaty skin like a paste.

Squinting my eyes against the bright light, I spin in a circle, looking for someone—anyone—to help.

But there might as well be a tumbleweed rolling across my feet for what I find. The loud sound of the ocean fills my head like I stuck a seashell up to my ear.

It must be a trick.

I look around, terror twirling, rattling inside my body.

Where is she? Where's Lainey?! Why did she go back inside that deathtrap?!

The empty street mocks me. I imagine hordes of people waiting to grab me hiding behind every corner and shrub.

I—I don't know what to do. I can't just leave her in there, but I can't go back in. Terror sticks my shirt to my skin, stamping the fear to my soul in a way I'll never forget.

My chest heaves, and my face feels wet. My fingers come away stained with my blood and tears, and there's something so final about the sight of the bright color against my dirty fingers.

I know deep in my gut that if I go back inside that building, I'll never come out.

I drag my fingers through my hair, spinning in a circle again, looking for help—something to guide me to my next move. My hair whips across my face as a hot breeze winds through the abandoned industrial neighborhood.

"Think, Maddie, think," I mumble. My thoughts are a jumbled mess, but I know I need to call someone. I can't call Mary. I don't even know where my sister is, but I know I want her far, far away from here.

And Mom is—shit, I don't even remember if she's in the city. And even if she were, and assuming she'd want to help, she'd never make it in time.

I wipe my brow again, ignoring the bright slash of blood on the back of my dirty hand. And then it hits me. I don't even think twice about it.

"Matteo."

I know he'll come for me.

I thank fate for small miracles when I realize my phone is still wedged inside my small crossbody purse, which is still draped across my chest. With trembling fingers, I pull it out and go to my contacts, looking for the number I never thought I'd call again.

Pressing his name, I bring the phone to my ear and listen to it ring once before the line connects. Before he says anything, I say, "Matteo." My voice cracks on his name.

"Where are you?" His tone is firm, his words quick and urgent.

A sob works its way up my throat. "I—I don't know. I'm in trouble, Matteo. I'm at a warehouse. And it's collapsing, and I—I'm scared."

"Get the fuck outta that building, Madison, right the fuck now!" His voice is loud, and it clears some of the fog I'm wading through.

"I—I am. I'm outside the building."

"That's good, Cherry. Stay right where you are, okay? I'll be right there." Some of the harshness leaves his voice, but the urgency is wrapped around his clipped words.

Relief hits me hard, and I sink to my knees. Pebbles press into my skin, but I don't move. It gives me something to focus on instead of the crumbling building in front of me.

"How? How will you know where I am?"

"I'll always find you, Cherry. Always. Stay on the phone with me, yeah?"

"Hurry, Matteo. I don't know if he'll come back . . ."

"Who? Who's going to come back?"

The ringing in my ears gets louder, and I have to press my palm to my ear to block it out. I can't really make it out, but it sounds like Matteo's barking orders at someone.

I pivot on my knees, trying to place the noise. It sounds almost like sirens, but I can't tell where it's coming from.

"Cherry? Are you still there?"

I tilt my head to the side. The rocks on the road cut into my skin, but I can't make myself move. If I move, then Matteo might not find me. And I have to stay here to wait for him. And Lainey.

"I swear to God, Madison, you better be okay when I get there or I'm going to burn the city down in retribution." His words are a growl.

It's one of my favorite things to hear—the way his lips curve around each syllable and the deep, throaty almost growl that pushes through.

I can't be sure, but I have a sneaking suspicion that I'm in shock. And I just know that I'm going to kick my own ass for not soaking up Matteo's voice and protectiveness, but no matter how much I want to, I can't make myself snap out of it.

"I'm here."

"I'm coming for you."

His promise reverberates in my body, imprinting on my soul.

CHAPTER SIXTEEN

MADDIE

SHOCK.

I'm in shock.

And even though some part of me recognizes that, I can't seem to snap myself out of it.

It's like I blinked and all of the sudden, I'm in the back of an ambulance. Someone's shining a light in my eyes, and I can see the EMT's mouth moving, but I can't quite make it out. It feels like someone shoved cotton in my ears, muffling all the noise.

I turn my head to look for Matteo, the movement feels heavy and fast. He promised that he'd be here, and I stayed on the phone, but then the cops and ambulances and firetrucks got here. And I couldn't hear anything over the sirens.

Two cops rushed me, asking too many questions that I didn't have answers to.

What happened?

Who blew up the warehouse?

Are there others inside?

An EMT pushed the cops aside and helped me off the ground and over to her ambulance. And I guess that's where I've been for the last few minutes, sitting on the back bumper and scanning the area for Matteo. The EMT tried to get me to lie down on a stretcher, but I wouldn't budge until I saw Lainey—and Matteo. I could've sworn I saw a glimpse of him.

I can't believe he actually came.

And I really can't believe that I called him. It was almost fateful —the entire day. It feels like something out of a movie script, not real life, and definitely not *my* life.

Finally, I spot him. His dark gray suit stands out in a sea of destruction even if he's looking a little dusty and dirty. Anxiety prickles my senses with him so far away from me.

The notion doesn't even make sense, considering I've seen him more in the last week than I have in the last two years combined. I shouldn't be dependent on him—or anyone—for my comfort. My mom taught me that lesson a long time ago.

And yet, here I am.

My heart races and my adrenaline spikes when the building shudders in the background and a chunk collapses. I flinch when the crash reverberates through the industrial park.

I watch him as he shoulder-checks a cop, snarling something in his face as he passes him. He holds my gaze as he weaves around the people separating us, getting to my side a moment later.

"Madison." His eyes tighten as he scans me from head to toe.

"You came," I breathe the words out. I tip my head to the side, as if seeing him at this angle will offer the insight I so desperately need right now.

He takes two steps closer toward me, the fabric of his pants brushing against my shins. Sitting up on the back of the ambulance like this puts us at a closer height than normal.

He tips my chin up with one finger and leans in. "I'll always find you."

Out of the corner of my eye, I see the EMT stiffen at Matteo's words, but she keeps cleaning the cuts and scrapes on my arm.

Any other day, and I might be creeped out by that sentiment. But not today. Today, I'm grateful. I reach out and wrap my fingers around his hand that's not touching my face and give it a little squeeze. "Thank you, Matteo."

He holds my gaze long enough that I hope he can read the sincerity in it. "It was nothing," he murmurs, sweeping his thumb back and forth over my jaw.

"It was everything. I—"

I feel adrift. Lost, floating down river while everything I thought I knew is another county away. How does someone just snatch a girl in broad daylight on a busy street? Somewhere in the back of my mind, I realize that I got lucky. Really lucky.

If it wasn't for Lainey, I know I wouldn't be sitting here. And I know I need to make sure she's okay, but I just need another moment. One more moment where I don't have to be the strong one, where I can lean on someone else, even just for a few seconds.

I lean my forehead against Matteo's chest and let my lashes flutter closed. I'm exhausted. Mentally and physically tapped dry.

With slow movement, giving me plenty of time to pull away, he slides his hand up my arm and settles it against the back of my neck. He holds me pressed to his chest, and something about the simple gesture opens the floodgates.

I can't stop the tears from silently trailing down my cheekbones, landing against the soft fabric of his white shirt.

"I'm going to get blood all over your shirt," I murmur.

His response is instant. "I don't care about a little blood, Cherry."

His hand on the back of my neck both soothes and commands, such an interesting juxtaposition. It's exactly what I need.

"Anything serious?"

"I can't talk about another patient's injuries," the EMT replies, her words clipped.

"You're not being asked to violate your Hippocratic oath, you pretentious fuck," Matteo snarls. "I'm asking if my girl needs further immediate medical attention."

"Sir, I don't appreciate being talked to—"

I sigh and tune them out. I don't feel like wading in, and I trust Matteo enough in this moment to look out for me.

Rolling my forehead to the side, I look at the wreckage that I was inside less than an hour ago.

My anxiety spikes again when I don't see my cousin. I honestly didn't think I had any left, but I suppose anxiety is one of those bottomless-pit things.

As if conjured by my thoughts, I see her. Like a phoenix rising from the ashes, Lainey walks out of the building, flames at her back.

FOR THE SECOND time in twenty-four hours, I rouse from unconsciousness unnaturally. I should be in my dorm, in my bedroom, snuggled under my favorite summer quilt.

But I don't feel the morning sun on my face, and I don't hear the low whir of the A/C tower unit in the corner, and I don't smell coffee brewing. Which means either it's cloudy and we lost power, or I'm not at home.

I let myself wake up slowly, just like I do in Shavasana pose at the end of every yoga class. I wiggle my toes first, then feel the energy move through my body, climbing higher and fluttering my fingers.

I don't hear anything—not even a sound machine or hushed conversation or the hum of the city that never sleeps.

I crack open my lids and wince at the brightness of the room. The sunshine isn't beaming over my face, but it is shining through cream-colored, gauzy drapes into the room through a wall of floor-to-ceiling windows with glass French doors in the center.

I quickly slap a hand over my eyes, squeezing them shut in a lame attempt to ward off the throbbing in my head.

After a few minutes, the pain subsides enough to be tolerable. I blink a few times to clear my blurry vision and realize that I have no idea where I am. I vaguely recall going home with Matteo last night.

Like the thought of the warehouse conjured it, sharp pains shoot throughout my body.

With hesitant fingers, I reach up and touch the side of my face that's throbbing in beat with my heart.

I suck in a breath at the contact. It's swollen and sensitive, and I can only imagine how it looks if it feels this bad.

Pushing myself to my elbows, I look around the spacious room. The walls are pale gray with white crown moulding. The cream-colored carpet looks plush and the charcoal throw rug in the center of the room looks thick and soft.

A low-profile white dresser takes up one side of the room with a huge mirror mounted to the wall above it. A picture frame TV hangs above a small fireplace on the other wall with two overstuffed chairs strategically placed around it.

I peel the stark white down comforter off with reluctance. The soft, fluffy material makes it feel like I'm cuddling a cloud, and I know as soon as I leave this bed—this room—everything changes.

Right here, right now, I can pretend that I didn't just get kidnapped off the street as easily as someone buys a newspaper. That I didn't get tied up to a chair in the middle of an abandoned, exploding warehouse. That I didn't get beat up at the hands of some psychopath. That I didn't call my ex-boyfriend to come rescue me because he's instinctively the first person I reach for.

Great. Now I'm dealing with guilt creeping up along my spine too. I probably shouldn't have called him yesterday and dragged him into this mess—whatever *this* is.

I bite my lip as I contemplate what to do next. I know I'm supposed to be doing something, but the idea of doing anything feels really hard right now.

I vaguely remember seeing Lainey yesterday, and I think we spoke, but everything else is just outside of reach.

I need to find my phone and call my sister—and Lainey. Tears fill my eyes as my emotions threaten to spill over. Residual fear, relief, and anxiety war inside me, but I shove it all down, way down deep, inside a locked box, and tossed into the abyss of stuff I don't think about anymore.

The last twenty-four hours feel like the plot of an action movie that Lainey would drag me to. I would always try to barter for a romcom since that's what everyone expects of a girl like me, but I think she secretly knew the action movies were some of my favorites.

A gust of breath leaves my lips on a sigh. Swinging my legs off the bed, I realize that I'm not wearing the same clothes I was in yesterday.

In fact, all I'm in is an oversized black tee. I pinch the fabric near the collar between my thumb and index finger and bring the material up to my nose for a sniff.

"Something wrong?"

The voice startles me enough that I jump and flinch, dropping my hold on the fabric. I press a hand to my thundering heart. "Jesus, you scared me."

Matteo Rossi stands inside the doorframe with his back against the wall and his hands in his pockets. Black pants, black shoes, and a crisp button-down shirt. The sleeves are rolled halfway up his forearms, displaying all his tattoos—some of which I don't remember seeing two years ago.

His dark-brown hair is longer on top and styled into that artfully messy look that most men spend thirty minutes on. I bet Matteo doesn't even spend a tenth of that on his. I know from firsthand experience that handsome asshole comes by his charm naturally.

His hazel eyes look more green than brown today. A five-o'clock shadow covers his jaw, and damn if it doesn't look incredible on him.

I look him over again, wishing not for the first time that I could read him. "I mean, I was kidnapped, beat up, and left inside a building that was crumbling."

He pushes off the wall and strolls toward the bed with his hands still in his pockets. "Yeah. We're going to have a chat about that today. How are you feeling?"

I tip my head back to hold his gaze. "See my previous statement."

The corner of his mouth tips to the side, and I swear his eyes twinkle. "Good enough for snark then. Yeah, you'll be alright."

He slides his hand out of his pocket, the whisper of fabric rustling loud in the quiet of the room. Tension builds, the chemistry crackling in the air. Slow enough to give me time to move away, he brings his hand to my face. With the back of his middle finger, he slides my hair off my face, revealing my injury.

My breath catches at the contact, and my voice comes out a rasp. "I'm sure I look a mess."

"You're beautiful."

There's a moment of silence. It's weighted, and I resist the urge to shift on the bed. I look away first, letting my eyes unfocus on the comforter next to me.

I let the compliment roll off my back. I don't have the mental capacity to deal with it right now. "What am I doing here?"

He cocks his head to the side, his eyes narrowing. "Don't you remember yesterday, Cherry?"

I wet my lips, wincing when something painful tugs at the corner of my mouth. "I, uh, think I do, but some things are a little blurry, and I don't remember coming here."

"That's probably because you passed out in the car—mostly from the adrenaline crash. The EMT warned us about that, remember? Then I carried you inside."

"And where am I exactly?"

"My home."

My eyebrows climb up my forehead at his answer. In all the time we were together, I never went to his house, and I desperately wanted to.

I watched this movie once where they explained how your home environment can tell a person more than words can. Something about seeing someone's most comfortable place offers the best insight. I glance over his shoulder at the room with a fresh, different perspective.

"It's brighter, lighter than I imagined."

He smiles a genuine smile, and something about the sight turns my insides to goo. He always had such a nice smile, so charming and deceptively disarming.

Shit. I'm so screwed.

He takes another step toward me, and I instinctively widen my legs so he has room. He's close enough to touch, but outside of his fingertips still in my hair, we're not touching. "Yeah? And how did you picture it?"

"Dark. Rich woods, distressed metals, clean lines."

He chuckles, the noise low in the back of his throat. "This is my guest room. My room's down the hall. You're welcome to check it out and see if your theories are correct."

I hear the teasing in his voice, and I'm tempted to take him up on his dare just to see his face when I march into his bedroom.

Then I remember that this isn't some trip down memory lane. I'm only here because someone kidnapped me yesterday with plans to torture me inside an abandoned warehouse. My mood plummets, and my smile along with it.

"What else happened yesterday?" My gaze searches his. I'm desperate for answers, but I'm not sure that he would give them to me even if he could.

He smooths my hair back, shifting his gaze to his hand. "You have a connecting bathroom. It should have everything you need, but if it doesn't, just let me know, and I'll make sure someone gets it for you."

A kernel of frustration simmers in my gut at his subject change. "That's very kind of you, but I should probably get going. I'm sure my sister is beside herself, and Lainey——"

"Your sister is safe. She's staying with someone else." He holds up his hand when my lips part, a protest on my tongue. "At her request. And Lainey's with the boys of the Brotherhood. I've already taken the liberty of checking up on both of them."

I snap my mouth shut and think for a moment. It feels weird to experience so much gratitude for him. Outside of the last couple weeks, my last memories of him were less than glowing. The kind that imprints on a young girl and stays with her for a long time, affecting every relationship she has after that.

"Take your time, and when you're done, join me for breakfast in the kitchen."

The pounding in my head makes it hard to focus, but maybe a hot shower would ease it a little. And after that, I'll thank him again and I'll be on my way. Mind made up, I nod.

"I have all your favorite foods."

My breath hitches at the admission. It's intimate in a way I wasn't anticipating. "You don't know me anymore, Matteo," I whisper.

He slides the hand tangled in my hair along my jawline and tips my chin up with his fingertips. His movements are slow and far more sensual than they should be.

"Don't I?" He flashes me a smile and steps backward, his hand slipping from my hair. "I'll see you in the kitchen."

He holds my gaze as he walks backward, only severing the connection when he closes the door. I stay on the bed long after he leaves, my mind spinning.

What the hell have I gotten into?

CHAPTER SEVENTEEN

MADDIE

"WHAT'S . . . all this? Are you expecting company?" My eyes widen as I take in the breakfast spread laid out on the island in the middle of the kitchen. A platter with bagels and different flavored cream cheeses, all the ingredients to build your own yogurt parfait, Belgian waffles, fresh fruit, and omelets.

"Espresso, latte, freshly squeezed orange juice, or tea?" Matteo asks as he brings a red espresso cup to his lips.

My hair is still damp, curling wildly at the ends, but my body feels a little less achy after the steaming-hot shower I took. The bathroom was large and luxurious—and surprisingly stocked with products similar to the ones I use.

I avoided my reflection, the aches and tender skin enough of a reminder. I don't want to see myself like that, and if I just pretend hard enough that I'm okay, maybe I'll actually start to feel *okay*.

It's a weak plan, but it's all I have right now, so I'm going with it.

I found a stack of new clothes on the vanity, and oddly enough, I didn't even think to question why he had women's clothes in my sizes with the tags still on. Until now. I cock my head to the side, looking at him in a new light. Something's not adding up here, and I know I don't have all the information to figure it out.

"Matteo, what's going on?"

He sets his cup down on the counter behind him, the fabric of his black shirt stretching tight across his chest. His shirt sleeves are rolled twice—just enough to glimpse the tattoos inked to his wrists.

Without a word, he pours the tea over ice and adds a dash of sweetener.

Exactly how I like my tea.

A shiver of something foreign rolls through me.

He adds a paper straw and slides the glass across the counter before leaning back against the sink and taking another sip.

The glass is cool against my fingers, and I take a drink to quench my thirst.

Mango Ceylon. One of my favorites.

"While you're here, I want you to treat my home as if it were yours—"

"*Your* home?" I can feel my eyes widen, and I turn my head from side to side, taking everything in with fresh eyes.

It's an open floor plan, not even big archways to separate the rooms like you find in so many penthouses. The kitchen bleeds into a dining room. A wrought-iron chandelier with dimly lit Edison bulbs hangs above a blonde, wooden eight-chair dining room table. It gives the room subtle warmth.

The table is bare except for a laptop at one end. I imagine Matteo sitting there, sipping espresso with the rising sun and working on . . . whatever it is he does.

The dining room transitions into a living room that sort of wraps around the outer perimeter in a U shape. One entire wall is floor-to-ceiling windows, as is the fashion for so many apartments like these.

I always thought the word *apartment* felt too small, too plain for homes like these. Ones where the couch costs more than a car.

A staircase to the second floor is on the far side of the apart-ment, and another hallway goes beyond that. I haven't really gotten the full tour, but I doubt I'll be staying much longer, so my curiosity will just have to chill out.

"Did you think I'd bring you to a stranger's home?" A frown

creases his face, somehow just enhancing his good looks. "Is your head alright? I already mentioned that I brought you to my house earlier."

That five o'clock shadow really works on him, and I lose a few seconds just admiring his strong jaw and powerful aura. I refocus on him. "What? No. I guess I thought this was your parents' house or something . . ."

"Like I said, I wouldn't bring you to a stranger's home."

The ice in his voice is noticeable, and I wrack my brain, trying to remember if he ever mentioned his parents when we were dating. We were young and stupid, and we were both more interested in other things than deep dives into our parental issues.

"Okay. So this is your house. That you live in by yourself? I thought I counted like ten rooms upstairs."

He shrugs. "I have a few trusted . . . roommates, most of whom don't primarily live here."

What a cryptic response.

"So in light of what went down yesterday—what's been going on surrounding your cousin—you have two options. Either you can have twenty-four seven protection by no less than four bodyguards."

"Or?" I raise a brow when he pauses. I've never known him as dramatic, so there must be another reason.

"Or you stay here. With me." He finishes his espresso and places the cup in the sink before meeting my gaze once more.

I know he alluded to as much earlier, but I guess I didn't really think much about it. I was distracted by physical pain and anxious thoughts about my girls.

"What? Why? Lainey's with Wolf now, right? So she's okay."

"You're right, she's with Wolf, and they're protecting her. But I spoke with him earlier, and Lainey might still be in danger. And since the two of you look so similar, it's in your best interest to lie low until everything's passed."

My brows furrow as fear shoots through me, swift and sharp. I'm not the only one who could pass for Lainey. "Where's my sister?"

"She's safe, but you can call her and talk to her for yourself. I have a couple guys watching her from afar."

I inhale a quick breath. "I thought you said she was safe?"

"She is, but I don't know the Blue Knights like Wolf does. And we're still not sure if all the events are tied together or coincidental."

I hold up a hand, my brows scrunching in confusion. "Whoa, whoa. What events? The stuff with Lainey? And what's the blue knights?"

He nods a couple of times, folding his arms across his chest. "The Blue Knights are an MC upstate."

Panic bubbles up my throat, propelling me toward hysteria. "You shipped my sister off to *wannabe Sons of Anarchy* fanboys?! What the hell is wrong with you!"

"I can assure you they're not *wannabe*s. They're the real deal—the one-percenters." Matteo says it so casually, like he's not ramping up my anxiety with each word out of his perfect mouth.

"That doesn't help," I growl out the words through clenched teeth. "I want to talk to my sister. Where's my phone?" I hold my hand out, palm up. I didn't see my phone earlier, and the last time I remember having it was to call Matteo.

He slides a phone that was hidden behind the fruit bowl across the island toward me. "Use this one. We had to disable your old one temporarily."

"I copied your information over, but nothing that can geo-locate you. Your location has to stay hidden for now. Do not share where you are, under any circumstances."

The unfamiliar voice stops me in my tracks. I turn to face the newcomer, my reaction time almost embarrassingly slow. "I don't even know where I am," I mutter.

"Madison, meet Dante Esposito. He's family, and he'll be hanging out with you while you're here. I trust him with your safety, so I'm asking you to trust me."

"I don't understand. I thought you said if I stayed here I wouldn't need bodyguards."

"Think of him more like your friend." Matteo leans back against the counter behind him.

I feel his stare on my face, but I'm too preoccupied looking at

Dante and trying to figure out how a man his size can move so quietly.

I scan Dante from head to toe. He's the same height as Matteo. His black hair is long on top, enough to grab a good handful to keep him right where you need him. It's messy and tousled like he just rolled out of bed, but unless he sleeps in suits, that can't be true.

The light gray suit looks like it was made for him, and judging by the kitchen I'm standing in, I wouldn't be surprised if he has a whole closet of tailored suits. Just like I'm sure Matteo does.

Dante's dark-brown gaze is patient as I give him another once-over. There's no question as to what I'm doing—I don't think I could be subtle now if my life depended on it.

My face flushes with heat when Dante clears this throat. It's a small, quiet noise, not one intended to embarrass me.

I trail my gaze up to his again, catching the edge of a tattoo peeking over his white-collared shirt. "Nice to meet you, Dante," I murmur.

He nods, a smirk ghosting across his lips. "Madison."

The low timbre of his voice coasts over me like a wave, slow and soft. I watch him for another moment. He moves around the kitchen with a level of familiarity that backs up Matteo's family claim.

His muscles bunch as he grabs a mug from the cabinet next to the sink and makes a latte. The simple action is anything but as the fabric stretches along his back and around his biceps. Tattoos peek out from underneath his collar and shirtsleeves.

There's something so alluring about a man who knows his way around a kitchen. And dressed like that? It's like I just discovered a kink I didn't know I had.

I look between the two men in front of me as I take another sip of my drink. I suddenly found two very big perks to staying here for a few days. There are far worse places to be than sharing a kitchen with these two. Wait until I tell Lainey. She's going to love it.

"So how long are we talking? I need to stop at my suite to pack a few things." My mind already beelines to a packing list of things to bring.

"You're taking it all surprisingly well," Matteo says.

"Well, considering my cousin is in a heap of trouble, I've decided that staying here *temporarily* might be a good idea."

The truth is I leave here now, I'll be alone, and I don't think I particularly want to be alone right now. Lainey's with her men and apparently my sister is living out some motorcycle club fantasy. Though, knowing her, she's probably curled up in a chair with a book.

"Good. There are a few ground rules we should go over," Matteo says. But my mind already shoved all the loneliness inside that box marked *do not open* and buried it deep. Now, I'm thinking about all the things I'll need if I'm staying here for a little while.

I'll need my normal skincare routine, my makeup bag, a few different outfits, some sleepwear—maybe even something skimpy. Oh! I have that lacy black piece I got with Blaire a few months ago. I've only ever tried it on, but I can just imagine wandering the house in the middle of the night and finding one of them in the kitchen. And then I'm bent over the island and—

"Madison? Are you okay?"

Matteo's voice snaps me out of my daydream. I let the smile slip from my mouth.

Warmth flushes my cheeks, and I clear my throat. "I'm sorry, what did you say?"

Matteo's brow creases as he looks at me over the feast laid out between us. "Maybe you should grab something to eat. I said to plan on staying here indefinitely."

The last word stutters around in my brain and I end up choking on the iced tea I just drank. "Excuse me—did you just say indefinitely?!"

Sitting on the end of the bed, letting the plush comforter offer me some comfort, I think about the events of the last however many hours. I recline on the pillows and stare at the ceiling. Without conscious thought, a memory of my childhood comes to mind.

"Maddie. Maddie, are you awake?" my sister whisper-shouts.

I crack an eye open and see her shadowed form at the end of my bed, illuminated by the glow-in-the-dark stars stuck to the ceiling.

I pull back the comforter and scoot over. "Come on in, Mary."

She climbs in beside me, snuggling into the other pillow on my queen-sized bed. I turn over to look at her with a wide yawn.

"Are you okay?"

She burrows underneath the comforter further. "Yeah."

"Bad dream?"

She nods, the movement creating a scratching noise that makes the hair rise on my arm. I close my eyes, exhaustion pulling back into dreamland. "Wanna talk about it?"

Mary's had a bad dream almost every night since we moved into our home for the next seven years—longer if we go to college together here. We're in a dorm suite with our cousin, Lainey, while we attend St. Rita's All-Girls Academy. I like the change, the freedom, but she's struggling a little to adjust.

"It was about Dad. He was being eaten by a shark, and I couldn't save him. But then this shark morphed into Mom, and I don't know . . . I woke up then."

I squint at her, but she's so bundled up, I can't see much more than her eyes. "I'm sorry. You can stay with me tonight."

"Thanks, Maddie."

"Of course. You're my sister." My words trail off as sleep overtakes me.

Blinking out of the sudden memory, I take it as a sign to check-in with my sister.

I dial her number, and right before I'm ready to end the call, she picks up.

"What?"

"Mary, it's me."

"Oh." Her voice softens. "I didn't recognize the number."

"Yeah, it's, uh, not my phone. It's just a friend's."

She scoffs. "You mean Matteo?"

"Yeah. About that, where are you? Why didn't you want to stay with me? And are you okay? What the hell happened?"

"You mean, why didn't I want to stay with you and your ex-boyfriend, who I didn't even know you were talking to again?"

The scorn in her voice has my shoulders tightening. "Jesus, when you put it like that, it seems—"

"It's exactly like that. Look, I don't want to be around anyone right now. It's not personal, okay?"

I fiddle with the comforter, brushing the fabric between two fingers. "Okay. Matteo said you're safe, but I want to hear it from you. Do you feel safe wherever you are?"

She laughs, and it's so far from the carefree laugh she used to have that I flinch.

"Sure, Maddie. My sister got kidnapped, my cousin's into dangerous shit now, and I stupidly gave personal information to some stalker. Yeah, I feel safe now."

Panic grips me by the throat, and I force the words past tight lips. "I don't understand. Can you start from the beginning? Let me help you."

She exhales. "I don't even know where to begin. I messed up, Maddie. But we're not little kids anymore, and you can't fix me, okay? So, just stop—just stop trying to fix everything all the time."

Tears prick my eyes at her dismissal of me. "I'm not trying to *fix* you. I just want to help."

"Well, I don't want your help, sister."

I roll my lips inward and nod, not that she can see me right now. "Okay. You, uh, stay safe. And I'll see you soon, I guess."

"Bye." She ends the phone call without another word.

I stare at my phone for a moment, wondering how the hell everything got so turned upside down.

CHAPTER EIGHTEEN

MADDIE

"CAN I ASK YOU SOMETHING?" I don't look at Dante as I ask him. Instead, I pop a kernel of popcorn in my mouth and chew it with slow bites.

I feel his eyes on me, but I keep my focus on the giant projection TV in front of us. There's an eighties movie marathon playing this weekend, and Chunk just got left in the freezer with the *stiff*, as he calls him. I remember when I was terrified that I'd get locked in a freezer with a dead body for a month after I first watched this movie. We were too young, but Mom's boyfriend at the time put it on when he was supposed to be watching us while she recovered from some cosmetic procedure.

"Sure."

"What do you think happens when you die?"

He doesn't answer me, but I can feel the intensity of his gaze on my face. I imagine what I must look like to him. This girl who he's never met is suddenly everywhere all the time. In his home and on his couch and in his life twenty-four-seven, if Matteo is to be believed.

"Why do you ask?"

I resist the urge to smooth back my hair, freshen my appearance as I debate how to reply. It's almost an unconscious tic I have, instilled by my mother and reinforced by my classmates.

I still wonder how Lainey and Mary both escaped St. Rita's seemingly unscathed. In some ways, I've always been envious of them. Neither one cared much about gossip or the trendiest fashion or maintaining any sort of relationships—fake or otherwise. Both of them are always content to do their own thing.

Lainey's always been busy. I think it was her way of coping with life, and somewhere along the way, it morphed into her personality. She was more likely to be working or volunteering, which is something so many of our classmates turn up their noses at.

And Mary was always in the library, studying the days and nights away. And maybe initially, it was a habit born from fear of failure, but I think it turned into her refuge.

She was convinced that if she didn't study so hard, she'd fail school. But she's always been good at it—a natural, Mom says. I don't think she ever received anything less than an A. On anything. Ever.

And me?

What do I do? What's my thing?

I sigh, my soul feeling the exhalation just as much as my lungs.

I'm nothing like them, not really. I'm not as smart as Mary— and I'm definitely not that good at school. And I'm not as naturally charismatic as Lainey. She doesn't see it, but people flock to her just to be in her proximity. I mean, Jesus, she has three guys vying for her affection right now. Three!

And I can't seem to snag one.

My mind involuntarily conjures three very different smirks. Three very different men who have all affected me in ways I haven't experienced before.

Okay, so maybe I can capture someone's attention, but I can't keep it. Or them.

I'm not jealous of Lainey. Of either of them. I love them.

I just wonder where I fit into our triangle. Our bond feels stretched and misshapen lately. We're closing the chapter on one part of our life, walking into the next journey, and I can't help but wonder if I'll be taking a different path than either of them.

Who am I without them?

I pull myself out of my thought-spiral and refocus on Dante's question.

"I asked because when that guy took me, and I woke up alone, tied to a chair in the middle of a warehouse, I swear I saw my life flash before my eyes."

I toss another buttery kernel in my mouth as tears well in my eyes. I keep my gaze trained on the screen, determined not to make eye contact as I crack my chest open and bleed out in front of this stranger.

Maybe that's what makes this easier. He doesn't know me from a stranger on the street, so his opinion isn't weighed down by his judgment of my past.

A self-deprecating laugh bleeds from my mouth. "And you wanna know the most ridiculous thing? It wasn't much of anything. A highlight reel of summer vacations with a mother who was more interested in prowling for her next boyfriend than mothering and pretentious events and parties with classmates in fancy dresses who don't give a shit about me. And then the fun memories with my cousin and sister." A wistful sort of smile tips the edges of my mouth upward.

"And then I had a strange thought: How many people would mourn me if I was gone? *Really* mourn me?" I pause, my hand halfway to my mouth, a few kernels clenched between my fingers. "Not many. My cousin and sister would, but they're fighters. They'd move on eventually. Friends? Nah. Girls like me are more inclined to have frenemies than actual friends. My father's dead, my maternal grandparents, too. I haven't seen my paternal grandparents in so long, I'm not sure I'd recognize them if I passed them on the street."

He doesn't respond, and the silence stretches between us, heavy and accusing. An apology is on the tip of my tongue, but I swallow it down. I think I'm allowed to be melancholy and introspective on this, so soon after everything happened.

It's hard, but I resist the desire to fill the silence. Instead, I focus on the screen to see Mikey and the rest of the goonies crawl through some tunnels. The sight eases some of the weight on my shoulders. There's something about movies from your childhood that offer you sweet nostalgia.

When I was younger, I used to fantasize about going on some big adventure like this. I had a wild imagination that only grew with my father's bedtime stories of faraway lands.

Without a word, Dante leans forward and sets his bowl of popcorn on the coffee table in front of us. I watch from my peripheral as he pushes off the plush midnight-black U-shaped couch and walks around it to leave the room.

Well, damn.

I guess he wasn't in the mood for introspection and a mild existential crisis conversation. That's alright. I'm good at being alone.

I'm sure he's regretting his offer to have a movie marathon with me. In fact, he's probably texting Matteo right now, requesting he send me away.

After Matteo dropped his *indefinitely* bomb earlier, I retreated to the room I woke up in, hoping for clarity. Instead, I had a less-than-great phone call with my sister and then fell asleep on the bed. I only woke up when Dante knocked on the door and asked if I wanted to watch a movie.

Before I can toss another kernel in my mouth, a pint of strawberry frozen yogurt is in front of my face. I don't immediately grab it from him. Instead, I trace the tattooed fingers wrapped around the frosty carton with my gaze, turning my head to follow the ink up his arm. I have to tip my head back to see his face, so it rests against the back of the couch.

I feel a little foolish looking at him upside down like this, but I'm so thrown by this gesture, I don't know what to do exactly.

After another moment of silence, I ask, "What's this?"

"This conversation deserves ice cream, don't you think?" He moves the carton in his hand from side to side, the motion catching my attention in my peripheral.

I lift my head and grab the pint from him, our fingers lingering longer than necessary. Or maybe that's my imagination.

"This is froyo." I meant it as a question, but it didn't come out that way. I turn the carton to the side, surprise wrinkling my brow. "Strawberry Surprise, actually. This is my favorite."

I look from the pint to him, watching him walk around the over-sized couch with a pint of ice cream in his other hand. Chocolate chunk.

"Huh. Must've been fate, then, yeah?"

His lip twitches when he says fate, and I can't tell if it's sarcasm or an inside joke I'm not privy to or a trick of the light. The floor-length soft-vanilla-colored window treatments are closed, their blackout feature living up to their name.

I open the carton, get a spoonful, and enjoy the bright taste of strawberries on my tongue. I barely suppress a moan. "Ugh. I'd forgotten how good this really is."

Dante chuckles, this deep, masculine sound that sends pricks of awareness across my neck. I feel my answering smile before I even realize it.

"So, you're one of those."

I take another bite before shifting to face him, bending one leg under the other and leaning back against the armrest. The movie is all but forgotten as I give him my attention. "One of what?"

"Those girls that audibly enjoy their food." He spoons another bite of his ice cream in his mouth, a smile still playing around the edges of his lips.

I shake my head a few times to the side. "I don't know what you mean . . ."

His tongue peeks out to lick the back of his spoon, and I lose my train of thought. I sweep my hair off the back of my neck in a futile attempt to cool my neck off. It's suddenly warm in here, which doesn't make any sense, all things considered.

"If you say so." He smirks this dirty little smile, and I feel like something inside snaps. Suddenly, I'm looking at all six-foot-three of him casually leaning against the couch, legs spread in that way that sounds so stupid but looks hot on the right guy. And Dante? He's definitely the right guy.

His tattoos are dark in the dimly lit room, a sharp contrast to his crisp-white tee. Slim-fit black athletic pants mold over his legs, and I feel like I might have to reevaluate my stance on the classic gray sweatpants look. Because, damn, these pants are really working for me.

He must've changed while I was napping, and I can't decide if I like him better in lounge wear or suits. Honestly, I'd take him in either.

His dark hair is pushed back over his face in that haphazard way that makes even the smartest girls do stupid things.

Not that I'm the smartest girl, because I'm not. But even I know enough to read the trouble written all over him.

I don't know what the hell is going on with me, but it's like fate decided to place all these men in front of me lately. It's like she's daring me to do something about it.

"To answer your question: I'm not sure."

It takes me a moment to remember that I asked him what he thinks happens when you die, but that was four spoonfuls of my favorite froyo and black athletic pants ago, so I'm going easy on myself.

"I like to think there's something after our time here on Earth. But there's no way of knowing. What if this is all we have? Would you do anything differently? Would you live your life with no regrets?"

"No regrets," I murmur, my gaze distracted and thoughts far away. I'm sure I've said these words before, but I'm not sure that I've ever said them—or thought of them—quite like I am now. Something about the way Dante explained it resonates with me.

Do I live my life with regrets?

"It's such a funny thing. Regret. By the time you regret something, the moment has already passed. There's no time machine to go back and make a different decision." I turn to face him again, watching the way he sits with such ease and confidence.

"Ahh, she gets it." He smiles, his eyes nearly sparkling with interest.

I tap the back of the cold metal spoon against my lips as I think. "So, you have to have the capability to recognize a potential regret while you're making a decision or make peace with the ones you have," I muse with a raised brow.

"You live your life with no regrets."

I set my spoon down and look at him. "Is that what you do? Live freely?"

His gaze roams over my face for a moment. "It's a luxury not everyone has. And in my line of work, it's easy to lose sight of what matters. Easy to get tangled up in the messiness of greed."

"*Line of work*? What're you—forty? Who even says that?" I tease him around a mouthful of frozen heaven.

He places his spoon in his ice cream carton with deliberate slowness, settling it on the couch next to him. Tipping his head back against the back of the couch, he looks at me with a raised brow. "Do I look forty to you?"

I shrug one shoulder and squint one eye like I'm trying to see him clearer. "I'm not very good with ages."

He smirks, his eyes darkening even further beneath his long, sooty lashes. "I bet you could figure it out."

I let the froyo melt on my tongue as I give him a very obvious once-over, twisting my lips to ward off the smile threatening to bloom.

Is he flirting with me?

I hope so, because I'm here for it.

Flirting is the lost art form. Too many people want to skip over all the good stuff—the thick tension and crackling energy in the air. The longing glances and subtle touches.

So many of the assholes my friends associate with are short-sided and only concerned with one thing. And listen, I'm not a prude. I like orgasms just as much as the next girl, but I also like my men to be respectful and not complete slimeball douchebags.

And givers. I like 'em generous.

Unfortunately, that seems to be a tall order. Hence why I haven't dated much in the last couple of years. Looking at Dante now, I can admit to myself that I'd date him, among other things.

In a New York minute.

In fact, an idea percolates. One that I think my progressive cougar of a mother would approve of.

I open my mouth, a flirty retort on my tongue, when his phone rings and vibrates against the coffee table. I can't help my curiosity, and I lean forward to see who's calling him. Could it be Matteo checking in on me?

All I see are numbers, so it's not someone in his contact list. Huh.

"I gotta take this," he murmurs as he gets up off the couch and walks around it, leaving the room.

"Okay." I follow him with my gaze, my interest piqued. I don't really know anything about Dante, but I think I want to get to know him.

No regrets, right?

CHAPTER NINETEEN

MADDIE

DANTE DOESN'T COME BACK for the rest of the movie or the next one, but I saw him poke his head in the room a few times.

I'm laying down on this couch, and I've decided that it's maybe the most comfortable surface I've ever slept on—including the mattress in my suite.

I've been dozing on and off for the last hour or so. It's hard to tell the time in here with the curtains drawn and the lights low for the movie.

A buzzing sounds, and it takes my brain a few moments to wake up enough to realize that it's the new phone Matteo gave me. Rolling over, I stretch my arm out as far as possible so I don't have to get off this cloud masquerading as a couch.

It's Lainey. That perks me up a little, maybe a video chat is just what I need. I roll to my back and scoot up a little, answering the phone just as a yawn spills from my lips.

"Hey, Lainey."

"Maddie? Oh, thank god you're okay. You are okay, right? Wolf said you were, but I haven't had a chance to call you until now. I'm so sorry I didn't call last night. Sully got hurt—really hurt. And once he was patched up, we came to their apartment here in the city, and

I just . . . crashed. But Maddie, I'm so, so sorry for dragging you into my mess." Her words come out quickly, strung so close together I'm not sure she took a single breath. Her eyes tear up, and she blinks, sending a tear running down her cheek.

My eyes well in response to seeing her, and I know I'll lose the battle to hold the tears in. Not only do I have a tendency to tear up when I see someone crying, but my emotions are all over the place and so close to the surface right now.

"Oh, Lainey, it's not your fault. Is Sully going to be okay?" My throat feels thick, and I swallow down the unshed tears. I can't imagine how scary that would be to see someone you care about get hurt. And I don't care what Lainey says, she definitely still has feelings for Sully.

"I think it is though. I don't understand what's going on, but I— I'm pretty sure they were trying to get me, but took you by accident." She clears her throat and looks to the side. "It was the same guy from my birthday, the one with the red eyes. And I just—you have no idea how sorry I am that you got hurt. And Sully, he'll be fine."

"That's good, about Sully, I mean. And I'll be fine, so don't worry about me. I'm more concerned about you. Why would someone want to kidnap you? I—I don't understand."

She shakes her head, her hair swirling around her tear-streaked face. "I wish I knew."

I nod a few times. "Would you tell me if you knew anything? Because I don't understand why all of a sudden, some psycho is trying to snatch you off the streets of New York City." I shrug a shoulder and run a finger underneath my left eye, catching a stray tear. "I'm not sure what exactly to be scared about, but it's like my body does. I've been on high alert since I woke up."

Lainey nods, a grimace slashing across her beautiful face. "I know, and I'm sorry for that too."

"Lainey." Her name comes out on a sigh. I hadn't accounted for how she'd feel after everything, even though I really should have. It was careless of me to not realize she'd agonize about everything.

"You're not responsible for something someone else does, and you're not responsible for my feelings."

She nods, a tear sliding down her cheek with the movement.

I bite my lip, hesitating on how to phrase what I want to say. Screw it, Lainey and I don't have that kind of relationship where we have to tiptoe around each other. I blow out a breath and look her in the eye.

"If that guy actually got you and not me, I don't think we'd be talking right now. I think they would've done something horrible to you, Lainey. And if me getting taken by mistake stopped something awful happening to you, then I'm glad it was me. I'm worried about you."

Her lips tip up into a rueful smile, and she chuckles. "Always the mother hen, Maddie. I'm okay. Or I will be. I have people watching over me now."

I nod and return her smile. "Good. And how are those Fitzgerald boys, hmm? Are they treating you well? Because if they aren't, they have to answer to me. And my new friends." I waggle my eyebrows at her, knowing how ridiculous I look when I do it. It never fails to make her laugh, and today is no exception.

I think about my *new friends*, and even though I said it to tease her, I wonder what they would do if I asked them to rough those boys of hers up. Matteo seems like he'd be on the fence, but I bet Dante would.

I have a sneaking suspicion that Dante would be down for some classic intimidation. He sure has the muscles for it.

"New friends, you say? Where are you, anyway?" she asks around a laugh.

"I'm—" A hand appears in front of my face, tattooed fingers covering my phone entirely. I startle, my shoulders flying toward my ears and my body tensing out of instinct.

"Shh. It's just me."

I crane my neck back, and once again, I find myself looking at an upside-down Dante.

"Jesus, you scared me." His hand holding the phone is the only thing keeping it up. My muscles unclench in an instant, adrenaline fleeing my body.

"No locations." His voice is firm, at odds with the small smile on his lips.

I feel my eyebrows scrunch together as I tilt to the side to see him better. He gives me room to move without removing his hand from my phone. "Are you serious right now?"

"As a heart attack. No locations, Madison. Do we need to go over this again?"

A scoff slips past my lips before I even think about it. "Oh, come off it, Dante. That's my cousin we're talking about! She's the one who saved me. She's already seen Matteo!"

"I don't care. If you can't stick to my rules, then I'll take your phone privileges away."

He somehow manages to look intimidating in his position, bent over the couch, less than a foot from my face. He's close enough that I can see the silvery flecks in his eyes. They remind me of my favorite constellations, and I allow myself a moment to get lost in them.

I refocus my gaze, his plush lips stealing my attention next. They look soft, like he'd be an excellent kisser.

He clears his throat, and I blink several times, mentally chastising myself to get it together. Finally meeting his gaze, I see his amusement. Out of the corner of my eye, I see his lips twist in a smirk, and it takes all my willpower to hold his gaze.

I feel unlike myself. Restless. Searching. Unrestrained.

"See something you like?"

A small gasp escapes me. I'm not sure if I'm more surprised that he called me out on my ogling or that I'm thinking about telling him *yes*.

Fake it 'til you make it, right?

I tip my chin back and hold his gaze. Channeling Blaire, I tell him, "Give me my phone back, or I'm calling Matteo."

"Who do you think gave the order, princess?"

Something about the way he growls the word *princess* makes my insides wobble. A moniker hurled at me with disdain for years shouldn't sound so good coming from his lips.

I don't falter, raising an eyebrow in challenge. It's not much, but I'm not in a position to do much more—literally and figuratively.

He hooks a thumb over his shoulder. "I'll be right outside that door. Don't do anything stupid. This is for your safety."

I bite back the urge to snap at him. I'm *not* stupid. But I don't understand what the hell is really going on either. I nod at him, my gaze locked on his.

Whatever he saw on my face must tell him as much. He lets go of my phone, his fingers lingering along mine for a moment before he straightens up. With one last look at me, he turns on his heel and saunters out of the room.

That's honestly not a word I'd ever use to describe the way someone walks out of a room, but it fits Dante to a T. Walk is too tame of a word for the way he just moved.

A noise from my phone steals my attention, and I turn to see my cousin's smirking face.

"Sorry, girl. Dante's a bossy asshole." I yell the last few words, taunting Dante, who I'm positive can hear me.

"Who's Dante?"

I huff with a roll of my eyes. "Just some asshole Matteo's friends with."

She quirks a brow. "Girl, I felt that sexual tension through the phone line however many miles away I am from you."

I feel my face warm and shrug. I was trying my best to not ogle the man, but damn, did he make it tough.

Lainey's eyebrows meet her hairline. "What about Matteo?"

I tip my chin up and look down my nose at her, a smirk on my lips. "Yeah, well, maybe I picked up a reverse harem novel after you told me all about your *situation*. And if you can do it, I thought I might try it. And what better time than when I'm cooped up in a safe house with some hot guys?"

CHAPTER TWENTY

MADDIE

HER ABRUPT LAUGH is the balm I didn't know I needed. I join her, both of us laughing like a couple of school girls.

"You're too much, Maddie."

I mock-gasp. "Me? I'm only trying to follow in your footsteps."

Lainey opens her mouth, but someone calls her name before she can say anything. She glances behind the camera with a roll of her eyes. "Hang on, Maddie. I'll be right back."

She must set the phone down, because the next thing I see is what looks like a ceiling. Despite straining my ears, I don't hear anything on her end. I'm sort of dying to see what her relationship with those boys is really like, you know, when they don't think anyone is watching.

I let my mind wander back to the whole idea of me entertaining *something* with multiple men.

It wasn't something I'd really thought too much about beyond the pages of the books I read. But I can't deny the lure of having a harem of men—especially if it's anything like Lainey's shared.

If being plucked off the street like a cheap slice of pizza has shown me anything, it's that life is short.

For years I've done everything expected of me.

I've volunteered for every charity function, navigated the shark-infested waters of high society, weathered all the hateful comments spewed by arrogant boys playing as men. I put my sister and cousin first in almost everything. I've played wingman to my own mother while she prowled for men closer to my age than hers, for goodness's sake.

And I did it all with a fucking smile on my face.

I've lived my life according to others—*for* others—for years. Shame licks at my skin when I realize that I would've continued to live that way had a psychopath not intervened.

How ironic is that?

What kind of person does that make me if I feel gratitude for the man who kidnapped me?

I don't even remember a time when I wasn't this way. A people pleaser.

But something has changed inside me since that moment I was dragged to a shitty van, kicking and screaming.

I've sacrificed so much for so many, and in a cruel twist of events, no one was willing to sacrifice five minutes of their time for me.

No one.

And that might be the hardest pill to swallow right now. I'm not naïve. I know there are terrible people on this earth. With how many people live in the city, the odds of some of them being awful humans are high.

But I didn't expect everyone to look the other way—or worse, be indifferent. I'd like to think that if the situation were reversed, and I saw some girl being taken, I'd do something. Get help.

I know in my heart if Mary or Lainey were there, they would've stepped in. But they love me.

And I also know that they'll support me in my choices—*whatever* they may be.

Well, Lainey will.

And Mary would too, if she wasn't in the middle of her own shit right now.

Even though my sister feels a thousand miles away, you don't break a bond like ours so easily.

So why not? Why shouldn't I start a collection of men? I'm not expecting a ring. Just a summer fling. Some honest, steamy fun with some seriously hot guys. Something to think fondly of when I'm stuck inside the stifling walls of a classroom in the fall.

I can bury my unresolved feelings for Matteo and leave only the attraction. The chemistry and lust.

In an uncharacteristic move, I don't have a detailed plan for what to do. I'm going to try something new.

Spontaneity.

The idea is more daunting than having more than one boyfriend.

Four different men come to mind, without even conscious thought. Perhaps my subconscious has been steering me in this direction all along.

I mean, I nearly had sex with a stranger in the middle of a charity gala—a *stranger*! My version of a one-night stand was making out with a guy I went on a double-date with.

I was sheltered by choice, if that makes sense. Someone had to look out for the three of us. And in a city this size, it would be all too easy for something to go wrong, so I did my best to keep my head in the game.

And that's worked really well for me—for us. The only time I let the ball slip was a couple years ago when Matteo and I dated. We were kids then—I was fairly innocent. But I was into him with a fierceness that scared me a little.

And when I look at him now, some of those butterflies feel a whole lot heavier, demanding even. Curiosity thrums inside my veins at the idea of rekindling *something* with Matteo.

I bite my lip when a fantasy scrolls across my vision. Me sandwiched between my mystery man from the gala—my Aries—and Matteo.

That's assuming I ever see Aries again. I'd probably have more of a likelihood of adding Charlie Hunnam to my harem than seeing him again.

Mesmerizing green eyes materialize in this fantasy.

Leo.

Tall and tattooed with that goddamn dimple. He'd be the perfect addition.

And damn, without my phone, I don't know how to get in touch with him.

I hear muffled voices from the hallway, and I glance in that direction. I don't see anyone, but I imagine Dante leaning against the wall, crossing his huge arms across his well-defined chest.

Yeah, I could definitely add Dante too.

Huh.

I guess maybe I've been slowly accumulating my own harem after all.

I'm not exactly sure how to go about it. I have to imagine it takes a very specific type of man to be open to this kind of relationship.

And what better person to solicit information from than my very own cousin, the one who planted the idea, unintentionally, I'm sure.

"Maddie? Earth to Maddie."

Lainey's shout rips me from my thoughts. "Hm? I'm sorry, I must've spaced." I shake my head a little to the side.

Lainey's brows crease and she leans toward the camera. "Are you sure you're okay? Maybe you should call that Dante guy back in. I'm not sure if you should be alone."

I wave her concern off with a few flicks of my wrist. "I'm fine, I promise. I was just lost in thought, and I didn't realize you were back."

She nods, the movement measured and slow. "If you say so."

"Everything okay with you?"

The tops of her cheeks pinken and she clears her throat. "Mm-hmm. Wolf just, uh, needed to tell me something quick."

"If you say so." I tease her with her own words, and she smiles in response. I bite the edge of my lip as I think about how I want to phrase what I want to know. "How do you do it? Three boyfriends, I mean? Do you use like a rotating schedule or?"

"It's unconventional. And spontaneous, I guess. Sully and I, we're"—she shakes her head and bites her lip—"complicated."

There's that word again. *Spontaneous*. I can't decide if it's fateful or if it's like that green car experiment I read about last year and I've tricked my brain into highlighting it.

I never thought about spontaneity except in the sense that I'm decidedly *not*. But now that I've not only thought about it, I considered actively being spontaneous, it's like I opened Pandora's box.

And I'm not sure if it'll ever shut.

"It's not clear between us yet, but I'm hopeful. As hopeful as a girl can be in my position."

Her eyes are pinched in the corners, and I can't tell if it's from her words or the events from the last few days. Honestly, it's probably both.

"Damn. I'm sorry." I'm still rooting for that asshole to get his head outta his ass, but I'm not sure if he ever will. She hasn't given me a clean segue yet, so I'm just going to dive in and hope for the best. "Does that mean there hasn't been any group activities yet?"

My cousin just stares at me with the blankest look I've ever seen on her face, and if I wasn't so invested in the answer, I'd laugh.

"You know. You and at least two of them—oh my god! Has the bed seen all four of you at once yet?"

My excitement climbs the longer she's silent. She's holding strong to her blank look, but I see the corner of her mouth twitch upward. I feel my eyes widen and I raise a fist in the air for a celebratory fist pump.

She holds out a hand, palm facing me with a shake of her head. "No, no. There hasn't been much of that." She trails off, looking offscreen for a moment.

I can't stop the eager grin crawling across my face. "That sounds like a *but* statement."

She chuckles and shrugs a shoulder. "But I wouldn't be opposed to it. We haven't exactly had a lot of time lately."

"Ah-ha! I knew it! Yes, girl. Damn the patriarchy!" I fist-bump the air again and then bring it toward the camera. She obliges me and brings her closed fist to the camera for a virtual fist bump.

"I don't think I was thinking about the patriarchy, Maddie," she says with a roll of her eyes. "But I'm not ashamed. All three of them are incredible."

"Even when Sully's being an asshole?" I waggle my eyebrows at her.

"Yeah, even then." She sighs, a small smile playing along the edges of her lips.

We're both quiet for a moment, but it's a comfortable silence. She looks away from the phone for a moment, and I stare at her profile. She looks tired. Sad. Her shoulders seem heavy, her soul battered.

My heart aches for her and everything she's been through. Not only in the past few weeks—but her entire life. She's one of the strongest women I've ever met, and I'm always in awe of her.

"I'm sorry about everything, Lainey." My voice is soft, smooth in the still air.

She looks back at me, her eyes welling up with tears. "Me too. Me too."

"I wish I could be there with you. But when you're ready, I'm here, okay?"

"Love you, cousin."

"Love you too."

Her sniffles turn into chuckles. "Always bringing some joy to the conversation. I don't know what I'd do without you and Mary. I pray that I'll never have to find out."

My own heart squeezes at the thought of the three of us being separated in any kind of way—let alone a permanent one. "Well, I can speak for the both of us when I say you'll never have to find out!"

"Where is your sister, anyway? I haven't had a chance to talk to her since the diner, and I want to check-in."

I tilt my head to the side. "Didn't you hear? She's with some biker dudes. Apparently, Wolf vouched for them. And she didn't want to stay here with me. Said she needed 'space' whatever that means." I play off my hurt feelings with a scoff and tell myself that if I act like I'm not offended, then maybe I'll will it.

Her head jerks back at the mention of *biker dudes*. "No, I . . . must've missed that somehow. I'll call her after we hang up."

"Don't bother. Her cell reception is nonexistent where she is. But I talked to her earlier, and she was okay. Told me about that creep she met online. Honestly, it's probably a good thing that none of us are in our usual routines right now." I shudder. The thought of another man following one of us freaks me out more than I let on. "That Max guy sounds like a creep."

"Oh, okay. I'll have Wolf look into it."

"Call me later, okay? Don't leave me hanging or I'll worry!"

"Always," she says with a smile. "Be safe, Maddie."

The two words we've uttered to one another more times than I can remember suddenly take on new meaning after both of us have had our run-ins with the evil and deranged men of this world.

"You too, Lainey. You too."

She smiles at me one more time before ending the video call. I stare at my phone for a moment before I decide against calling my sister. If she wanted to talk to me, she'd pick up the phone or call me back. Maybe she really does have bad service. Or maybe she's ignoring me.

I lock my phone and toss it on the coffee table before leaning back to settle into the cushions and mindlessly watch the next movie.

CHAPTER TWENTY-ONE

MATTEO

FIVE DAYS.

She's been in my apartment for five goddamn days.

And the world hasn't exploded.

Yet.

I'm not positive that the rug isn't going to get pulled out from underneath me and murder me and everyone I care about.

It's not a matter of if but when.

That's why I have contingency plans all over the city. Like a garden, I've planted seeds all over this city and a few others, watering them appropriately with alliances, rumors, and money among other things.

We have enough enemies as it is without total dissension within our family. The cracks are widening, sides are being taken, and anyone who doesn't end up on the right one won't be here soon enough.

That's one thing my father and I agree on: If a man's loyalty can be bought, then he's a liability. And liabilities are dangerous in my life.

If the heads of the five families really knew how bad it was, they'd cut their losses and wipe our line from the board. It's a delicate dance, overthrowing your father to take his place. If I push too hard, one of his little rats will scurry to him and inform him of my plans, fucking everything up.

Brute force won't work simply because we don't have the soldiers for it, not when I don't know where allegiances of the other families lie.

That leaves subtly, patience, and duplicity.

Something my father doesn't seem to understand. His arrogance is going to be his downfall.

My chair creaks as I lean forward to pull up the security footage of my house, settling on a video from a few days ago.

I watch in fascination as Dante follows Madison all over my house. She's like a little butterfly, always floating around from one room and one thing to the next. She never sits still for too long unless it's to binge-watch a movie or two.

Eighties adventures and action movies seem to be her favorite. But I already knew that. I remembered that from our time together years ago, and even if I didn't, I've had tabs on her for longer than even Dante knows.

They're at the table playing some card game. Dante's mouth moves, but I don't have the volume on, so I have no idea what they're talking about. The need to hear their conversation is nearly overwhelming. Especially when Madison tips her head back and laughs. Dante smiles at her, and even from this tiny screen on my computer, I can see it in his eyes.

He's into her.

The urge to wrap my hand around her throat and take her lips as a reminder to her—to everyone—that she's mine rides me hard, and I clench my fists on my lap.

I close my laptop with a click, and the silence of my office bears down on me. I sent my few employees home hours ago, the hazy dusk of the setting sun illuminating the spacious office. I've been spending too many hours here lately.

It's one of the few places I know doesn't have any little rats running around. And since my apartment is now housing a red-haired temptress, my office is the next best place.

I stare at the diagram in front of me. It's basic enough, but the visual reminder of what happened and list of possible culprits helps me focus.

All I know is that there have been several targets, and no one's claimed it yet.

If it were the local street gangs, not only would they be bragging about it to everyone with ears, but they know they'd be signing their deaths. The only reason they're even around is because the five families allow it.

We're on good terms with the Irish and the local MCs, no thanks to our boss. The cartel doesn't usually fuck with us this far north, but it's possible a new faction is trying to make a name for themselves.

There are a few different families it could be—Russian comes to mind.

And the other possibility is that it's one of the five families. Or an outlier.

Families have been trying to infiltrate the five for generations. It's not that simple. There's a reason these five families are the ones —the top of the food chain.

Order is paramount, and as much as I dislike certain structures from the five families, without them, we'd devolve into chaos.

My phone vibrates on my desk, pulling me from my swirling thoughts. Dante's name flashes across the screen, and a moment of fear licks down my spine.

I press accept and the words fly out of my mouth before the phone is even to my ear. "Is Madison okay?"

"She's fine."

I blow out a breath, the relief hitting me harder than I anticipated. "Okay. What do you need?" I spin around in my chair and look at the city lights twinkling below me. It's like I'm in the clouds this far above the city.

"Marco called. One of his soldiers went missing the day before yesterday. His body was delivered to Marco's front lawn twenty minutes ago."

"Motherfucker." I pinch the bridge of my nose and wrack my

brain for any correlation. "First the robberies, then the arson, then more robberies, and now outright murder. And dumped on our capo's lawn, no less. The escalation doesn't follow a typical pattern. Could it be a coincidence?"

"It's possible. Someone dumped him in the one blind spot in Marco's yard, so his cameras didn't pick up anything. It seems personal though. This kid had two to the chest, and his eyes were gone."

"Gone?"

"Plucked from the sockets."

"Jesus Christ," I say through gritted teeth. "It's a goddamn message."

"That's my guess, too. Marco's ready to go on a rampage, and only calmed down once I promised him retribution." Dante sighs, the sound loud in my ear.

"Did he say anything to suggest it was personal to him or the kid?"

"Nah, said the kid was well-liked. Young and smart, would've been a good earner." He pauses, the silence heavy and oppressive. "What do you want me to do, boss?"

"Fuck." The curse leaves my mouth on a hiss. "Whoever is behind this isn't fucking around. He'll want to retaliate."

My dad didn't keep his title as boss of the five families because he sat idly on the sidelines. Nah, he's much more the *shoot everyone and ask questions never* type of leader. It's useful in some situations, but I fear that without an inkling of who's responsible, the streets are going to run red with the blood of the innocent long before any of this ends.

"Against who though?"

"He'll no doubt start with whoever pissed him off last. No one is safe from his manic rage."

"I'll call it in, but be prepared for anything. We don't know how much information our enemies have."

"Understood."

"Oh, and Dante? It's time our roommate came home."

"You sure? What about Maddie?"

I let the use of her nickname from his mouth roll off me like water on a duck's back.

"What about her?"

I mentally pat myself on the back for the growl of anger I kept from my voice. I'm not jealous, exactly. I trust Dante with my life— and hers. And I'm thankful he can be there to protect her when I can't.

"How long are you planning on keeping her here? I can't watch her every day for the rest of my life, and she can't stay here forever." I just imagine him rolling his eyes at me.

It's like he doesn't know me at all. Of course, I can fucking keep her there forever. When she runs out of clothes and whatever, I'll just buy her new things. I rather enjoy the idea of coming home to her every night, even if she's already sleeping. It's strangely comforting just knowing that she's sleeping down the hall from me.

The most obvious answer keeps flashing in front of me like some neon diner sign. I know Dante's thinking the same thing I am right now.

Marriage.

I don't answer him, which is answer enough. The fact that he's acting like he's not having the time of his life with my girl is a little insulting. I know he knows I've been watching them together. Not that there's anything to watch really, but just their interactions are hardly purely platonic.

He huffs, the noise loud and frustrating. "We really need to talk about this. You can't marry her."

I shrug and stare at the twinkling lights, letting my eyes unfocus. "We can talk about it later. I'll be home tomorrow night."

"Yeah, okay." He disconnects the call before I can say anything else, and that little show of anger is almost as bad as it gets between us. Dante's always been my best friend and my advisor. The kind of guy you call when you need to dismember and dispose of a body.

I know there's reason in his point, but I can't see another way, not yet, at least. And I'll be damned if my father attempts another shoddy marriage arrangement. That shit might work on my younger brother—not that I'd let it happen—but I'm a made man now. I don't abide by that sort of contract, not for anyone.

I sigh, raking my hands through my hair as I mentally prepare myself for this phone call. Two fingers of whiskey later, I call my father and deliver the news.

CHAPTER TWENTY-TWO

MADDIE

I'VE BEEN HERE for nearly a week, though the first day or two was kind of foggy. My head feels good now, and most of my aches have dulled to something way more tolerable.

I've settled into a routine of sorts. It still feels a little like I'm on some extended vacation—but one where I'm stuck inside a house with someone I only recently met. Given everything that happened recently, it's a bit of a surprise that I agreed to it.

There's just something about Dante that makes me feel safe. Protected.

Of course, I thought I'd be with Matteo when I originally said I'd stay here, but I don't mind Dante pulling bodyguard duty. A lot of people I know have part-time bodyguards, and given that I just had my own for a few days courtesy of Lainey and her men, it's not as odd as it could be.

Strangely enough, I haven't seen Matteo since that first day when he told me my life was changing—even if only temporarily. I'm not sure if I'm disappointed or not.

I can't deny that I've enjoyed the last week getting to know Dante. You can tell a lot about a person in those small moments of quiet. And I've learned that while Dante is a man of few words, the ones he does speak hold plenty of weight. And I like it.

I like him.

The smell of fresh popcorn rouses me from my room. In the back of my mind, I wonder how Mary and Lainey are. I've had little contact with each of them—just a few text messages with my sister.

I idly wonder if I'll have any missed messages when I get my phone back. Maybe a few from Blaire.

And Leo.

I'm not sure how I'm going to explain my sudden radio silence to him. I don't want to lie to him, but I'm not sure how well the truth will go over. I have to hope that he'll understand why I didn't reply for however long I've been here.

Time loses all meaning when I'm indoors all day and sleeping at weird hours. The floor-to-ceiling windows welcome the sunshine each morning, but the blackout blinds in the room I'm staying in make it feel more like midnight than noon.

Glancing at the clock, I'm a little embarrassed it's nearly eleven o'clock in the morning. I'm not used to sleeping so late. Usually, I'm up pretty early, but either I really needed the rest or those blinds are messing with my circadian rhythm.

Or maybe it's because Dante and I stayed up until three o'clock in the morning watching *Game of Thrones*. I still can't believe he'd never seen it. We have two more seasons to go, and I haven't made it a secret that I'm dying to see his reaction to everything.

It's almost like I'm watching it for the first time again. I enjoy seeing it through his perspective. He has a lot to say about the Starks, and I can't wait to see what he thinks about the last couple seasons.

Rounding the corner to the kitchen, I'm not surprised to see Dante at the stove, stirring the popcorn maker. The noise is loud and the smell is delicious. What's surprising is he's not wearing a shirt. Outside of the first time we met, he's been casual in athletic shorts and sweatpants and tees.

I feel my mouth part as I take in the wide expanse of his back.

Tattooed designs swirl and cascade over his muscles, telling a story with each stroke of ink.

I don't realize I'm moving until I'm right behind him, a hand hovering over his back. Desperation to touch him bounces around inside me, the feeling both foreign and right.

I hesitate for a moment, giving both of us time to move or speak, but when neither one of us does, I reach forward, my fingertips trailing down his back. He doesn't flinch, instead, staying perfectly still. I get the feeling he's letting me explore.

I follow the ink with my fingertips, staring in fascination at the goosebumps they leave in their wake.

We've grown close over these last few days, outside of a few innocent things. I think that's bound to happen when you spend nearly every waking moment together.

I take another step closer, and the fabric of my tank top brushes against his back. I'm more aware of what I'm wearing—and not wearing—than I've ever been.

And I can't decide if I'm delighted or distraught that I'm only wearing a loose, lightweight blue tank top with a cute dark-blue bralette and a flirty white skirt that hits mid-thigh.

My exploration stalls on a beautiful detailing of a rose. The pads of my fingers brush against the inked petals. The details are so life-like that wonder clogs my throat. I wonder what it would take for a guy like Dante, whose body tells a story of turmoil and dark days, to get a beautiful, almost dainty flower on his back. The rose wraps around his ribs, the stem leading into his shorts.

I'm so lost in my exploration that I don't realize the popcorn stopped popping. He turns the burner off, the soft click loud in the quiet kitchen.

Slivers of soft sunshine cut across the room from the nearly closed blinds, creating a shadowed pattern in the kitchen.

My heart pounds in my ears, and nervousness climbs up my throat as I slowly bring my other hand to his back. When he doesn't protest, I smooth both palms up his back, my touch light on his warm skin. Pricks of electricity spark in the space where our skin touches, and I gasp at the feeling.

"What are you doing?" His voice is low and warm like freshly spun caramel, smooth and rich.

I lick my lips and trail both hands around his ribs. "Exploring."

"I'm not a map, Maddie." His voice is low, my name rolling off his tongue like he's been saying it for years, not days.

My fingers tingle with anticipation as I take the final step forward, my front now pressed against his back. I lean forward and place my lips on the edge of one tattoo.

He sucks in a breath, letting it out in a hiss. I skim my lips over his skin and place another kiss, and like a rubber band snapping, he springs into motion.

In one second, he spins around to face me, his hands clasped around my wrists suspended midair. His grip is gentle and firm as he walks me backward until my back hits the island. But I'm honestly not even paying attention because his chest is in my face.

It's like I've died and gone to heaven. Holy . . . I didn't even know abs could *look* like that. I swear to god, I lose a few moments in time where I'm just zoned out on his incredible body.

Intricate inked designs take up most of the space on his chest and abs. He has small areas of blank space, and I want to know what he's planning to put there. A guy like Dante doesn't leave space like that unless he has plans for it.

My view cuts off when he steps closer. Holding my wrists loosely, he lowers them to the island behind me, and my back arches with the new position. My nipples tighten, my body flushes with desire.

His scent invades my senses—something woodsy like vetiver. He's all around me right now, warming me up in more ways than one. I bite my lip to keep myself from doing something bold, like pushing onto my toes and sealing my lips against his.

That'd be crazy though, right?

I mean, it wouldn't be that crazy. He wouldn't be standing this close if he wasn't interested, a voice reasons. It sounds a lot like Lainey, and since she's the brainiac of our little trio, I decide to trust her judgment.

Without a word, he lowers his head and sinks his teeth into my bottom lip with just enough pressure for me to take notice.

And believe me, I freaking *notice*.

My breath hitches at the feel of his lips so close to mine. My mouth parts on an exhale, and he slowly releases his hold on my lip. I curl my fingers over the edge of the counter to keep them still. Eagerness thrums in my veins.

His teeth ghost over my lip again, gently scraping, and I feel the pressure in my clit. It feels a lot like a promise—one I intend to keep.

"You shouldn't bite your lip like that," he says against my mouth, his lips just barely brushing along mine.

My chest rises and falls with quick breaths, the anticipation suffocating. "I might need another reminder." My voice is breathless, and if I wasn't so close to seeing how Dante kisses, I might be a little embarrassed about it.

He pulls back, and my lashes flutter open. I don't know when I closed my eyes, but butterflies soar inside me.

He smirks as he steps back, his hands sliding off of mine with each step. "I had a feeling you might. But for now, let's watch a movie. It's my pick."

He turns around and finishes the popcorn, giving me a few moments to get myself together. That might be the best non-kiss kiss I've ever had.

The swirling fog of lust is palpable, like I could reach out and curl my fingers over it in the air.

If I thought I was desperate for him before, after that small taste —a tease, really—I'm downright determined now.

I place a hand over my beating heart, willing my breathing and libido to slow down. Once I feel like I can look at him without jumping him, I grab the large bowls off the counter behind me and help him divvy up the popcorn.

CHAPTER TWENTY-THREE

MADDIE

AN HOUR LATER, and I'm barely paying attention to the movie. It's honestly freaking me out. It's not jumping-at-you scary but psychologically, and those always freak me out way more.

It's not that it's a bad movie, but I'm probably not the best person to watch it. I'm a baby when it comes to psychological horror films, especially the new ones. I don't watch them often, but when I do, I'm looking over my shoulder for weeks afterward.

The credits roll and the room darkens with the black screen. The white letters provide the only light, and I realize I have no idea what time it is. It's easy to lose track of time here.

I roll my head along the back of the couch to look at Dante. His gaze is already on mine, his face open, but I can't read it.

The empty popcorn bowls sit discarded on the other side of him. He's leaning back against the couch, his legs spread casually wide and feet firmly planted on the floor. His chest is still bare and I can't make out the details of his tattoos in this dim lighting. He's close enough to touch if I stretch my arm out, but far enough away where any brushes of his hand along my shoulder are intentional.

"What did you think?"

"I thought it was fucked-up. In a good but scary as hell way." I bite my lip and face the screen, thoughts of the scene where you realize what's actually going on scrolling in my head. The horror on the actors' faces was tangible.

His thumb presses down on my bottom lip, freeing it from my teeth. "What did I say about that?" His voice is low and smooth, and it sends a wave of warmth through my body.

The pad of his thumb rests against my mouth, and I have a moment of indecision. I talked a big talk to Lainey, but for all my bravado, so far it's been nothing but hot air. I haven't been spontaneous at all.

Well, I kind of was in the kitchen a few hours ago, but I sort of thought he would take the opportunity I gave him and kiss me. But maybe he needs another little push.

I swipe my tongue across my bottom lip, catching his thumb in the process. He hisses at the contact, and it's the reaction I didn't know I was waiting for. I run my teeth over the pad of his thumb, holding his gaze the entire time.

His eyes darken to nearly black as he slides his hand down the front of my throat, using his thumb to tip my chin up.

"You're playing with fire, baby girl," he murmurs, his voice like gravel.

I look at him through half-lidded eyes, my breaths coming faster and deeper. Something about the way he's holding my neck started an inferno inside me. "Maybe I wanna get burned."

His fingers flex against my neck, and I can't stop the groan that spills from me. I don't know who moves first or if we lean in at the same time, but in the next moment, his lips are on mine.

It's surprisingly gentle, tentative even. Just his lips pressing against mine for a single moment. I swear it feels like my soul sighs in contentment with the contact. He barely pulls back, just enough to brush his lips across mine.

Once, twice, three times, never taking his hand from my neck. His grip isn't firm, more careful, reverent.

I feel the smile curl across my lips at his cautious exploration, my body humming in approval.

When he places another chaste kiss on my lips, I decide to play. I love that he's giving me soft and gentle, but I want to feel him lose control a little. I want to taste his desire.

So, I lean forward and capture his lip between my teeth. And I bite down—hard.

He's like a caged beast, and I just waved a big, juicy steak in front of him. And then unlocked his cage. His answering growl sounds like lust personified. Low and deep, he groans against my mouth before he captures my lips in an earth-shaking kiss.

His hand leaves my neck and slides down to grip my hips, and with both hands, he lifts me up, placing me on his lap. A startled squeak escapes before I can stop it, but it quickly turns into a soft groan at the feel of his thick erection underneath me. I sink onto his lap and wrap my arms around his neck, losing myself in the tingles radiating down my spine.

"Yo! You called me home, so here I am. Man, you're never going to believe it, but I think I actually got stood up for the first time." A man laughs, the sound self-depreciating.

It takes a moment for the voice to filter into my lusty fog. I pull back from Dante's kiss-swollen lips, tilting my head to listen for more voices. I haven't seen anyone else the entire time I've been here, and I don't remember Matteo mentioning anyone else living here.

Someone's rummaging around in the kitchen. The fridge opens and the clinking of glass jars and bottles filter into the living room.

"Who is that?" I look over his shoulder, keeping my voice quiet. Surprisingly, no fear dances along my spine. The fact that Dante makes me feel safe is both enlightening and heavy.

Dante tilts his head back with a sigh. "Matteo's brother."

"Bro, did you hear me? I said I got stood up by that chick I was telling you about. Damn, I thought you'd be out here laughing at my expense by now."

My brows furrow as I look back at Dante. His mouth distracts me, my legs involuntarily squeezing against his hips. "Matteo has a brother?"

The hiss of a bottle opening pulls my attention from Dante. I crane my neck to look over the couch, but all I can see from here is the darkened living room and the single light on over the stove. I don't know how long we've been locked away in here, but I think it should still be daylight out. Unless someone closed the blinds.

I spare a second to think of the ramifications if Matteo was in the kitchen right now. I wonder what his reaction would be to finding me straddling Dante, his best friend and the guy he put in charge of watching me.

I roll my hips and a strangled groan sounds behind closed lips but his gaze never leaves the place where our bodies are touching, separated by a few pieces of cotton. My mouth quirks up on one side. Yeah, I'd say he's watching me alright.

Dante's fingers flex against my waist. "Fuck," he says on a sigh. He tilts his head forward and skims his lips against the column of my throat. "To be continued, yeah?"

I nod before he even finishes talking. Despite wanting to push boundaries, I don't actually want to hurt anyone. And I have a feeling Matteo is more of a shoot-first-ask-questions-never kind of guy.

I open my mouth to reply, but before I utter a single syllable, the lights come on, lighting up the darkened room to nearly high noon. I close my eyes, tucking my face into Dante's neck for a moment as white spots dance behind my closed lids.

"Damn." Matteo's brother whistles. "Bringing a chick back home to bag her on Matteo's couch? I'm impressed."

Dante grunts, sliding up and down my ribs in a distracting motion. "Fuck off."

There's something familiar about his voice, but it's just outside of my reach. I pull back from Dante, blinking my eyes a few times to let them adjust to the bright light after being in the dark for so long.

I let my red hair shield my face from this newcomer—this brother I'd never heard of—as I feel the couch cushion depress next to me.

"She looks pretty from this angle, man. In what world do I get stood up on the same night you get lucky? Is there a full moon or something?"

Irritation coils around my limbs as anger holds me immobile. This guy sounds like a prick.

"C'mon, baby doll. Let me get a good look at you before my brother loses his shit on your boy here. He doesn't like strangers in his house," Matteo's brother says with a click of his tongue.

Someone tugs on a lock of my hair, and the move is so reminiscent of playground politics that I forget my manners for a moment. Shrugging his hand off my hair, I roll my shoulder back and turn to face this mysterious brother I never heard about.

Time seems to freeze as I stare at a familiar face. My mouth drops open and a sudden dizziness blankets me. I shake my head to dislodge it, my eyes blinking overtime like one blink will magically change who's sitting next to me.

I feel the weight of Dante's stare on my face, but I can't pull my gaze from the man in front of me.

"It's you," I breathe.

CHAPTER TWENTY-FOUR

MADDIE

HIS BROW SCRUNCHES and his mouth parts, but no words fall from his lips. Lips that I've tasted—lips that I want to feel again.

Shock tightens my throat as fate plays yet another unexpected hand.

"I . . . I don't understand."

My gaze flies between his eyes, searching for answers to questions I haven't even formulated yet. But he offers me nothing more than his own disbelief.

"That . . . is a very good question," he murmurs, his brows slanting low over his eyes.

"I didn't ask a question." I trail off as my heart slams against my ribs. In my mind's eye, I'm second-guessing every interaction with him, wondering if there was an obvious sign and I missed it.

"Why are you here?"

I tilt my head to the side and counter, "Why are *you* here?"

"I live here—"

"Sometimes," Dante interrupts him.

Somehow, I'd forgotten that I was sitting on his lap having this bizarre conversation. I scramble off Dante's lap, my movements clumsy and awkward as I put distance between us. I stop halfway to the projection screen, but the need to flee rides me hard.

I clench my shaky fingers as I look between the two men on the couch. I can feel how wide my eyes are, and I'm sure I look ten shades of crazy, especially with the credits scrolling on half of my body.

I take a deep breath and expel it, lowering my hand to hang at my side. "Okay, so you sometimes live here. In this house."

Leo nods. "That's right. And why exactly are you here?"

It's not an accusation exactly, but it's not the warm and fuzzy way I'd grown accustomed to from him.

"I'm staying here. Temporarily," I offer as I cross my arms. Suddenly I feel like I need to defend myself.

Leo nods again, the movement slow and somehow sarcastic. "Cool. So somehow you moved in with my brother. *Temporarily*. And you didn't bother to tell me."

I tighten my arms across my chest and square my shoulders. "I didn't know you two were brothers. Otherwise, I would've never agreed to see you."

His lips curve downward in displeasure for a single moment. Then he plasters an obvious fake smile on his face. "Right, right. 'Cuz you've got something going on with his best friend here. I see."

I rear back in shock. "What? No. It's not like that—"

"Then what's it like?" Leo interrupts me, his face hard and unreadable.

I glance at Dante for the first time since I saw Leo, pleading with my gaze. His face might as well be carved from stone for all the emotion I see on it.

My heart sinks.

Dante leans back and spreads his arms across the back of the couch. Tipping his head to the side, he regards Leo with a smirk plastered on his face. "It's none of your fucking business, kid."

My shoulders sag in relief that he shut him down, that he's on my side. My mind stumbles, drunk on the overwhelming confusion and coincidence.

Only, I don't much believe in coincidences. No, fate's playing one of her games again, and I can't tell if it'll end up being for my benefit or against it.

"That right? Then I bet my brother would be delighted to know what I walked in on. You and I both know he doesn't just invite people to stay here." Leo stares at Dante, challenge tightening the skin around his eyes.

Dante tenses, his muscles tightening with tension as he stares at him. "Don't act like you give a shit about your brother. Besides, I know he watches the cameras—and he knows I know, which means you *don't* need to do shit."

My brows scrunch at Dante's words, and immediately, I scan the corners of the room for these alleged cameras. I don't know what I'm expecting, but I don't see anything that screams *camera*.

Leo drums his fingers along the back of the couch as he stares down Dante with a smirk. "We'll see."

"So you two know each other?" Dante asks.

"Yeah, we know each other, alright. Dante, meet my date I told you about. Madison, meet my cousin, Dante." Leo settles against the back of the couch, his chin tipped upward and his eyes locked on me.

"You're cousins?" My gaze bounces between the two of them. Twin beacons of masculinity and power. They sit on opposite ends of the couch, all forced nonchalance, but the tension in their arms gives them away. They're practically vibrating with energy, and neither one wavers, their attention solely on me.

A plain black tee molds over every dip and strains around every muscle on Leo's chest. His tattoos look dark in the low light, swirling down his arm. His green eyes look darker than I remember, or maybe they've just never looked at me with such contempt.

It's a little messed up, but his angry smolder is turning me on.

I know it's not the right time—I know that—but I can't stop the thoughts from forming. Whether by accident or not, they left a space between them—one just big enough for me.

Just call me Goldilocks.

I rake my teeth over my bottom lip and squeeze my fists for a moment, letting the tension rise. It balloons between the three of us, rising and expanding to suffocate the oxygen until only desire remains.

I'm sure they're not feeling the same thing as me, but it's like a switch in my brain was flipped, and I can't get the idea out of my head.

The one where I get to have them both.

"Not really. Our parents are close, so we grew up together," Dante explains.

I nod like I get it. And on paper, sure, I do get it. But staring between the two of them, I don't really.

When did my life start feeling like fiction?

The silence stretches, leaving nothing but emotions and feelings to fill the space between the three of us.

I shift on my feet, indecision thick on my tongue. I bite my lip to stop myself from blurting something—anything—to ease the tension. What would I even say though?

I'm in uncharted waters, and I selfishly don't want to mess anything up with either one of them.

"Ah, Leo, you're here. Sorry I'm late, I got caught up," Matteo says, scaring the daylights out of me.

I visibly jerk at the sound of his voice. Jesus, he's like a ninja with his silent moves. I'm sure it didn't help that I was preoccupied by the two men in front of me.

"No worries, *brother*. I just got here." Leo stares at me, his lips twisted in a smirk.

"Everything okay?" Dante asks, without taking his eyes off of me. I'm not sure who he's asking, but I nod a few times, anyway.

Matteo walks in the room, stealing my attention from the other two. Black button-down shirt, dark pants and shoes, tousled hair in a way that tells me he had his hands in it not too long ago.

He's a bad boy fantasy come to life.

He walks into the room and stops a few feet away from Leo. He casually rolls up his sleeves, revealing his dark tattoos inch by delicious inch as he looks between the three of us with a raised brow.

"Madison, meet my brother Leo. Leo, meet Madison Walsh, my ex-girlfriend."

A scoff slips from Leo's mouth, his lips twisting into a cruel smile. "Your ex-girlfriend, yeah? That's just fucking rich." He pins me with his gaze, the contempt lashing at my skin.

In the corner of my eye, I see Matteo freeze with his hand on his sleeve. I don't move my attention from Leo, though.

"Is there something you want to say, little brother?" Matteo's emphasis and inflection on the words little brother prick my ears, but I'm locked in a battle of sorts.

Leo's eyes harden, and he tips his chin back. I recognize the vengeful look, and I bolster myself for the impending damage he's about to inflict. I shake my head, the movement small and quick. He raises a brow with a smirk as if I'm asking him not to tell Matteo about our time together.

I'm not.

I straighten my spine and drop my weight into my back leg. Folding my arms across my chest, I tip my chin right back at him in the universal elitist-prick language I'm sure he'd recognize. *I'm not scared.*

His mouth spreads into a ghost of a smile, but it's gone before I can blink. He settles into the couch and looks at his brother with a shrug, the picture of nonchalance.

"Just telling Dante about the girl I was seeing, you know, the one I took to Aunt Louisa's place. I haven't been able to reach her for a week, and she bailed on our last date. Total no-show. Which is so fucking weird, because this girl." He pauses to drag his teeth over his bottom lip, looking from Matteo to me. "She was fucking thirsty for my dick, bro."

My cheeks warm with his insinuation. I lean on my years spent with Blaire and her minions and sharpen my tongue on my frustration.

"Don't get it twisted, Leo. I wasn't the one who cornered you and stole a kiss underneath a willow tree."

His jaw clenches and he pushes up from his faux relaxed position to stand in front of the couch. "Stole? *Stole* a kiss?"

I lift a shoulder and an eyebrow but keep my mouth shut. It's a dare, and I'd bet my inheritance that he'll rise to the challenge.

He eliminates the space between us in three steps. Some of the rage in his body visibly deflates. But I'm not sure if it's another act or not. He leans toward me, close enough to feel the heat from his body. Leo's like the sun he throws off so much heat. One of these days, I know I'll get burned.

But not today.

"Oh, baby, we both know it was a mutual meeting of lips," he murmurs.

I stare at his lips for a beat, imagining them against mine. "And teeth."

He takes another step toward me, and I hold my ground even though the urge to back up pounds at my legs. You know that feeling when your instincts kick in, when they flip their switch and yell at you to run because there's a predator in your vicinity?

It kind of feels like that right now. Surprisingly, I don't hate it.

He steps into me, his big body brushing against mine in the most tantalizing way. Leaning down, he grazes his nose from my collarbone to my ear and whispers, "And we also both know that I could've taken you underneath that tree if I wanted to."

My lashes flutter and my breath hitches at the imagery he just offered, and my voice wavers. "No. Never."

His big palms slide around my waist and settle on my lower back, pulling me flush against him. My back arches, and I gasp at the contact. My eyes flash open, connecting with Dante's first. He captures my attention, and I miss whatever Leo whispers against my skin.

My blood pounds in my ears, drowning everything out. All I can do is focus on the way Leo feels against me and the way Dante looks at me. It's a heady combination, and I let my imagination run wild for a few precious seconds. My body feels both heavy and dizzy with lust.

Dante's expression shifts so drastically that it takes me a moment to catch on. His brows drop low over his eyes and he stands up faster than I can blink.

"Matteo." Dante's voice cracks like a whip through the room, dissipating some of the haze.

I feel Leo stiffen, his muscles bunching underneath my palms. Jesus, I don't even remember sliding them up his chest like that. I can't see Matteo from this angle, but a thread of anxiety punctures my desire.

"That better not be a fucking gun in my back, or we're going to have a fucking problem, *brother*." Leo practically spits the words through gritted teeth a few inches from my skin.

Tingles race down my spine, and I can't tell if it's from Leo or the mention of a gun.

"Oh, we already have a problem. Get your fucking hands off of my girl," Matteo growls out.

Leo pulls back and whirls around, getting in Matteo's face. "*Your* girl? You miss the part in story time where I had *my girl's* pussy rubbing against my cock last week?"

"Shut the fuck up, or I swear—"

"What? You'll what? Shoot me? Go ahead, motherfucker." Leo's words are coated in venom and dripping with derision. He holds his arms out to the side, taunting Matteo.

I stare between the two of them in disbelief, my jaw dropping. I step in the middle of the three of them, their testosterone-filled triangle standoff suffocating.

"Jesus, what is wrong with you guys?! And why the hell do you have a gun out?" I pin Matteo with a scathing glare. "I don't care how mad you are, that's no excuse to point a gun at us."

Matteo clenches his jaw and tips his chin up. "I'd never point a gun at you. I was giving my brother a warning."

My eyebrows hit my hairline. "Next time, try using your words instead of throwing a temper tantrum. And you." I spin around to face Leo. "Your little flex was unnecessary. You didn't need to tell them like that."

Leo narrows his eyes, and after a moment, nods once. I guess that's all I'm going to get from him right now. One more to go. Turning to face Dante, I put my hand on my hip and say, "And you could've intervened and dissolved it."

I look at each of them one more time before giving in to my desire to flee the situation. I don't really know what else to say, and with the way my hormones are ruling over my common sense, I know that if I don't get out of here now, I'm going to do something I'm not quite ready for.

At the hallway, I look over my shoulder and see that they haven't moved yet. All three of them stare at me with an intensity I wasn't expecting.

A shiver works its way down my back, and I can't deny it any longer. I enjoy having their attention on me.

CHAPTER TWENTY-FIVE

MADDIE

IT'S three o'clock in the morning, and I can't sleep. I've been in my bed for hours. In such a short time, I'd gotten used to staying up late to binge-watch TV and movies with Dante, but I just wasn't up for it tonight.

I excused myself after our big introduction, and I haven't really left my room since. I know it's a cowardly move, but I'm trying to be extra forgiving with myself. I've never tried to date more than one person at a time before—and I didn't account for the familiarity.

Someone placed dinner inside my room while I was in the shower—a big, juicy cheeseburger and a side salad with an iced peach black tea. My bet is on Dante. I've seen firsthand how quiet he can be if he wants.

I tried to call my sister, but I got her voicemail. Again. So either she's still screening her calls or she doesn't have service. Or I guess her phone could be dead too. So there are several possibilities, but I know her. So I know she's just ignoring me for one reason or another.

I was going to call Lainey just to chat, not even about this new development, but then I remembered all the shit she's wading through, and I can't bring myself to dump more on her. Even if mine pales in comparison to what she's dealing with.

So that left surfing some streaming channels for the last few hours. Nothing is holding my attention, and I can't stop thinking about the conversation earlier.

I can't believe Leo and Matteo are brothers. *Brothers!*

What are the odds? No, really, in a city this size, that's gotta be less than one-tenth percent, considering I didn't even know Matteo *had* a brother until today.

Looking around this luxurious room with the crown moulding, fancy fireplace, floor-to-ceiling windows with blackout blinds, and the connecting custom bathroom, I think there's probably a lot I don't really know about Matteo.

I roll onto my back and throw an arm over my eyes, letting my hair fan out around me. Some action movie plays quietly in the background. It's one that I've seen dozens of times, but it's my go-to movie when I need a pick-me-up.

It's not working tonight.

I move my arm back to my side and blow out a breath, stirring the flyaways on my face. It was supposed to be easy. Just date and flirt with and kiss who I wanted, when I wanted. Easy peasy.

Then why am I sitting awake in the middle of the night with angry moths churning in my gut? The look on Leo's face won't leave my mind. Sure, he eventually talked a big game, but his whole show was exactly that—a performance. His initial reaction is the one that keeps playing across my vision.

I war with myself, worrying my bottom lip. But I know sleep won't come until I talk to him.

I still want to have my own harem of men, but I don't want to trample anyone in the process. That's not who I am.

"Screw it," I murmur. I sit up, toss my legs over the side of the bed, and slide to the floor.

I don't give myself any more time to think about it—or chicken out—and leave my room. Now that I'm in the hallway, I realize my mistake. I don't really know which room is Leo's. I turn left first and slowly walk down the hallway, listening for—well, I don't know what I expect to hear in the middle of the night.

The first door is a bathroom, the second is an empty guest room, and the third, I remember from the brief tour when I first arrived, is Matteo's room. Turning around, I walk back and pass my room. The one across from mine is Dante's, so that leaves three options. Tiptoeing down the hallway, two doors are open—spare bedrooms. Which means the last one must be his.

Standing in front of the closed six-panel wood door, I raise my fist and knock quietly twice. Squeezing my eyes shut, I can't decide what would be better: he's asleep so I can abandon this hair-brained idea, or he's awake and I can make him listen to me.

The hinges creak and my eyes snap open. Dark green eyes peer at me through the partially opened door.

"What?"

I twist my fingers together in my hands, my nerves clogging my throat. "Can we talk?"

He sighs. "It's the middle of the night."

I nod a couple of times. "I know, and I'm sorry if I woke you. But I can't sleep, and I wanted to talk to you. So here I am."

He runs a hand through his hair, his biceps flexing and straining against his shirtsleeves. It's distracting.

"It's fine. I wasn't really asleep yet either. Come on in," he says as he opens the door wider and steps backward. I follow him to his bed, sitting on the end next to him. He leans forward, placing his elbows on his knees and his chin on his fist.

The room is large, a California king platform bed taking up central space in the room. A fireplace with a black mantel and black and white photos above it are on one side of the bed and a large TV and overstuffed cream-colored chair are on the other side.

A giant area rug warms up the space, vanilla-colored with just a hint of blue. His sheets are messed up, like he was tossing and turning too. Quiet instrumental music plays from a speaker somewhere, and soft light spills into the room from lamps on both bedside tables.

"So you live here, huh?" I cringe as soon as the last word leaves my lips, keeping my gaze casually scanning his room.

"Did you really come in here to ask me that?"

I lift a shoulder up and laugh, the sound quick and quiet. Looking at him over my shoulder, I say, "No. I don't know why I said that. I'm nervous, I guess." I blow out a breath and shift to face him with one leg bent on the bed. "Look, the circumstances behind me ending up here are wild and unexpected, to say the least. But I like you, Leo. And I never would've stood you up if it wasn't an emergency. I had no way of getting in touch with you. I'm sorry."

He keeps his gaze forward and nods a few times, the only sign he heard me.

When the silence stretches to uncomfortable lengths, I brush my hands down my cotton sleep shorts and thighs and stand up. "Okay. I'm going to head back to my room then."

One step toward the door and his hand latches onto my wrist. "Wait."

Pausing mid-stride, I look down at him. At this angle, our faces align near perfectly. Tilting his head up a little, he pins me with his green-eyed gaze. Intensity and determination line every inch of his body, and my heart skips a beat in response.

"How long?"

I lick my lips, my response immediate. "Since the day we were supposed to see that group in the park."

His thumb brushes back and forth over the sensitive skin on the inside of my wrist, snagging my attention from his intoxicating eyes. This close, I can see swirls of sea green and amber in his irises. They're unlike anything I've ever seen before.

He shakes his head slowly, his gaze unwavering. "No. How long has it been since you were my brother's?"

"Years." It feels like a lie, sour and sharp on my tongue. I've always been Matteo's. But how can I feel like Leo's and Dante's, too?

And Aries's, a little voice reminds me. As if I could forget the way he handled me like I belonged to him.

Or maybe they feel like *mine.*

214

With his gentle grip on my wrist, he pulls me forward so I'm standing between his spread legs. He sits back, putting his face close enough to mine that I could brush my lips across his with a tilt of my head.

"And Dante?"

"I just met him when I came here." I breathe the words against his mouth.

He cocks his head to the side, jaw clenched and eyes blazing. "So you just hop on any guy's lap, then?"

Jealousy colors his words, and I'm momentarily surprised at my reactionary response. A perverse sort of pleasure flows through my veins, sluggish and warm. It gives me an idea.

With my free hand, I smooth my hand up his chest and over his shoulder, pushing his body back. We both know he wouldn't budge if he didn't want to, but he goes willingly.

The light from the lamp behind him casts shadows on his face at this angle, making his green eyes stand out. They're such an unusual shade, I can't stop my gaze from straying to them. His angled jaw, strong brow, and tousled hair paint a tempting image. One I plan on seizing.

With one hand on his shoulder and the other still captured in his grip, I put one knee on the bed. Before I can settle my other knee on the bed, his grip on my wrist squeezes just hard enough to get my attention.

"What are you doing exactly?" he murmurs.

"Whatever the fuck I want," I whisper against his lips before I swing my other knee on the bed and sink my weight on to his lap.

The thin fabric of his athletic shorts does absolutely nothing to conceal his hardening dick. I swivel my hips a little, and my shorts ride up, exposing my legs.

One light tug on my wrist and my torso moves forward, enough for Leo to capture my lips in his. He teases me with soft kisses, pulling back every time I try to deepen the kiss. I answer his taunt with a rock of my hips, grinding against his dick.

I twist my wrist around, ready to shove my own fingers inside my throbbing pussy to ease the tension. He halts my movements and places my hand on his neck.

"Don't move your hand until I tell you." His words are rough with lust.

I lick my lips and nod too many times to be anything less than eager. "Okay." I keep my hands on his shoulders, but I don't stop rolling my hips over him, hunting for the perfect amount of friction I need.

Soft fingers slide the thin straps of my tank top off my shoulders, the fabric pooling low and exposing more of my breasts. My breath hitches and my nipples tighten under his gaze. He runs a finger along the top of the fabric, stopping in the middle to tug it down.

The cool air caresses my skin, such a sharp contrast to the feverish way I feel inside right now.

"Such perfect tits," he murmurs, skimming his lips around my nipples. He takes his time exploring, flicking his tongue out to taste me.

My fingers dig into his skin hard enough to hurt, but he doesn't even flinch. I can't stop my hips from flexing against him, his cock hitting my clit at just the right angle each time.

He pulls my nipple in between his teeth, tugging and sucking. It feels like a direct shot to my clit, and I can't stop the moan that spills from my lips. It's loud and drenched in want and need.

"Please, Leo," I beg, my lashes fluttering closed.

His hands slide up my leg, his thumbs tracing a path along my inner thigh and leaving goosebumps in their wake. While his lips and tongue tease me, he hooks a finger in my shorts and pulls them to the side. Cool air hits my exposed pussy, the sensation only turning me on more.

I never sleep with underwear on, and even though I wasn't planning on doing *any* of this in here tonight, you'd have to physically force me away from him right now.

I know the moment he realizes I'm bare underneath my shorts. He chuckles against my skin, his breath whispering against me.

"You tryin' to kill me, baby?" His words end on a groan, his lips on my skin. Fingers flexing on my hip, he holds me still against him.

He runs his knuckle up and down, over and over, slow enough that I can practically taste my impending orgasm.

"Stop teasing me," I pant between breaths.

Without a word, he swaps his knuckles for two fingers and plunges them inside me. My breath stutters inside my lungs, the feeling of his long fingers inside of me short-circuiting my brain for a moment. Then he starts moving, and I swear it feels like I'm astral-projecting, rising higher and higher.

My hips rock involuntarily, and I know I'm close. As if he can read my mind, his hand leaves my hip to tangle in my hair at the back of my neck. He slams my mouth on his, our tongues at war with one another. He fucks my mouth in time with his fingers, and when he grinds the palm of his hand against my clit, I detonate.

Stars blind my vision, my breath stalls, and I go weightless.

His fingers slow but don't let up, and my orgasm won't fucking end. It's like he's prolonging it somehow. Him and his magical fingers.

Finally, it ebbs, but I don't feel any less boneless.

My lashes flutter open, and I pull back from his mouth to rest my forehead against his. "Holy shit. That was incredible," I breathe out with a laugh.

He withdraws his fingers slowly, and I lean back to give him some room. I watch with reignited lust as he slides his fingers in his mouth, licking them clean. Then he steals my lips in another kiss, one that has me reaching for the band of his shorts.

A loud cough startles me enough that I jump. Leo clutches me to his chest in a protective move I wasn't anticipating.

"Enjoy the show, brother?"

CHAPTER TWENTY-SIX

MADDIE

POSSESSIVENESS DRIPS from Leo's words, and desire flares inside my veins. I kind of want to smack some sense into myself because of it. Leo's hand snakes up my neck to grab my hair and tilt my head to the side. Normally, that's the kind of dominant move that gets me hot, but I have a sinking suspicion he's doing it for someone else's benefit.

And while I think I might like to explore the idea of a little audience, this is not exactly what I had in mind.

I uncurl my fingers from his waistband and place a chaste kiss against his lips. His gaze flicks to mine for a moment, long enough for me to see the victory shining in his darkened green eyes as he stares down our guest.

I fix my tank top and adjust my shorts so I'm covered. Then, with efficient movements, I slide off Leo's lap. He folds his arms across his chest with a quirked brow, and I vow to take his shirt off at the next opportunity. That man's chest feels like it's carved from marble, and I'm dying to get a closer look.

I flash him a small smile, one that I know just tips up the corner of my mouth, and walk backward toward the door. I imagine how I look to him right now—hair tangled and mussed up from his hands, clothes rumpled, cheeks flushed.

The smirk he flashes me is pure carnal sin, his damned dimple peeking at me.

The smell of sandalwood invades my senses. Matteo's close. I wasn't sure if he would've bailed the moment Leo called him out, but I should've known better. I don't think Matteo's backed down from a challenge in his life. Why should this be any different?

I keep my eyes on Leo until the last possible moment. Only when I'm standing right next to Matteo do I shift my attention. Dragging my fingertips across his chest in a featherlight touch, I murmur, "Don't you know it's polite to knock, Matteo."

He halts me with a hand around my fingers. "I did. Twice. I could hear you moaning, and I thought you were in trouble."

Pushing onto my tiptoes to get closer to his face, I whisper, "Liar."

"Did you need something or did you just come to cockblock me?" Leo asks, voice hard and louder than it needs to be.

I slide my fingers from Matteo's grip and walk around him out of the doorway. I hear their voices as I make my way down the hall-way, but it's too quiet for me to make it out. I can hazard a guess that some of it is at least about me.

But Leo really shouldn't worry about Matteo. It's been years since we were together. I know that I called him when I was panicking and scared, but I'm choosing not to examine those feelings right now.

Instead, I'm focusing on how good Leo and Dante—and *Aries*—make me feel. Hell, if Matteo plays his cards right, I might even be persuaded to let him join in on the fun.

And that's all it'll be—*fun.*

Something to remember when I'm married to some douchebag with a side piece and more money than decency. Or you know, when I'm old and gray.

I can't afford to have feelings for all these men beyond a general caring. Anything more than that would be emotional suicide for me. Once feelings get involved, then everything goes to shit.

And then they leave.

They always do.

So this time I'm wrapping my heart in a thick layer of bubble wrap and burying it under a mountain of lust.

That's a much safer emotion.

I make it to my room before my adrenaline crashes and the trembling comes. Holy hell. I kind of can't believe I just did that. I feel like a badass bitch who can conquer the world.

Damn. Is this how Lainey feels all the time? Or Blaire? They just take what they want and actually *enjoy* it?

It's a whole new world, living for yourself and not others. I press my fingers to my lips to smother the giddy, post-orgasmic laugh that's bubbling up my chest. I didn't really have a plan when I went knocking on his door, other than to make sure he understood. Honestly, I'm not really sure that he does. One thing led to another, and before I knew it, his fingers were inside me and I was riding that bliss.

I collapse on my bed back-first with a smile on my face. The quiet hum of the bathroom fan lulls me into that space between sleep and wake, where my thoughts tangle up between four very different men.

My eyes drift closed, thoughts slowing down into a pleasant thrum, and I slip into a peaceful sleep.

Matteo

BLOOD THUNDERS IN MY EARS, mimicking the rage pounding my veins. I clench my hands, murder in my gaze as I face my brother. Finally, I hear the click of Maddie's door, my signal that she's out of earshot.

I'm across the room in seconds, fisting Leo's shirt and hauling him off the bed. A cocky smile that looks a lot like my father's spreads across his face, and I shove him back down. He lands on the bed with a laugh.

"That's it, old man? That's all the fight you got?"

His taunt hits the mark, but it serves as a reminder that I'm not my father. I won't use my fists instead of my words.

Not first, at least. If he doesn't calm the fuck down with his taunts, I won't be held liable for what I do. And last time I checked, Dante was out running an errand, so he won't be intervening this time either.

I back up a few steps, running my hand through my hair and staring at my little brother. "What the fuck are you doing?"

The laughter falls from his face so fast it's like I imagined it. "Me? What the fuck are you doing creeping inside my room when I have my girl in here? And don't even think about feeding me that bullshit line about thinking she was in trouble, because we all know it's a fucking lie."

I nod, straightening my shoulders and fixing my sleeves. It's a bullshit power move, and we both know it. "You're right. The truth is that she was mine long before she was yours." I stare at him for a moment, giving him a moment to prepare for the weight of my next words. "And she'll always fucking be mine."

He holds my gaze, ever the fucking challenger. "She doesn't feel like yours, brother. She feels like a sunflower in a sea of crabgrass— soft and delicate and *mine*."

My fingers twitch, itching to inflict pain on anyone or anything to stop the pain from lancing through my chest at his words. I lock down my emotions, trapping them underneath layers of chain to deal with another day. Or never.

He tips his chin up with a sneer. "Though I suppose Dante feels the same."

A chain snaps, the rage erupting up my throat like lava. "The fuck's that supposed to mean?" My words come out as a snarl, but my brother doesn't even flinch. If anything, his eyes sparkle with satisfaction.

"You should really ask your best friend, man. Or better yet, watch the camera feed."

I shake my head, disbelief turning the motions slow. My stomach clenches, a running reel of all the times we spoke about Maddie flashing across my vision.

No, Dante wouldn't make a move on her. He's too loyal. He knows my feelings toward her, he's said as much himself. And he knows the ramifications of getting involved with someone right now. It's a perilous time, especially with the recent move by our instigator.

No, this must be some twisted power play by Leo. Dante doesn't have the balls to go for Maddie, especially not under the roof we share.

I shake my head with a frown, staring at my brother and trying to find the crack in his lie.

He holds my gaze, expressionless. "Ask him, man."

I wave a hand in the air as if to dissipate this conversation. "I don't have time for this. We're at war, Leo."

He freezes, his eyes blinking rapidly. "What? With who?"

I stare at him, admissions on the tip of my tongue. It would be so easy to unload some of this on him. He'd be an asset, but maybe more importantly, he'd be informed. He would take my warnings more seriously.

And he'd help me keep Maddie safe.

I pace, a few steps to the right and a few to the left. After two rotations, I've made up my mind.

"All you need to know is that we're at war with an unknown enemy, and the safest spot for you is here."

"Is that why Madison's here?"

Running my hand over my face, I sigh. "No. That's unrelated and not my story to tell, so you'll have to ask her about it."

He nods like he expected that answer. "I still don't understand how I never met her before if you two supposedly dated."

"That's a story for another time," I say as I turn around and head for the door.

"Wait, that's it? This is such bullshit, man! Why don't you just tell me what's *really* going on?"

"You know it doesn't work like that. You're not made yet," I tell him over my shoulder.

"And who's fucking fault is that?" He advances on me in three steps, his finger pointing at me in accusation. "You were already made by the time you were my age."

I turn around and step in his face. "Don't fucking push me, Leo. And you know why. I joined the family early so you didn't fucking have to. So you could live a *normal life*."

He laughs, the noise caustic and dripping with disdain. "Oh, you've got to be joking. You think living at some boarding school year-round and never seeing my family is a *normal life*?"

"It's better than the alternative."

He steps backward a few paces and scrubs his hand down his face. "Whatever you tell yourself to sleep at night. I'm sure I'm not the only one who feels fucking abandoned—"

"Don't bring him into this," I interrupt with a growl, my shoulders bunching in anger. I take a half step backward and stretch my neck from side to side. "We're getting off topic. Look, it's going to get bad before it gets better. But it *will* get better, and then we can talk about you joining the family. I have . . . plans in place."

I don't know how I feel about my brother joining the family. A part of me, the older, protective brother part, doesn't want him anywhere near it. But realistically, I understand that he can't change his last name. And the Rossis have been in the five families since the beginning. It's in his blood as much as mine. And I don't have any right to take that from him, but at least I can protect him from the darkness of this life for a little longer.

He thinks this is what he wants, but if he knew how it really was, he'd run and never look back. In some ways, I envy his ignorance of the dark and depraved details of the families. It's a luxury many of us didn't have.

"And Madison?"

I pause in the doorway, my chest seizing at the mention of her name from his mouth so soon after I saw them together. "You know where I stand."

"I'm not giving her up. I mean it, man. You'll have to pry her from my cold, dead hands," he growls through gritted teeth.

I don't turn around, leaving him facing my back. I don't trust myself not to engage if he takes a swing at me. Because I know he wants to. He's too green, too young to understand the ramification of taking a shot at the undeclared underboss of our family.

I'm sure I could spin it as a family thing, which it is, but it'll make both of us look weak. And that's not something I can afford right now. Instead, I face the hallway, protecting us both, and deliver the thinly veiled threat to the person I spent most of my life shielding.

"Don't make promises you don't intend to keep, brother."

CHAPTER TWENTY-SEVEN

MADDIE

I WAKE up with a belly full of anxious caterpillars squirming around. I don't know what to expect today, and I've never really done well with the unexpected. The soft cotton of the sheets feels cool against my legs as I stretch my limbs out. There's something about a good stretch to start the day that energizes me .

Unbidden, images of last night drift across my consciousness. Hot pricks of shame poke at my bliss, threatening to pop my good mood like a balloon.

Last night was . . . a lot.

And it'd be easy to let pop. To let polite society's norms taint what were two of the best kisses I've ever had the pleasure of experiencing. Though, all the kisses between Leo and I have been amazing, so maybe it's more like two of the best kiss*ers*.

But spending the week away from those expectations and those people has freed me from those restrictions—at least temporarily.

I don't have any regrets, and if given the chance, I'd pick up right where Leo and I left off.

And where Dante and I left off.

My lips tip up in a secretive smile. In a weird way, I'm kind of proud of myself. And I know once I tell Lainey, she's going to be giggling right alongside me.

Who knew following my own North Star would feel so rewarding? And *orgasmic?*

Ugh, my eyes roll of their own accord at my cheesiness.

My stomach rumbles, reminding me that this new schedule I've been on isn't conducive to breakfast before ten o'clock. I'm used to eating before seven most mornings, and usually something light like yogurt and organic, grain-free granola or egg whites.

But here? Here, it's like a gourmet breakfast with omelets and muffins and all the kinds of food my mother warned my sister and me away from when we got boobs in middle school. That's when I first really started understanding what it means to count calories.

Not everyone is meant to be a parent, and unfortunately for us, our only living parent falls into that category.

With that depressing thought, I haul myself out of bed and get ready for the day. I want to have a conversation with Leo and Dante, clear the air a little. When I went in search of Leo last night, it was with the intention to talk. But things escalated, and we didn't do too much talking.

Not that I'm complaining.

But I want to be clear with them. I'm not trying to hurt anyone. That's not my goal here.

I'm sure there will be a few questions. And depending on how it goes, maybe the best thing would be for me to head home. It was so kind of Matteo to offer up his home to me to lie low in, but I'm okay now. It's probably time for us all to get back to our daily lives.

It's been a wild week, the least of which is finding out that Leo and Matteo are related. You'd think that with the week I'd had I couldn't be surprised, but I was.

My emotions ping-ponged from desire to shock too many times last night that the details are a little fuzzy.

Caffeine. I need caffeine to think everything through.

I quickly get myself ready, dressing in one of my favorite summer dresses. It's a knee-length, linen, A-line dress with a delicate halter neckline. Soft blue and white flowers cover most of the fabric, and the skirt is swishy and flirty.

I add a little concealer underneath my eyes, apply a few coats of mascara, and bronze my cheekbones to complete the look. Leaving my hair down might be a mistake in this humidity, but I can always twist it up.

The unmistakable smell of cooking bacon wafts down the hall, and I let my nose lead the way to the kitchen. Before I'm anywhere near, I hear voices—male voices. Slowing my steps, I tilt my head to listen. I'm not going to eavesdrop, but after yesterday's surprise, I don't want to be caught off guard by another *roommate*.

My footsteps are quiet on the distressed plush runner rug in the hallway, the soft fabric absorbing the noise. I hear Leo and Matteo for sure. There's at least another voice too, but it's too quiet for me to tell if it's Dante or someone else.

Then I hear it. My name.

My ears prick when Matteo says my name in that deep baritone of his. It's like it's tied to those memories from years ago, and it brings me back to those good times. They say you never forget your first love, and I can attest that it's true for me.

I pause inside the hallway, so only the barest hint of me is visible. But fate's on my side today, because Leo, Matteo, and Dante are standing around the island, absorbed in a conversation. None of them are facing me, and that almost makes it too easy.

I feel a little guilty about listening to their conversation, but then Leo opens his mouth, and my guilt flees.

"Oh, so you get to fuck her but I have to stay away?" Leo throws his hands in the air, anger rolling off of him in droves.

"Yeah, that's exactly right, little brother, so back the fuck off," Matteo growls without taking his concentration from the espresso machine.

"I'm so sick and fucking tired of listening to you tell me what to do all the time. I always do what you ask, but not this. I won't do it."

"Is that right?" Matteo goads, nodding his head.

I can see the fury building inside him, and it only proves to pour gasoline on my indignation. Who are they to tell me who I can and can't have sex with? And why are they all sitting here and talking about me like I'm not right down the hall? It's like they don't care if I walk in on this little pissing contest.

"Yeah, that's right. I'm tired of always taking your orders. How about you listen to *me* now, yeah, old man?"

"Watch it. I'm only three fucking years older than you," Matteo interrupts with a growl.

Leo ignores him and continues, "How about *you* stay the fuck away from her, yeah? Trust me, brother, I take *very* good care of her. But you already got a front-row seat for that, yeah?" The implication is there in every word and the smug smile on Leo's face. I fight my knee-jerk instinct to feel shameful about it, and instead, wrap it around me with pride. I hold on to my empowerment with a vise grip.

Like a train wreck I can't look away from, I watch in perverse fascination as Matteo's face totally shuts down and his body goes still.

"The fuck you say to me?" His voice is low, and I think that only makes it scarier.

Dante wades in with his arms raised in the universal calm down gesture. "Alright, c'mon, guys. Let's remember we're a fucking family, and it's the twenty-first century, Maddie can fuck whomever she wants."

Three things happen at the same time: Dante realizes his wording, Leo grins in satisfaction, and Matteo loses all semblance of control.

"The fuck you just say? Don't think I don't know what the fuck you were doing with her, Dante." Matteo glares at his best friend.

Dante, for all his bravado, doesn't even blink in the face of Matteo's ire. His chest puffs out, his muscles looking impossibly bigger, and he tips his chin up, almost like he's daring Matteo.

I know I need to step in, but I'm just not sure how it's all going to play out. I take a deep breath and push off the wall in the hallway, stepping out of the shadows and into the bright lights of the kitchen.

"Stop."

One word and all three heads whip toward me. The sense of power infuses my veins, but I easily dismiss it. I didn't step in here for that, even if it is a nice ego boost. I did it because the thought of the three of them fighting—really fighting—over me makes me sick to my stomach.

I'm human and I'm an avid romance reader, so of course, I want them to fight a little bit. But not to the level I know they're heading for.

I lick my lips and look each of them in the eye. "I'm not a prize to be won."

"Sure you're not, *Jasmine*," Leo says, crossing his arms and fighting a smile.

I roll my eyes and snap my fingers. "Focus, you *Disney prince*. I'm serious though. None of you have a say in what I do or who I do it with." I hold up my hand when Matteo's mouth opens. I can see his rebuttal written in his stiff posture. "I'm the only one who has a say in what I do with my body and who I share it with. That being said, I don't want to disrespect you in your home, so I think it's time for me to head back to mine."

A chorus of protests meets my declaration, but I hold up a hand, palm out, to stay their opinions.

I pause to wet my lips and smooth my dress out, taking a moment to gather my thoughts—and courage. I look at each of them from underneath my lashes. "I don't know how to go about this exactly, so I'm just going to rip the Band-Aid off. I'm attracted to each of you . . . in spite of our history," I murmur the last few words, narrowing my eyes on Matteo. "And I know it's unconventional and maybe unfair of me to ask, not when I'm basically telling you I'm . . . exploring—"

Leo barks out a cough to cover up his laugh. I cut him a glare and he raises his eyebrows in the very gesture of innocence.

"Anyway, I know it's not fair of me, but I'm asking it anyway. To not see anyone else, I mean, if you're seeing me. And if you've changed your mind, then okay." I twist my fingers as I look between Dante and Leo as I deliver my terms—that's exactly what they feel like. I idly wonder if Lainey ever had to lay it out like this . . . I should definitely call her and pick her brain on how exactly to avoid the Rossi and Esposito landmines.

And looking at Matteo now—his posture rigid, his jaw clenched, he looks like he's one wrong word away from exploding. I sometimes wonder what he would be like if he ever eased up on his control.

No one says anything, and then Matteo and Dante pull out their vibrating phones. They still for a moment, and trepidation tiptoes down my spine. "What's going on?"

"Goddamnit," Matteo curses. "That's the third one this week. Motherfuckers are getting bold."

"We need to figure out the problem," Dante offers.

"A meeting's been called for all of us."

"What?" I ask again. The shift in energy is palpable, and it's triggering my fight or flight response, which is such a weird reaction. I know I'm safe with them, so I'm not sure what wires are crossed.

"Nothing you need to worry about, Madison." His tone is dismissive, and he barely spares me a glance.

"Maybe I want to help," I offer.

Matteo scoffs. "I don't think so."

I bristle, his disbelief at my offer to help pokes at an old emotional wound. "I'm good at problem solving," I defend.

Matteo barks this sarcastic laughter that grates on my nerves. I just know whatever he's going to say next is going to hurt. "This isn't a charity dinner or a school dance, this is a real-world problem with real-world consequences. It's out of your pay grade." He sneers, the words slithering from his mouth like poisonous darts.

My mouth falls open at his casual mention of a school dance, like he didn't absolutely shred my innocent heart at a school dance two years ago.

Then he pours salt on the wound.

I roll my lips inward and nod my head a few times. It's more to buy myself a few extra seconds than anything else. I hover by the entrance to the hallway, my mind already planning how I'm going to pack my stuff and leave the second I leave this hallway.

My sinuses sting, warning me of impending tears, but I shove

232

them down. I'm not going to give him the satisfaction of knowing he struck a nerve.

I should be thanking him. I was starting to look at him differently, think of him differently. I guess I needed the reminder of who he really is, and who he thinks *I* am.

Not a partner or an equal.

But as someone who's only good for one thing: arm candy.

My steps are hurried as I walk down the hallway toward my room.

"Madison. Wait."

I stop in my tracks and spin around, my hair whirling with the sharp movement. My jaw hurts from how hard I'm clenching it—in anger and in a weak attempt to hold off the tears that want to break free.

"What, Dante? I think your silence said enough."

He stops a foot in front of me and holds my gaze without flinching. "Don't leave."

I fold my arms across my chest and look to the side as anger and embarrassment hold my tongue hostage.

"I won't speak for anyone else, but I want you to stay." His voice is low, persuasive and earnest.

Like some sort of spell caster, his voice eases my immediate anger and smooths over the rough edges of embarrassment. I turn my head to look at him, inhaling his woodsy scent.

He searches my gaze, and after a few moments, he nods. I'm not sure what he saw, but whatever it was satisfies him. He nods again and takes a backward step.

"Dante," Matteo calls from the kitchen where I left him.

Dante looks at me for a moment before he turns around and stalks toward the kitchen.

I exhale a breath I forgot I was holding and decide it's time for some air.

CHAPTER TWENTY-EIGHT

MADDIE

I WALK AROUND FOR AN HOUR, casually browsing a few shops around Matteo's apartment. I know I need to go back to my dorm, but I'm not ready to go back to Matteo's apartment and get my stuff. I needed a little space from them.

Dante asked me to stay, but I'm not sure it's the best idea. I like the idea of exploring more with him—and Leo. But maybe a change of scenery is better.

The walls felt like they were closing in on me, and I needed some air to clear my head. Walking around and admiring beautiful things usually helps calm me down. A byproduct of shopping with my mother for so many years, I'm sure.

I suppose I could always just leave now, head to my place without a word to any of them. But something about not saying goodbye has my soul aching in a way I don't understand.

I'm a little surprised . . . and maybe even disappointed that none of them followed me, even just watched over me to make sure I wasn't snatched off the street again. But I suppose that threat is gone now, Lainey and her boys are taking care of it.

Still, the hopeless romantic part of me thought they'd catch up to me. Maybe this is fate's way of telling me it's time to move on. That or I read too many romance novels.

I walk toward a coffee shop I spotted about a half block down. It's hot today, and the sunshine and humidity make it feel ten degrees warmer. An iced tea would taste amazing right now.

I open the door and welcome the cool, air-conditioned air. A bell chimes, announcing my arrival.

"Welcome to Mocha Lisa!" someone greets me from behind the counter. I can't see them from this angle, but I smile in response.

I look around as I walk toward the counter, taking in all the decor. This place is incredible. Bookshelves line one wall with brightly colored spines facing outward. Mismatched overstuffed chairs, vintage-looking tables and chairs, flowers in tall, skinny vases as centerpieces, overflowing bakery case.

Mocha Lisa might be my next favorite coffee shop.

"Hey, what can I get you?" the barista asks with a wide smile. Her black hair is pulled back into a messy bun on the top of her head and black, wide-framed glasses sit perched on her nose, framing ice-blue eyes. They've got to be the palest blue eyes I've ever seen, and they're so mesmerizing, it takes me a moment to respond to her question.

I laugh, embarrassment warming my cheeks. "I'm sorry. It's just, I've never seen eyes like yours before. They're so unique."

She waves a hand in the air, her smile never wavering. "You're fine. I get that all the time. So, what'll it be today?"

"Oh, uh, how about an iced tea? Something with caffeine. Lots of caffeine, please."

She nods her head as if she's commiserating with me. "One of those days, huh?"

"You have no idea." I smile and let my gaze wander as she gets my drink together. I look over their bakery case in interest. Home-made cookies, coffee cakes, mini cupcakes, biscotti, fudgy brownies. You can usually find some hidden gems in the bakery case of a good coffee shop.

"Well, this should give you that boost you need. It's a loose leaf black tea with a hint of apricot. It's one of our bestsellers and one of my favorites. The timer will beep in a few minutes when it's done steeping, then I'll pour it over some ice for you." She places the mini French press of steeping tea and the timer on the counter. "Four twenty-three today."

"Perfect, thanks." Looking down, I reach into my crossbody purse. My fingers curl over my wallet when a familiar voice rolls over me.

"Here."

Lifting my head, I notice a familiar hand holding a familiar black card. My muscles tighten at his proximity, and my heart betrays me by skipping a beat.

"I'll take an Americano too, please."

The barista takes her time taking his card, her gaze asking me if I'm okay. I nod twice before tipping my head to the side.

Sun-kissed skin, a five o'clock shadow, and pouty lips are the first things I see. "How did you find me?"

"A coffee shop with vintage books and mismatched chairs? Where else would you be?" His response is immediate, and it thaws a little of my ire. "Okay, that's not entirely true. This is the twelfth coffee shop I've been to in the last hour. Pretty sure the last place was going to call the cops on me for asking about you." He shrugs, unbothered by the prospect of the cops showing up for him.

I step to the side to see him clearly. Charcoal-colored V-neck tee, shorts, and designer sunglasses covering his green eyes, he looks the part of casual wealthy like so many others in this area. "What's with the sunglasses inside?"

The timer goes off, stealing my attention from him. The barista places Leo's Americano on the counter, shuts off the timer, and pours the tea over ice.

He murmurs his thanks as he takes a sip of his coffee, his little noise of appreciation stealing my attention from the French press.

I gasp before I can think better of it and take a step toward him. "Jesus, Leo, what happened?" I brush tentative fingers over the skin underneath his eye. It's darkening and puffy, and I've been around enough to know a black eye when I see one.

He grabs my fingers in his hand and brings them to his lips. He places a kiss on each of my fingertips, murmuring, "It was nothing."

My breath catches at the tenderness of it, my anger melting away further. "It sure looks like something. What happened?"

He smiles against my hand. "You should see the other guy."

"Ha-ha. Don't use that cliché line on me, Leonardo," I scold him.

"Ooh, baby, you know what happens when you say my name like that," he murmurs around a smile.

"Keep it in your pants, Casanova. We're in the middle of a coffee shop," I hiss in a hushed voice.

He lifts his head from my fingers, piercing me with his intense gaze. "You never minded an audience before."

I pull my fingers from his hand, my cheeks pinking under his reminder. "That's different. Plus, you're in the doghouse, so stop being so charming."

Without another word, I grab my drink, thank the barista, and make my way toward a little table along the wall. I pause before I sit down, looking over my shoulder with a raised brow.

Picking up on my cue, he follows me to the table and sits across from me. He leans forward, arms on the table and gaze on me. I take a sip of my iced tea just to give myself something to do. Deja vu hits me hard, my head dizzy, mind scrambling. I squint an eye to stop the spinning feeling. It lasts long enough to remind me why I don't like those spinning rides at amusement parks.

"Hey, what's wrong?"

I wave a hand in the air as the feeling passes. "Nothing, I'm fine. Why are you here, Leo?"

"Ouch," he says with a grimace, clutching his chest with one hand.

I wait him out with a raised brow.

His teasing grin falls from his lips, his expression open. "I needed to find you, to apologize, and, fuck, I don't know, fix it."

I raise a shoulder in a half shrug. "How can you fix something your brother feels?"

"That's just it. I don't think he really feels like that. Matteo has a hard time, uh, expressing himself. He spends too much time wrapped up in here." He taps his temple with his index finger.

I bite my lip and look him over. "I don't understand. Earlier you seemed, I don't know, jealous. And now you're here championing for Matteo? Apologizing on his behalf? I don't get it."

He drums his fingers on the table. "When I win your favor, it'll be because I'm the better man, the better choice, not because Matteo fucked up before we could really begin. I'm not a default choice, baby. I'm the only choice."

His words feel like a promise, spinning around into the air and branding themselves on my soul. A shiver skates down my spine, and my cheeks flush at his intensity.

"What if I don't want to choose though?"

He rakes his teeth over his bottom lip, his eyebrows low and fingers drumming faster on the table. "Then that's something we talk about."

I nod and take another sip, surprised by his answer. It's what I wanted to hear, but still, I'm surprised he seems so . . . at ease.

"And that stuff you overheard, that wasn't about you—not really. My brother and I have . . . a complicated family."

"Doesn't everyone?"

He nods a few times as he fiddles with the sleeve to his paper coffee cup. "But most families aren't in the mob." His words are barely above a whisper.

His words roll off his tongue with such ease that I second-guess what I heard. "I'm sorry, did you just say the—"

"Yes," he interrupts, looking over each shoulder. "Don't say it again. The five families have eyes and ears everywhere."

My mouth parts as I search his gaze for any amusement or tease, but all I find is resignation.

"You're kidding, right?"

He shakes his head. "And Matteo's in the thick of it. So I'm here on all of our behalf."

"I don't understand."

He drums his fingers on the table, his knee bouncing to the same tempo. "There's a lot I'm not privy to, but I just thought you should know."

My cheeks heat and my eyes narrow, suspicion coating my words. "If this is some attempt to warn me off—"

"It's not. I swear." He sighs. "I'm not sure if he would've told you, but I'm so fucking tired of all the secrets. And I like you, Madison. So, I, uh, wanted to let you know."

The tops of his cheeks flush pink, and I decide he must be telling the truth. I don't think I've ever seen him less than confident. But this guy sitting in front of me now, fidgeting and blushing? This is a new version of Leo. And I can't say I don't like it.

"Okay. What does that mean then?"

He blows out a breath and runs his hand through his hair, mussing it up in a distracting way. "I don't know. Will you come back to the apartment with me though? Matteo will be better at explaining things than me."

CHAPTER TWENTY-NINE

MADDIE

"ALRIGHT. I'm going to use the bathroom first." I sling my purse across my body and crane my neck, looking for a restroom sign.

"Back corner. I'll wait here for you, yeah?" Leo takes a sip of his Americano.

In one movement, I stand and push my chair in. And on impulse, I lean over and brush my lips across his before pulling back.

"What was that for?"

Rocking back on my heels, I offer him a half shrug and a smile. "Felt like a good time for it."

"Always. It's always a good time for a kiss from you," he murmurs, flashing those distracting dimples at me.

"You're too smooth for your own good, you know," I tease him. "I'll be right back."

I spin on my heel and head toward the back of the coffee shop. I kind of love it here. It reminds me of my favorite one by my dorm. All cozy, overstuffed chairs and eclectic tables between them. Three bookshelves of books and games to borrow. Big windows that let the sunlight in, and decor that straddles the line between vintage-chic and gaudy.

The antique glass door handle squeaks when I twist it to open the bathroom door, but the inside is modern with three stalls, two full-length mirrors, and two sinks.

I wash my hands and use this delicious mango-scented hand scrub after I finish, admiring the vintage cross faucet handles. I haven't seen anything like these before.

I turn to grab a towel from the stack of well-loved hand towels, and the lights go out. It happens in an instant, the switch from fluorescent lights to pitch-black startling.

I freeze, water sliding down my arms and terror licking my nerve endings. My breathing picks up, and I can't stop blinking like that's going to help me see better.

Maybe they blew a fuse. That happens in these older buildings all the time.

Or it could be a rolling blackout. It's hotter than Hades outside still, and I can't remember the last time I watched the news. It's definitely possible for this to be a planned thing.

No need to panic.

I abandon the towels and swipe my hands down the fabric of my dress. Reaching blindly, I pat tentative fingers in the space in front of me and shuffle my feet forward. I'm so thankful I wore sneakers today. I'm sure I would've broken an ankle if I was in my red soled shoes this afternoon.

A few steps later, and I feel wood beneath my fingertips. Smoothing my hands down the wood, I find the handle. Relief blankets me when I palm the door handle.

But it's short-lived because it's not turning.

Why is the handle not turning?

My body flushes from head-to-toe, and my heart starts hammering against my ribs. I try again, but my hand keeps slipping off. It wasn't fully dry, so I take a few precious seconds to really dry it on my shorts.

You're fine, Maddie. It's just a bathroom. No one's going to grab you from inside a bathroom.

My mental pep talk does jack-shit to calm me down. I feel the terror bubble up my throat, lodging itself there.

My phone vibrates in my pocket, and I want to facepalm so bad, but with my luck, I'd miss and give myself a black eye. I should've realized this sooner. I can just call Leo, and he'll open it from his side.

Crisis averted.

Blowing out a breath of anxiety, I slip my phone from my back pocket and open it to view the new text message. It's from a number I don't have saved in my phone—I don't recognize it at all, actually. It has a plus-three-nine-three area code, which must mean it's international.

Oh, *duh*, I bet it's Lainey. I know she's been using all sorts of different phones lately, so I'm not really surprised. I blow out a breath, already feeling calmer about everything.

I open the text message, intent on sending her an SOS and then calling Leo. But what I see has my heart stopping.

It's not Lainey.

I don't know who it is, but I can't stop the feeling of dread crawling down my throat.

Unknown Number: You're in danger. Run.

I flip open my flashlight app and spin around, widening my eyes to try and see anything. The last stall is closed, and suddenly, I can't remember if it was closed when I came in here.

Sweat coats the back of my neck, and I toss my hair to the other shoulder to cool off.

I give myself another pep talk and walk toward the closed door with my fist clenching the phone. It's the only logical place anyone could be hiding. Not that I necessarily think anyone is hiding in here for me, but someone sent that message. I'm praying it was a bunch of punk kids playing pranks on unsuspecting people.

Bending over at the waist well before the door, I look underneath the door for any feet.

Nothing.

Inhaling a deep breath, I blow it out and kick open the door. It swings on squeaky hinges, opening wide to reveal a toilet and nothing more.

Oh, thank god.

Relief makes my knees weak, and I tip my head back to exhale the breath I didn't realize I was holding. Okay, time to get the hell out of here. I knew watching that scary movie with Dante the other day was going to come back to bite me.

I jiggle the doorknob again, twisting it left and right, but it still won't budge. These vintage doorknobs are beautiful but a pain in the ass to work. With one hand, I pull up Leo's phone number and hit the call button, and with the other, I slap it against the door. I'm hoping between the two, someone will be able to help.

"Madison?"

"Leo! I'm stuck in the bathroom. The handle won't open, and the lights are out."

"What? What lights?"

Dread tiptoes down my body, leaving its icy chill in its wake. "The power went out. I thought it was a planned thing. But then I got this creepy text. Leo, get me outta here, please."

Desperation claws out of my mouth, and I start pounding on the door. The feeling of being watched coats my skin, oily and hazardous.

"Don't hang up. I'll be right there. Ten seconds." He's firm, commanding, and it settles the topmost layer of panic. "I'm here. Step back, okay?"

"Okay." I jog a few steps backward with a nod.

The handle wiggles for a moment before I hear a loud bang and see the door wobble in its frame. Three more loud bangs, and the door opens, pieces of splintered wood flying into the bathroom.

Back-lit by the hallway light stands my savior, my knight in shining armor. Shadows curl around his black V-neck and dark-colored shorts, holding him in their grips like he belongs there.

"Leo!" I sprint toward him, jumping at him and wrapping my arms around his neck at the last second. Arms open, he catches me with ease, pulling me in tight for a hug. "Thank you. I-I don't know what's going on, but I think we should leave."

He slides me down his body and laces his fingers with mine, tugging me toward the front of the store. The first thing I notice is the power. As in, it's *on*.

Okay. So maybe it was a blown fuse. But that doesn't explain the weird text. I want to ask Leo if he recognizes the number, but I'm going to wait until we're out of here first. I can't shake the feeling of eyes on me.

I follow Leo to the front door, a half step behind him and to the left. I side-eye every single person I pass, looking for . . . something that could tell me what the text message or bathroom was all about. I don't know what I'm expecting—maybe a sign that says "I'm guilty."

But I don't find anything but smiling people drinking coffee. And that might be the scariest part of all.

CHAPTER THIRTY

MATTEO

I STARE at the faces of the men around the table. The five families have always been the same. Romano, Marino, Gallo, Vitale, and Rossi. Our families crossed the pond decades ago and formed this unbreakable bond.

Unbreakable. What a fucking joke.

One of these motherfuckers could be behind the attacks. I eye each one, keeping my shoulders relaxed and my fists unclenched. It takes fucking work to act so unaffected. I don't know how all of them sit here and sip their drinks as if some asshole hasn't declared war on us by dumping bodies of our soldiers at our doorsteps.

But to go after someone's woman?

That's the level of savageness that should shake even the sturdiest of men. How can they not see the face of their wife or girlfriend or fucking side piece on Rachel Bianchi's mutilated face? Sal Bianchi's a fucking made man, been in the family for generations. A good earner, trusted member of the family.

And this is the respect he gets when his wife's body is dumped on his front porch? Where's the urgency, the vengeance?

A bunch of egotistical men smoking cigars like it's a dinner party.

I can't stop thinking that it could've been Madison. I know it's irrational, and I don't think any of them are even aware of her existence. But my fingers itch to call her.

Dante said to give her space and let Leo go after her. And as much as it pained me to not be the one to bring her back home, I didn't have the time. We had to get here.

My lip curls as I scan the lot of 'em. There's no love lost between most of us. Half of 'em still can't get over my father naming me underboss and they take every opportunity to let their opinions be heard.

But could one of them turn on the five families like that? Going after someone's wife is a far cry from snide comments and underhanded deals. It's more than declaring a war.

It's burning down everything the five families originally stood for and pissing on the burning embers.

Doesn't matter if he's made or not, a man goes after your woman unprovoked like that—he's on borrowed time, and he fucking well knows it. Love doesn't factor into the vengeance for most of these assholes. It's about the disrespect.

I look at each of their faces—the heads of the families, a consigliere, their underbosses, and a soldier or two. None of them look overly distressed, but that doesn't mean shit. These men have been playing poker three times a week for ten to twenty years.

I push down the urge to run my fingers through my hair to push it off my face. I'm fucking exhausted and stretched thin, and I'm sure the bags under my eyes show as much.

I let my mind wander as idle chatter surrounds me. I don't really give a fuck about some petty bullshit between the families. The shit I need to know won't be given so freely. It's in the subtext and what people *don't* say.

And I know Dante has my back—literally and figuratively. I know without looking that he's standing behind me, back to the outer wall, hands crossed in front of him. He always leaves his suit coat unbuttoned, so should shit hit the fan, he doesn't have to waste time wrestling open a button.

At least when it comes to this, I know I can trust him.

There will be a conversation about his actions with my girl, but murder waits for no man.

So here I am, gut burning with jealousy at my best fucking friend and my younger fucking brother. I clench my jaw and try to ignore the acidic poison infiltrating my veins and focus on the conversation around me.

Ironically, if I could've, I would've sent Dante with Madison. The Brotherhood is handling their business now, so she shouldn't be in the same kind of danger. But I pulled off her check-in detail—which was mostly fucking Dante, a little detail I discovered only recently—since she's been safe inside my house. I was going to get one of my most trusted soldiers to watch her while we came here, but Leo insisted he'd take care of her.

At Dante's encouragement, I agreed. Let's see if he can really hack the family life. He thinks he wants in, but he has no fucking idea what's really required to be a member of this family.

Your goddamn soul.

I've been doing him a favor all these years, protecting him from this shit. And this is the thanks I get—he goes after the only girl I've ever cared about.

If these emergency mandatory five families meetings weren't nonnegotiable, I would've gone after Cherry. But they are and they change locations on a dime. And if my second and I don't show, the Rossis look weak. So here we are. Fucking miserable together.

It fucking burns knowing that she's not at my home right now, that she's off doing whatever with Leo.

I flex my hand underneath the table at the sudden surge of jealousy that shoots through my muscles, clenching them involuntarily.

I did the right thing, right?

I can't divulge these kinds of secrets to her, and pulling her into my web, even just a little bit, will only be her ruin. It's good that she wants to go back to her place. Fuck, it was stupid to even bring her to my place to begin with.

So why does it feel like I'm having a fucking panic attack at the thought of her leaving? I rub at the spot that aches inside my chest without conscious thought.

"Something wrong, son?"

The quiet of the room after Dominic Vitale's question settles around us like a hundred-pound boulder.

I turn to face him, taking my time to tilt my head. "What did you call me?"

My voice is low and measured. Rossis don't raise their voices— we don't need to. When we talk, people fucking listen.

Vitale finally shows the first sign of self-preservation. He licks his lips and drums his fingers against the table. "You were touching your chest, so I asked if something was wrong." He shrugs both shoulders high up toward his ears and tips his chin up. All three of his sons mimic his stance.

I nod my head twice, the movement sarcastic. "Tell me something, Ralph."

"What's that?"

"Who am I?"

His bushy eyebrows bunch together as he stares at me for a moment too long. "Matteo Rossi."

I hold his gaze and say, "Exactly. I'm not your fucking son. And the next time you forget, I'm going to break three of your fingers to remind you."

I see the wheels turning inside his mind, and when it all clicks, he explodes out of his chair. His sons follow suit, all four of them yelling nonsense while waving their arms around.

Dad holds up his hand, palm up, and they quiet down. I don't move. I'm not worried about Ralph Vitale. That fat fuck couldn't hit a target if it was hogtied on the ground two feet in front of him. And even though his sons are slimy scumbags, they idolize my dad more than their own. They'd never step against us.

"You gonna let him disrespect me like that, Angelo?" Ralph asks, a bead of sweat rolling down the side of his face.

Dad shrugs with his hands in the air. "You disrespected him. He's a made man just as much as you. Besides, he didn't even break your fingers yet."

I'm not the only one who hears the pride in his voice when he talks of me breaking fingers. It's one of his signature moves, after all. Do you know how easy it is to lie about broken fingers? It can happen doing the most mundane of things. I'm lucky Dante knew enough about first-aid from his ma to properly splint my fingers when I was younger, otherwise, I have no doubt that mine would be a gnarly mess.

"Now that everyone's done acting like a bunch of pussies, let's move on. Who the fuck is torching our interests and leaving bodies? Does anyone know?" Dominic Marino asks around puffs of his cigar.

"Could be Russian. Tommy caught some guys of Russian descent snooping around the docks two days ago," Tony Romano, my friend, offers.

"Russian descent? What the fuck do I look like, some genealogy test? The fuck does that mean? Was he one of Alexei's guys or not?" Dad raises his voice by the end, nearly yelling.

"Said he didn't give up his boss, just said 'my employer' over and over," Tony replies without missing a beat.

Nah, there's no way it's not tied to this shit somehow.

It's either them or those New Jersey fucks. Those assholes are always looking to slide into our business. They'd love to cut us out completely and assume our holding in the city.

We're holding on by a thread, which is exactly why we need a change.

"Okay. Could be Alexei's making a play for the city. What else?"

"Heard a new cartel is in town trying to rally some hands behind them for a hostile takeover. We sent a suitable message to the cartel to show our loyalty to him. Omar Villa now has the head of the new cartel in a donut box."

Dad smiles and chuckles. "I do love a good jelly donut."

"Listen, boss, I don't want to talk out of turn here, but I think we need to consider looking into Jersey," Ralph Vitale says.

"Is that right? What makes you think so?"

"Mikey heard from Paulie Amato himself that he's making moves to overthrow us. He can't act officially until his uncle Mario is out of the picture. Apparently, he's all but officially stepped down."

Dad nods his head and sips his whiskey. "I'll keep that in mind.

We might as well get our regular meeting out of the way since we're all here. Who has something to bring to the table?"

"He doesn't have sons to carry on the Gallo name, so why should he get to keep his seat?" Ralph Vitale spits, pointing at Victor Gallo, head of the Gallo family. He's rounder than he is tall, and he spits when he talks. Which is why I always make sure to sit the furthest away from him. His three sons mirror his movements, which feels like a shitty attempt at a power play. If he thinks anyone will be intimidated by them—including Victor Gallo—he's fucking stupid.

He's lucky his last name protects him. For now.

Once I take over, I'll take the concept of *spring cleaning* to a whole new level.

"Is that so, Ralph? And just what are you proposing we do? Add another family to the table?" Dad asks as he twirls a cigar over his fingers like a poker chip.

It's an act, the nonchalance. And if you know him well enough you can pick up on it easy enough. It's in the tightness around his eyes and the forced smile on his face. He's like a deranged cobra, and he's just sizing up his meal for the day.

He stares at Ralph, goading him with his questions as if we haven't heard this bullshit before. Vic's girls are just a few years younger than me, and he lost his wife two years ago. It's not like he's suddenly going to have a boy.

It's the same shit. Someone pops off and Dad has to flex his power over everyone. Surprisingly, Dad says nothing, which will probably be worse for Ralph in the long run.

"Anything else, gentlemen? Or can we get the fuck outta here and go fuck our girlfriends while our wives cook our dinners at home?" my father asks, a slimy smirk on his face. Everyone laughs at his lame attempt at humor, and the fake notes grate on my nerves.

Vic holds my gaze and says, "Actually, I do have something. I'm proposing an arrangement between my Liza and Matteo, contingent upon the Gallos keeping their seat."

I lock my shit down tight, my face never betraying my true emotions. Inside, I'm fucking raging at the audacity. That fucker brought it to the table to make me squirm, put me on the spot in hopes I'd cave under the pressure. What he forgot to factor in was the meddling men around the table.

"So you get to have two votes in the five? I don't fucking think so," Anthony Romano says, smacking his open palm against the table.

Dominic Marino scoffs. "There's a reason we don't mix the five bloodlines."

"Good thing it isn't up to you, then." Gallo shrugs and looks at my father. As the boss of the five families, it's his call. "What do you think?"

My dad stares at him for a moment, rubbing his thumb and index finger along the edge of his jaw. "I'll talk to Matteo privately, which is what you should've done."

The chastisement is hardly a slap on the wrist. He's done far worse for far less. And I just fucking know that if I let him have this talk privately, he's going to make me fucking agree to it. And since I'm not ready to take him out yet, I only have one option.

Sweat rolls down my spine, and for once, I'm fucking thankful for the ridiculous dress code of full suits. The corner of my left eye twitches—a sure sign my stress is rising.

Fuck it.

"I'm already engaged to be married."

Silence fills the room, laden with accusation and suspicion.

"You better not be acting like you're too good for my Liza. Made or not, I'll fucking put a bullet in your eye and toss you over Old Man Baxter's bridge. Let his crocs deal with you."

Gallo's threat isn't entirely idle, but I'm not too worried. Like I said, I have Dante behind me.

My dad pushes back in his chair, balancing two chair legs on the floor and two in the air. His gaze is sharp and calculating as it stares me down. "Interesting timing, boy. Who is the lucky lady who's going to be my daughter?"

The way he says daughter has my hackles up. I don't fucking like it. Not for the first time, I'm going to stare the devil in the face as I deliver a lie.

"You don't know her."

"You better remedy that, son. Yeah? I want to meet the girl who stole my son from a profitable arrangement," my dad growls out, the tone at odds with the deranged smile on his face.

"She Italian?" Romano asks.

That's all these assholes care about—keeping the five families bloodline *pure*. What a load of shit.

"No."

I grind my molars, fucking livid with myself for opening my mouth to begin with. There's only one person I ever wanted to entertain the idea of marriage with. And I'll kill every last one of them before I ever willingly give them her name.

"Not Italian? Who is this broad?" Vitale goads.

"What's her name, son?" Dad asks.

I stare at him and shrug. "You'll find out soon enough."

Dad stares at me, his face unreadable. Five years ago, I might've caved under the threat of violence that stare promises. But not anymore. I give him my best blank expression back, a big *fuck you* if there ever was one.

"What are we doing for Sal Bianchi?" Dominic Marino asks, breaking the standoff between my father and me.

While I'm glad someone finally brought it up, I can't shake the feeling that something's wrong. I can feel it in my bones.

Two seconds later, my phone vibrates, indicating a call. I let it go to voicemail. Only emergencies allow for answering calls during a family meeting.

The incessant vibration from my phone ringing nonstop dances on my already fried nerves.

Out of the corner of my eye, I see Dante slip his phone from his pocket and discretely check it. The hair on the back of my neck stands up at the coincidence.

His eye twitches twice, which is akin to screaming for anyone else not in a room with the five deadliest families. I quickly scan the room to make sure no one caught that. Not that I expect them to, they're a bunch of lazy motherfuckers who have their soldiers do all the dirty work. Most of them wouldn't know how to read a man if their life depended on it.

Dante steps forward and leans down, and in the quietest voice barely above a whisper, says, "Problem at Monroe. Code black."

I nod to him once, so he knows I heard him. Inside, I'm fucking shaking and sweating, but outside, I'm cool and calm.

Five agonizing minutes later, Dad dismisses the meeting, and Dante and I casually make our way out of the basement of the seedy strip club located in the middle of nowhere.

Dad has an uncanny knack for sniffing shit out, and I don't have time to pander to his ego tonight.

There's been a break-in at my apartment.

CHAPTER THIRTY-ONE

MADDIE

LEO SLIDES his hand in mine, linking our fingers together. Tingles race up my arm and settle around my heart, warming some of my earlier fear. The elevator ride is quick, and then we're walking down the hall toward Matteo's apartment. There are only two penthouse apartments on this floor, both of them two stories. The hallway is decorated in soft grays, almost as if it's part of the apartments themselves. I idly wonder what the other penthouse apartment looks like, if it's a mirror copy of Matteo's or something totally different. Dante said someone lives there, but I haven't seen them, not that I've left Matteo's place until today.

A Victorian-era painting of a man hangs on the wall next to me, and I get the same creepy vibes like I did from the paintings at The Grasshopper.

It's always the eyes. They feel like they're following me.

I bump into Leo's arm, too caught up in side-eyeing the painting. "Oh, sorry," I say on a reflex, wrapping my free hand around his bicep to stop my stumble. My voice trails off and my steps slow when I see the open apartment door. "Did you forget to close the door?"

"No." He shakes his head, his voice low and hard.

My adrenaline spikes, my heart rate increasing. Something crashes, the sound sharp. It frays on my already tender nerves, and I jump, squeezing Leo's hand.

"Stay behind me, yeah?" With a hand on my arm, he guides me behind him, forcing me to let go of his bicep. I tighten my grip on his hand, staying a half step behind him.

Our footsteps are quiet on the plush carpet, but the thundering of my heartbeat in my ears is loud. I quietly exhale the breath I didn't realize I was holding as we approach the door.

Leo squeezes my hand once. I'm not sure if it's a warning or encouragement, but I tighten my hold nonetheless.

Another crash rips through the air, the shrill sound of glass breaking followed by male voices.

With the toe of his shoe, Leo pushes the front door open the rest of the way, placing his body fully in front of mine. There's a moment of silence—no male voices or things breaking.

"Matteo?"

I peek out from behind Leo and see Matteo rush him, hair wild, eyes wide. "Where have you been? Where's Maddie?"

This doesn't feel right—Matteo feels off. I step out from behind Leo, but still hold his hand like the lifeline it feels like right now.

My nerves are shot, and if I wasn't sure before, I know now that I have some unresolved trauma from the kidnapping. Realistically, I knew I couldn't just pretend it didn't happen, shove it into a box and bury it six feet under. Can't blame a girl for trying, though.

"Matteo."

In two steps, Matteo's in front of me. His tattooed fingers curl over my shoulders, and he pulls me away from Leo and into the apartment. He holds me at arm's length, his gaze flying over me from head to toe several times. I don't think I've ever seen him so manic. Even in the face of a collapsing warehouse, he wasn't this rattled.

"What's going on?" Leo asks as he steps inside and closes the door. "Holy shit."

Matteo lets go of me and spins to face his brother, and I get my first unobstructed view of the apartment.

Or what's left of it.

The couch cushions are slashed open, the drapes torn off the rings, plates and glasses smashed on the floor. Gouges in the walls, cabinet shelves torn down, food spilling out of the fridge. Someone tore this place apart.

He gets in Leo's face. "Why didn't you answer your phone?"

Leo pushes him back a step. "It was on silent. What happened here?"

Matteo steps toward Leo again. "And Maddie's? Where were you two that neither one answered?"

I shoved mine in my purse when we left the coffee shop and haven't looked at it since. Nerves line my belly at the idea of another text message waiting for me from the unknown number.

"It was in my purse." My voice is quiet, but it might as well be a gunshot for how Matteo reacts. He turns around and rakes a hand through his hair. The movement jerky and harsh.

"Someone broke in, and we were worried about the two of you," Dante offers from his position leaning against the island in the kitchen.

"Jesus. Are you guys okay?" I ask, taking a few steps toward Dante.

He shrugs, wearing his nonchalance like a coat. "We're fine. We weren't here."

"Did they take anything, or I don't know, leave a message or something?" Leo asks.

Dante folds his arms across his chest. "No, so far it seems like nothing was taken, but almost everything is trashed."

Matteo turns to face away from us, rubbing the back of his neck. It's quiet for a moment, and I take in the damage.

"You have to leave." Matteo's voice is low, but the steel behind his words is unmistakable.

"C'mon, man, ease up," Leo argues.

I tilt my head, trying to see what he's looking at, but his angle blocks my view. "Well, I don't think anyone should stay here. I'm assuming the bedrooms weren't spared," I counter, looking around at everything again.

Matteo throws his arms out to the side, his eyes wide and his hair a mess. "Look around you, Leo. She doesn't belong here!"

I flinch, my shoulders jerking toward my ears. He's loud enough that if I wasn't sure this apartment was soundproof, the neighbors would've gotten a front-row seat to Matteo's rejection.

Because that's what this feels like. Again.

I cut Leo a look before focusing on Matteo. "I thought you were going to apologize, not tell me to leave again."

His face loses all expression, an impressive feat considering he was a ball of emotion thirty seconds ago. He stares at me for a few moments, his eyes void of anything recognizable, and I just know whatever he's going to say will hurt. "I don't want you here, Madison. Get out."

This rejection hits its mark, cracking the soft shell of vulnerability around my heart, leaving a crevice for cruelty and self-doubt to slither in.

My lip trembles, and I feel my eyes fill with tears, but I clench my jaw to keep them from falling.

Matteo slides his hands into his pockets, a statue of elegance in the middle of destruction and chaos. My traitorous heart leaps at the sight of him like this, commanding and powerful.

One glance at his eyes and the blankness shining from his gaze is enough for me to snap back to reality.

This asshole thinks he can keep toying with me like I'm a yo-yo. Well, I've had enough. And I'm calling bullshit.

I wipe underneath my eyes with my index finger to catch any stray tears and shake my head, the motion slow and heavy. "You're a coward."

He flinches, a small jerk, but part of me rejoices at even the tiniest bit of emotion shining through his blasé exterior. It gives me the courage to keep pushing, even though my skin prickles with his rejection.

I won't beg him to keep me. But I will try to get him to see reason.

"Don't do it, Matteo. Don't push me away."

"I'm not pushing you away." He slides his hands into his pockets. He looks the perfect part of the villain. "I just don't want you in my house any longer. I owed the Brotherhood a favor, and now I'm all paid up. Look, don't take it personal. I'm sure you'll make a lovely trophy wife one day, but I don't need any more trophies. I need a fucking queen by my side."

My jaw drops, my mind blanking for a moment. What in the actual hell is happening right now? Eyebrows low, I roll my lip inward, biting on it to bring me back to the present.

Adjusting the strap on my purse across my chest, I back up a few steps. Leo reaches out for me, but I sidestep him, tripping over a broken lamp on the ground.

Matteo halts my fall with a hand around my bicep, and I flinch away from him.

"Don't touch me," I hiss. He doesn't release me until I'm settled on my feet. I wrench my arm out of his hand, and calmly walk to the door, bottling up my embarrassment and distrust like Nana's rhubarb jam. I put a lid on it and seal it, shoving it to the back of my mind where I forget about it.

"Are you fucking kidding me? You're just going to let her go like that? What the fuck is the matter with you?" Leo storms up to his brother and gets in his face.

I don't bother to turn around to look. I'm in self-preservation mode now, and I've already given this whole situation enough of my time and energy. Stepping over broken plates and around shards of glass, I pause at the doorway and look over my shoulder at the three of them. "Mail me anything that survived the damage or don't. I don't really care either way."

"Madison, wait! I'll come with you," Leo says, shoving Matteo and crossing the room.

I hold up a hand, palm-out. "Don't. You should stay here."

"Fuck that. I'm coming with you." He stops right in front of me, his chest brushing against my hand. "Don't shut me out because Matteo's an asshole."

A sad smile tips up the corner of my lips. "He's your family, Leo. Besides, this isn't goodbye for us. Just a see you soon."

His gaze roams my face, his expression hard and closed-off. In a move too charming and quick, he snakes a hand underneath my hair and slides it up my neck to cup the side of my face. Lowering his head, he fuses our mouths together in a kiss that feels a lot like goodbye.

A single tear rolls down my face, but I hold onto his wrist, keeping his hand—and his mouth—against mine for as long as possible.

My lashes are slow to open when I pull back. He brushes his lips across mine one more time. "I'll be right behind you, yeah?"

I nod, sadness heavy in my limbs. I don't think he'll be right behind me. In fact, judging by the way Matteo and Dante just acted, I'd say there's a very good chance I won't see any of them again.

His hand slides down my arm to briefly lace our fingers together. I walk backward, letting our fingers touch for another few seconds, memorizing the way it feels to have his gaze on me.

My eyes well with tears again, more likely that they never stopped, really, so I spin around to walk down the rest of the hallway. I don't want any of them to see me cry, that feels like a privilege they lost the right to. Pressing the elevator call button more times than necessary, I fight the urge to tap my foot as anxiety pricks at my skin.

Finally, the doors open and I step inside. I keep my eyes on the floor as the doors close, but at the last moment I remembered the scene from one of my favorite romance movies.

The last time I thought about it was the night of the masquerade with Aries, and that night, he turned back.

My gaze lifts without conscious thought, and what I find has my breath stalling in my lungs.

All three of them stand in the doorway, faces solemn but intense, watching me, letting me walk away.

CHAPTER THIRTY-TWO

MATTEO

"YOU STUPID MOTHERFUCKER. Give me one good reason why I shouldn't knock your ass out right now," Leo murmurs.

I tip my head to the hallway and leave my apartment. My gaze stays on the elevator, remembering the look on Maddie's face. My useless heart clenches, spearing me with white-hot pain knowing that I'm the cause of hers.

"Let's go, kid," Dante says.

I don't hear them behind me—perks of the quiet hallway—but I know they're following. I bypass the elevator, following the hallway around until we're on the other side of the building, where the only other penthouse is. I flip open the keypad panel on the door, type in the code, and push open the door.

The apartment is nearly identical to my own. Spinning around, I lean against the island and shove my hands into my pockets. Leo's surprise is palpable and expected.

He folds his arms across his chest tightly. "What the hell is going on?"

I raise my index finger to my lips, and Leo clenches his jaw, but doesn't ask any other questions. We're quiet as Dante sweeps the apartment with a handy device Rush Fitzgerald, one of the boys of the Brotherhood, made for us. It detects cameras, mics, and any other spyware, for lack of a better word.

Dante joins us in the kitchen. "All clean."

I can see Leo itching to move, but I have shit to say, so he's going to have to wait to bitch me out until later. "This is my apartment. Purchased under a real identity, Thomas Connet, that a friend of mine created just for this reason, though he doesn't know that. I needed a backup in case something like this happened."

"Why not in another building?"

"It's the perfect place, really. Whoever it was that broke in planted cameras and mics. Dante took care of them, but we don't know who's behind it or what their real target was. They also attempted to steal our files, but those are so encrypted that they're virtually un-stealable—at least not by the way they tried."

"Okay, so if Dante took care of everything, then why didn't you tell me this there? Or shit, tell Madison?"

I shake my head. "It's been compromised. We'll never stay there again."

"And Madison?" Leo presses.

I blow out a breath. I'm at a crossroads here. If I pull him in any further, and Dad finds out, he'll consider him a liability. He'll enlist him or kill him, neither of which are good options. But if I don't tell him, then he could wind up dead next in an attempt to get at me.

"Sal Bianchi's wife's body was found on his front porch. Someone left her there. No note, and no one's claimed it yet. They can use her against me, Leo. And they will. They'll torture her without a second thought if they think they can get to me."

His expression fills with tension, his eyes narrowing. "So you're just going to let her think the worst of you then? Think the worst of *me* by association?"

"No. I'm going to tell her, come clean. As clean as I safely can right now. But I wanted you to know first, so you don't do something stupid."

He throws his hands up in the air. "What the fuck are you waiting for? Dante could've told me this while you went after our girl."

I tilt my head to the side, tension tightening my muscles. *"Our girl?"*

"Don't be a dick. You're wasting time, man."

I nod a few times with a smirk. I'm glad he feels comfortable enough to call me on my shit. He can't be too mad at me then. "I paid the doorman to hold her up for ten minutes under the guise of a car running late to pick her up, I've got another minute or two. Listen, you and Dante get anything that's priceless from the other apartment and meet us at the new place."

"You mean we're not staying here?"

"Nah, kid. We've got another safe house. One that only three people know the location of. We'll be alright there. It's fully furnished, we just have to grab food," Dante says.

Leo looks me up and down with a raised brow. "You sure you don't want me to get Madison? I'm not sure she'll want to see you."

I grit my teeth at the reminder that my brother has a relationship with my girl. Shit, is she even my girl anymore?

Technically, it's been years since she knew she was mine. But what she didn't know was that she's *always* belonged to me.

And she always will.

My words from the family meeting flash across my mind, and I know I need to fill Leo in. But it's going to have to wait until we're all settled. The itchy feeling of foreboding still crawls along my skin, and the longer I'm away from Madison, the worse it gets.

"I'll be fine. No stops anywhere else, yeah? And use the back exit. I'll see you guys soon."

They both wave me away as I leave the apartment, jogging down the hallway, and stepping on the elevator right away.

Exhaling a breath, I prepare to grovel.

Maddie

"I really don't need a car. I'll be just fine in a cab."

269

"I'm sorry, miss, but I already called the car. It should be here any moment now. They ran into a bit of traffic, you know how driving around the city can be," the doorman says. He's an older gentleman with kind eyes, but right now, he's getting on my last nerve.

I don't want to spend another second here. The need to move, to put distance between me and whatever the hell just happened is riding me hard.

I look over my shoulder for the twentieth time, expecting to see Leo's shaggy brown hair, but the lobby remains empty. Sighing, I look out at the street through the glass, mentally hurrying the car up.

Finally, a black town car pulls up to the curb and idles. It must be for me. I adjust my purse across my chest and push open the door, letting the thick summer air in.

"Thank you, Will. I appreciate it."

Looking over my shoulder, I spot the one person I didn't want to see.

Matteo.

He's all smiles as he pats the doorman, Will, on the shoulder, slipping him what looks like a twenty dollar bill. I don't spare him another glance, just hustle to the car idling at the curb. I open the door and slide in, my thighs sticking to the leather seats a little. I reach over to pull the door closed when it gets caught on something.

"Slide over, Maddie."

I don't release my grip on the door handle or look at him when I say, "Get lost, Matteo. This is my car, and I'm not into ride-sharing today."

"I need to talk to you." His voice is low, the rich tenor of it melting some of my resolve. "Please, Cherry."

With a huff, I release the door handle and scoot over to the other side. I cross my feet at the ankle, spread my skirt out to cover my legs, and stare out the window, pointedly ignoring him.

"Thank you," he murmurs.

I don't bother replying. What would I even say?

Matteo leans forward and gives the driver an address and he

settles back into the seat. I feel his gaze on me, hot and heavy, but heartache roots me to the seat, away from him.

"I need you to come with me. There are things I need to tell you."

"I'm listening," I say, watching the colors fly by as the driver takes a corner too fast.

"Not here." His voice is so low, I'm not sure if I imagined it or not. "Please, I need to talk to you."

My anger swells and I cut him a glare over my shoulder. "What about what *I* need, hm?"

As if he can read me so well, his eyes soften and he nods. "Leo will be there. Dante, too."

My shoulders fall a little, and I repeat the same words I said to him after the warehouse. "I'm tired, Matteo."

He reaches over and drags his fingertips down the back of my hand with a featherlight touch. "I know, Cherry. All I'm asking for is ten minutes. Then, if you still want to leave, I'll make sure you get home safely."

I look from his hand on mine to his eyes and back again before I look out the window once more. "Alright."

CHAPTER THIRTY-THREE

MADDIE

THE CAR PULLS AWAY from the curb with a squeal of the tires and I stare at the unassuming apartment building. It's a far cry from the fancy one we just came from. Big, gray, and nondescript.

Matteo tilts his head toward the building. "Come on, just this way."

I hesitate for a moment. I'm not afraid of Matteo, not physically, at least. He protected me when I was vulnerable and scared.

But he's dangerous for me emotionally. And that is what has my feet rooted to the cement.

He stops a few feet ahead when he notices I'm not behind him. "Leo and Dante will be here soon. But if it makes you feel more comfortable, take this." He hands me his phone. "Three one nine, four one two."

His phone feels heavy in my hand, like the gesture is more symbolic than the actual action. I slip it inside the pocket of my dress with a nod of thanks.

"Three one nine, four one two," he repeats, holding my gaze.

"Got it." Three one nine is easy to remember, my birthday is March nineteenth. It's the other three numbers I need to commit to memory. I repeat them three times in my head as we walk inside the apartment building and take the elevator to the top floor.

We walk down a short hallway in silence, the clicking of our shoes on the floor the only noise. There's a keypad on the doorframe, and I stop next to Matteo as he presses six numbers. A hiss and a click, and the door unlocks with a whirring.

I follow Matteo inside, stopping in the open-concept kitchen. The whole place is an open concept, but outside of that, it doesn't feel anything like Matteo's apartment.

"Whose place is this?"

He shuts the door, the lock re-engaging, and comes to stand across from me, the island between us. "It's a safe house."

My eyebrows bunch low on my face. "A safe house? Why am I here?"

"I brought you here so I could explain."

I straighten my shoulders. "I think you've already explained enough, don't you? If this is why you brought me here—"

"It's not," he interjects, sliding his hands in his pockets and looking toward his feet for a moment. He raises his chin, his gaze meeting mine. "I'm in the mafia, Maddie."

"Okay," I murmur.

He takes a step back and cocks his head as if to look at me from a different angle. "I said I'm in the mob, and all you say is *okay*? This shit tonight isn't a fluke. It's a direct attack—on *me*. It's a warning that could be from ten different people for twenty different things. This is my life."

I lick my lips and shift my weight. Looking into his tortured eyes, I say, "Alright."

"What—what do you mean, *alright*?"

I lift a shoulder. "I mean, Leo kind of already told me earlier. He didn't give me too many details, but you can't help who your family is, Matteo."

He takes three quick steps around the island to get closer to me. "It's not just a loser uncle we're talking about here. It's me. *I* am in the mafia."

I close my mouth slowly and swallow as I search his gaze. "I don't understand."

He closes the gap between us, standing close enough that if I inhale deeply, our chests brush together. "I've done deplorable things, Madison. And I'll continue to do them. This is the life I chose, but it's not yours."

Like a lightbulb slow to turn on, an idea comes to me. One so ridiculous that it's barely worth bringing up, but there's something about the way he's looking at me now. It's a one-eighty from how he spoke to me at his apartment not sixty minutes ago.

I think he's scared.

Of what, I'm not sure, but now that the seed has been planted, it's all I can see in the hushed tone of his voice, the way his eyes are wide and sincere.

"Tell me I'm crazy, Matteo, tell me you don't feel the spark, the connection between us still. Tell me I'm a hopeless romantic and it's all in my head." I hold his gaze as I talk, opening up to let him see all the hope I feel. "Don't push me away just because you think you know what's best for me."

He leans his forehead against mine, sparks of energy prickle my veins at his proximity.

I lean into him a little, giving him some of my weight. With a deep breath, I jump off that emotional cliff and pray that he catches me. "I think underneath those expensive suits and that alpha possessive exterior is a man who's afraid—"

He breaks our connection with a sharp jerk of his head. "Of course, I'm afraid. You're my ultimate weakness, Maddie. And now someone knows it! I had to push you away. Do you know what these guys do to weaknesses in a man's life? They exploit them," he hisses. "A man walked out his front door to get his morning paper today, and instead, he found his mutilated, dead wife. And he was a soldier, one in a million. I'm in line to be the next fucking boss of the entire outfit! And I don't know how to protect you!"

His words are loud, but his anguish is deafening. His eyebrows dip low and distress lines every inch of his face. His chest heaves and pain settles around his eyes at his admission.

My heart aches in tune with his distress, my eyes welling with emotion I'm not sure how to name.

"Why didn't you just tell me?"

He raises a brow. "You wanted me to admit that I couldn't protect you?"

I lift a shoulder. "If that's the real reason behind your one-eighty, then yes. Wouldn't that have saved us a lot of turmoil?"

He steps closer, sliding his palm around the side of my neck. "I'm an asshole, baby. I'm going to fuck up. How about I just buy you a diamond necklace now, one with a ridiculous amount of gems. One diamond for each time I mess up and hurt you."

I tip my head back and to the side to hold his gaze. "I don't want a diamond necklace."

He flexes his fingers against my neck, the movement sending shivers down my spine. He brings his face close to mine as he speaks against my lips. "Then what do you want?"

My heightened emotions from earlier morph into something darker, deeper. The air around us swirls, tensions rising.

Girls at school always bragged that making-up after a fight or argument is the hottest thing, but I've never experienced it. Until now. Something clenches low in my belly, and I can feel every place we're touching with heightened precision.

He's giving me the reins, and I'd be a fool to pass that up.

"You," I breathe into his mouth before I seal our lips together.

He grunts, this low, masculine noise that sends my mind spiraling to other things that have him making that same noise.

I fist his shirt, holding him against me as I push onto my tiptoes to feel more of him. I run my tongue along the corner of his lip before I sink my teeth into it, teasing him.

He answers my taunt how I expected and tips my head back with his light grip on my neck. Lust coils in my veins, tightly wound and desperate to release.

He's the first one to pull back, my lips chasing his for a second. I'm slow to open my eyes, my head foggy with lust.

With his gentle hold on my neck, he tips my head back even farther. "That's not exactly the truth, now is it, Cherry?"

My brows furrow. "What? Of course, it is."

His thumb strokes the sensitive skin on my neck. "You mean to tell me that you haven't been snuggled up to my brother while you were at my house? I *watched* you." His words slither out through clenched teeth.

Keeping my face carefully blank, I stand up straighter and bring our faces close enough to touch. I lean up and scrape my teeth along his bottom lip in response. "Don't forget Dante."

He growls against my mouth—honest to god growls—and tingles zip down my spine. Lust courses through my veins, and I can't resist pushing Matteo's buttons just to get this alpha-possessive response.

My stomach growls, the noise loud and garbled enough to break the lusty bubble we're in. We pull apart, matching smiles on our faces.

"Seems my girl has other needs that need to be met first," Matteo teases as he runs his hands up and down my arms. "I haven't been at this apartment in months, so I'll run out and grab us some food. I think there's a great sandwich shop a half block down."

"Okay, let me grab my purse, and I'll go with you." I try to turn around, but his palms on my shoulders stop me.

"Stay here and relax. Let me take care of you, Cherry."

Warmth slides over me like sunshine on a crisp fall day. If I were a cartoon, my eyes would literally be sparkling with joy right now. "Alright."

"I'll be back soon. The door will auto lock behind me, and don't open it for anyone, yeah? Leo and Dante will be here soon, but they both have the key code."

I freeze, the warmth gone in an instant. "I thought you said it was safe here."

His thumbs sweep back and forth over my shoulder. "It is. Only a few people know about it. But Dante tells me I need to work on my communication, and ask instead of demand."

My lips tip up at the idea of that conversation. I bite my lip and lift a shoulder. "I kind of like you bossy sometimes."

His gaze scans my face for a moment, one hand snaking up to grip the back of my neck. With a gentle tug, he pulls my mouth against his in a kiss that's anything but chaste. Teeth clash, our tongues war with one another. He tilts my head, deepening our kiss and taking control in a way that has my toes curling in my shoes.

If this is how he kisses me goodbye every time he leaves the house, I'm going to have to start making excuses for him to leave.

He slows our tempo and pulls back after a final brush of his lips. I have to blink several times to clear the fog of arousal from my vision. Matteo's smug smile spreads wide across his too-handsome face. I don't even have it in me to tease him for his arrogance.

Honestly, he deserves it for the way he just kissed me. It's easy to forget our past when he plays my body with expert precision like that.

I lean against the island and stare at Matteo's ass as he walks toward the front door. The unmistakable outline of a gun stands out underneath his shirt, tucked into his pants. I'm not sure if that's in addition to or in place of his shoulder holster. I was too preoccupied to notice earlier.

My heart's pounding like I just ran a marathon, and a trickle of worry invades my happiness. If he gets me that worked up over a kiss, what's going to happen when I finally get him on a bed. Or a couch. Or the counter.

As if he can read the dirty direction of my thoughts, he pauses with one hand on the doorknob and halfway out the door. "Be in the bedroom when I—"

Matteo's shoulder jerks backward, cutting off his words. I freeze, my feet rooted to the spot next to the island and my mind unable to make sense of what I'm seeing.

Matteo's body jerks backward again, and this time he stumbles.

"Matteo!" I shout, my heart hammering inside my chest. Everything after that happens in slow motion, like someone pressed the button to play out these events in half-speed.

The front door swings into the wall with a thud and springs back to slam into Matteo. He doesn't even flinch, his attention on the blood spilling down his chest near his shoulder. He presses a hand to the wound, and blood seeps between his fingers, coating everything. The color is too bright, it doesn't look real.

It's the color that snaps me out of my panic, reigniting my synapses. My focus zeroes in on him, and I rush to his side.

"Madison, get the hell out of here!" he roars as he shuffles toward the door. He throws a shoulder into it, pushing it closed, and I reach his side and help him.

Before it latches, a black boot wedges between the door and the frame, blocking it. There's a ringing in my ears, and nausea surges up my throat at the sight of blood blooming on Matteo's gray shirt.

Matteo reaches for his gun with one hand. The person on the other side of the door chooses that exact moment to push, overpowering us.

We stumble backward a few steps, and my fingers start to tingle like the feeling that you get after they fall asleep, but now they're getting more blood flow—that prickly pins-and-needles feeling.

Matteo throws an arm across the front of me, palms my hip, and pushes me behind him. I make a noise of protest, but he only grunts in return.

It doesn't really matter anyway, because in the next instant, two men in black ski masks fill the doorway. They're wide and tall and intimidating in all-black with huge guns pointed at us.

I grip the material of Matteo's shirt in my fist, my adrenaline flying so high my hands are shaking. My fingers brush against something cold and hard—his gun. He never had time to grab it, and from the way his right hand hangs, I'm not sure if he'd be able to grip it.

I know this is a defining moment in my life. I can be a spectator in my life, sitting back and letting it happen *to* me.

Or I can be in the driver's seat, making choices for myself and those I care about.

There's no time to waste, I curl my fingers around the gun and pull it from the back of his pants just as one of the guys steps toward us. I remember the docuseries Mary made me watch about weaponry, and I quickly unblock the safety. It's one of the only things I remember about it, and I've never been more thankful for my sister's obsession with documentaries. I step to the side of Matteo with my arm raised. I've never shot a gun before, but if I don't try to do something, we're both dead.

"Senator Hardin sends his regards," he says and fires a shot. The noise is so much quieter than I expected. But it's not silent like the name suggests. There's a whirring noise, but the sound of Matteo's grunts as he falls backward into me is a noise I'll never forget.

I pull the trigger, my shot going wide when Matteo bumps into me. I grab onto his arm to slow down his downward trajectory, but he's so much bigger than me.

He slides to the ground, leaving me standing in front of two strange men who're threatening to end my life early.

There are no images of my life flashing before my eyes, no sense of euphoria.

Only rage and cold determination.

I make my own fate.

And I'm not dying today, neither is Matteo.

With a battle cry Xena would be proud of, I grab the gun with both hands and fire at them.

"Fuck! That fucking bitch shot me," one of them growls as the other one advances on me. "What're you doing, man? He said just to get the guy. He didn't say shit about a girl."

I fire the gun again, and he ducks, narrowly avoiding a lucky headshot.

"Yeah, well, I'm not fucking leaving a witness. Do you want to do twenty-five to life?"

He advances on me, grabbing the gun in his big hand and wrenching it to the side, away from his body. I tighten my grip and focus on bringing the gun closer to this guy so I can take another shot. I know I only have a few seconds before he either wrestles it away from me or just fucking shoots me. I'm not sure why he hasn't yet, but I'm thanking fate for small favors.

I shut out Matteo's heavy breathing, shove down the overwhelming panic threatening to loosen my muscles. But the intruder is too strong for me.

"Fuck this." He huffs, the noise angry. He raises his palm high in the air before he backhands me with enough force to send me to my knees.

My hair flies into my face and my vision swims. I taste the familiar copper of blood in my mouth. I push up onto my feet, swaying and raising the gun again. Squinting to see straight, I try to fire, but the guy closest to me shoves the gun upward, forcing the shot to go wild.

"Do you have a fucking death wish, you crazy bitch. I'm trying to save your life," the guy hisses in my face as he squeezes my wrist hard.

I cry out in pain and despair when my muscles involuntarily flex and I lose the grip on the gun.

"Just bring her with us, we'll drop her at the messenger's house when we pick up payment. But hurry the fuck up, we've been here too long already."

The guy holding my wrist growls something unintelligible underneath his breath and tries to pick me up with an arm around my middle.

It's like something inside of me snaps, and I'm not in Matteo's secret apartment anymore. I'm on the street outside the Blue Lotus Café, and I fight like my life depends on it. Kicking and screaming and scratching. I dig my nails into any available soft surface, never stopping no matter how many times he fends off my hands or maneuvers me.

In my darkest moments, when I was all alone, I replayed the events of that day over and over again, agonizing over what I could've done differently, wishing I would've fought back harder.

It's like this secret part of me has been unlocked, and I'm no longer myself. I'm the very basest version of myself.

Survival of the fittest.

And I will not be dying today.

I was lucky last time, but fate is not granting me a boon today. My cousin is in another city and my savior is bleeding out in the entryway.

"Enough," the other guy yells.

But I don't stop. I'll never stop. It'll be a fight to the death, gladiator-style, because I know if they take me, I'll be as good as dead.

I catch it out of the corner of my eye, but not with enough time to move out of the way, and the other guy slams a gun into my head.

As fate would have it, I'm still no match for a gun.

Consciousness leaves me, and everything goes black.

CHAPTER THIRTY-FOUR

ARIES

I FORCE A CHUCKLE, a smile pasted on my face, as some hanger-on tries way too hard to earn approval from the upper echelon of society. She's pretty in that girl next door kind of way, but she'll never survive a summer season with this nest of vipers.

I'm in the ballroom of some charity function where drinks flow and the food is far and few between. The more people drink, the easier it is to get them to donate for whatever charity they're sponsoring tonight.

I resist the urge to loosen my tie as I pretend to listen to the conversation around me. I'm preoccupied, scanning the room for a certain redhead, my raven. I haven't seen her at the last two functions, and I know it's unreasonable, but I'm getting annoyed.

I thought she enjoyed our game of cat and mouse. I know I am. It'd be so easy to find out everything about her and track her down. But where's the fun in that? The anticipation and sneaking around would be lost. And I'm having too much fun with her to just stop now.

It's been so long since I've done something just for me. I've lost track of how long I've spent away from home, charming my way into the tight-knit groups of our country's wealthiest offspring.

East coast, west coast, the south, or overseas—they're all the same. Bored with more mommy and daddy issues than they can count and more money than god.

They're not all bad. I've made some genuine connections— friends, even. But most of them would throw you under a bus to get in favor with a laundry list of people.

I've made it my mission over the years to be that person—the one people crave to please. It makes my job so much easier.

I'm a collector.

I collect secrets and favors. These people are so self-absorbed that most of them never even bat an eyelash when their kids crashed private parties. I'm always amazed at how much people talk when they're surrounded by so many others. Alcohol always helps too.

I've been privy to the secret society parties and underground shit that I know for a fact Matteo doesn't know about. But he will soon.

Just one more summer and then I can go home. I've got a hunch that a few senators have some deep skeletons in their closets, and I'm close to figuring out what they are.

My phone vibrates inside my pocket, over and over. Finally, I excuse myself from the conversation and walk down a quieter hall-way. Pulling out my phone, I see an automatic notification that my alarm system has been disarmed manually.

"Strange," I murmur as I pull up my camera feed.

I watch as Matteo walks into my apartment with a girl. It looks like they're arguing, but it's hard to tell. Her back is to the camera, but something about the pixelated image pricks at my intuition.

I switch to a different angle just as he kisses her. Annoyance flares, and I clench my jaw.

Why the hell did he bring some chick to our safe house to fuck? It's called a safe house for a reason. I rub my finger across my eyebrow and expel a breath. Now I'm going to have to call him and give him shit about it. Then I'm going to have to get a new safe house.

My thumb hovers over the exit button on the screen when Matteo heads toward the front door, and I get the first clear glimpse of the mystery girl.

My heart stops.

Raven.

Matteo says something to her, but I don't have the volume up, so I miss it. My heart pounds, and my fingers jab at the volume button on the side of my phone. Just in time for all hell to break loose.

He opens the door and all I can see is a gun with a silencer pointed right at Matteo. He jerks to the side and there's a struggle, but two masked men eventually barge their way inside.

Nausea climbs up my throat, and I loosen my tie to get more air into my lungs.

I don't realize I'm moving until I bump into someone, clipping their shoulder. I don't offer an apology as I practically jog through the ballroom and outside. I don't wait for a car. The apartment is ten blocks from here, I can run there faster than waiting for a car.

I watch in horror as one of the intruders says, "Senator Hardin sends his regards."

The blood drains from my face as realization dawns.

This is a hit meant for me.

Matteo jerks to the floor, and that's when she fights. My raven unleashes all she has on these motherfuckers, but it's not enough.

One guy hits her over the head with a gun and she slumps to the floor like someone pulled her plug. I decide he's going to die a slow and torturous death just for that.

But first, I sever the camera feed and call an ambulance to my safe house. There's no way in hell my twin brother is dying today.

To be continued . . .

Read Twisted Queen, the next book in the Five Families series here:
books2read.com/twistedqueen

A NOTE TO READERS

Are you still with me? I know that cliffhanger is a little high, but I promise I won't leave you dangling there for too long! And my DMs are always open if you need to slide in there and proverbially throw your kindle at me! ;)

Maddie's story continues in Twisted Queen! Read it here: book s2read.com/twistedqueen

---

I would be honored if you had the time to leave a brief review of this book! Reviews are the lifeblood of a book, and I would appreciate it so much.

xoxo
—pen

Stay in the loop!
Join my newsletter
Join my Facebook group, Penelope's Black Hearts
Follow me on Instagram @authorpenelopeblack

WOLF EXCERPT

Keep reading for a sneak peak at Wolf, book one in the Brotherhood trilogy.

It follows Maddie's cousin, Alaina, and it takes place right before Gilded Princess! It's a slow-burn, angsty Irish mafia reverse harem!

The complete series is available on Amazon and Kindle Unlimited here: books2read.com/brotherhood1

"Kiss a stranger."

Those three words started off a series of events I could have never predicted. Fresh off graduation, I have my entire summer planned out: European vacation with my cousins, college courses, and picking up shifts at work.

But then my mom calls and drops the bomb: she's getting married to the rumored head of the Irish mafia. Even though I've been looking out for her for most of my life, we haven't lived together in ten years. So when she invites me to stay with her for the summer, I don't hesitate.

And I make a new summer plan: skip the vacation, take online courses, and dig up dirt on Mom's new fiancé.

What I didn't plan for was Wolf Fitzgerald--and his brothers. Dangerously good-looking with tattoos and bad attitudes.

And my new stepbrothers.

Available now on Kindle Unlimited

books2read.com/brotherhood1

CHAPTER ONE

ALAINA

"Kiss a stranger."

An involuntary cough wracks my body as my strawberry wine cooler gets caught in my throat. "Sorry," I say as I put a hand to the base of my throat and set my drink on my desk. "It went down the wrong pipe when I thought I heard you say I have to kiss a stranger." I pin my cousin, Maddie, with a glare.

"That's because I did." She quirks an eyebrow at me and flips her long, straight red hair over her shoulder. "Although I'm not sure why you're surprised, because this isn't my dare."

"Well, it's not my dare, so . . ." I turn to look at Maddie's twin sister, Mary, with a new appreciation. "Color me impressed," I murmur.

"What?" Mary huffs and crosses her arms over her chest. "We're eighteen now—"

"Ahem." I point at myself with a wry smile. "Some of us are almost nineteen."

"Well, we're eighteen"—Mary gestures to herself and Maddie—"and your birthday isn't for another week. I thought we could step up the game a little." Mary's cheeks are pink by the time she's done talking. "Plus, we just graduated!"

Mary and Maddie are fraternal twins, and while their physical differences are minor, their styles couldn't be more different. Mary wears her red hair in a lob—a longer bob—that she straightens every day, and Maddie wears her long and curled. With matching ice-blue eyes, they're total knockouts. And they're my best friends.

"I think it's a great idea, but you guys are going to be disappointed because I definitely added 'binge-watch Vampire Diaries' in there last week," I tell them with a laugh.

Mary's stiff as she sits on the end of my twin bed in our shared dorm suite at St. Rita's All-Girls Academy. Technically, we're no longer high school students here, but since we're enrolled in the sister school—St. Rita's College, we're opting to keep the same living arrangements.

Mary's arms are still crossed tightly across her chest, and she stares at the cream-colored carpet as if it's holding all her secrets.

I glance at Maddie and nod toward her sister. With a sigh, she sets the colored popsicle stick with the dare on it on my dresser and crosses the room to her sister.

"Babe. It's totally fine. And you know I'm all for you kissing whoever you want—whenever you want."

"Yeah, you can have this dare if you want, Mary," I offer.

"No take-backs, Lainey. You know the rules," Maddie interjects.

Mary lifts her head, a wry smirk on her face. "No worries, all five of my dares last week were 'kiss a stranger.'"

A giggle escapes my lips before I can catch it, and Maddie joins in. After a few seconds, Mary loosens up a little, and before long, she's giggling right along with us.

"Who knew we'd still be playing the silly game we made up with an extra mason jar and colored popsicle sticks when we were twelve?" I muse as I take a drink of my wine cooler.

"Me. I did," Maddie sasses, lifting her chin and leaning back.

"That's because you came up with the idea." Mary rolls her eyes with a smirk.

"And what a good idea it was! Besides, what else were we going to do? We couldn't leave the dorm, and we needed something fun to look forward to since they dumped us in the city and left without a backward glance." Maddie's smile is hard and forced, her eyes narrow.

"Ah-ha! I knew you cared that Mom left us here and went to Europe that summer!" Mary exclaims, her earlier tension long forgotten.

Maddie tilts her chin up. "Don't be ridiculous, Mary. I did not. I was only making a point. And Mom brings us with her to Europe every summer now."

Watching my cousins trade quick retorts is like watching a tennis match. I sip my drink and settle back into my chair.

"Exactly! Because you pitched a fit that one summer, so now Mom's afraid to leave us here. Honestly, I don't even know why you want to go over there anymore. Being a wingwoman to your middle-aged mother while she picks up guys fifteen years younger lost its appeal years ago." Mary practically sneers the word wingwoman, and I do a double-take. The expression is more Maddie than her. I feel like I'm missing something here.

"That one summer? You mean the one where we were attending summer courses, and you got your period in the middle of ceramics, but I pretended it was me, and Becky Parsons made fun of me"— Maddie jabs a finger into her chest—"for months. That summer?" Her lips flatten, and a flush of anger creeps down her neck.

This is a familiar discussion they've had many, many times over the years. The thing is, Mary always apologizes—again—and Maddie always accepts. They hug, and then they move on. I'm not sure what it is about that one instance that has Maddie still hung up, but it's time for me to step in, like usual.

I stand up and face them, hands on my hips. "Alright, girls, are we going to kiss some strangers tonight or what?"

Both girls stop and turn to face me, their cheeks pink, arms crossed, and eyes guarded. I swear, they're so alike sometimes, it's like they're the same person.

This time, it's Mary who deflates first. She turns to face Maddie. "I'm sorry, Maddie."

Maddie turns toward her. "I'm sorry too. Don't worry about it. I'm just getting hangry, I guess." Maddie leans into Mary and wraps an arm around her shoulders. "Okay, let's pick our dares for tonight."

Maddie leaves her twin on the end of my bed and walks to the mason jar on my dresser. Somewhere along the years, we started keeping the dare jar in my room. The colorful popsicle sticks nearly fill the jar. We pick from the jar once a week, sometimes more, but always when we're together. Now that I'm working at the coffee shop a few blocks away, tutoring a couple of middle school kids in the afternoons, and singing for fun with the girls nearly every Friday, we have to be a little more strategic.

Maddie closes her eyes and pulls a stick from the jar. "Alright, tonight, Mary's dare is dance with a stranger." Her voice rises higher with each word, her eyebrows following suit.

My lips tip up in a smirk. I added that dare months ago. Ever since I started noticing the same guy show up to open mic night at O'Malley's Pub. Tall, chestnut-brown hair, and a cloud of danger surrounding him. He watches my set every time I sing, but he never stays afterward, and he's always alone.

I thought I'd give myself the push to approach him and ask him to dance, but it looks like Mary will be tearing up the floor tonight. I look at her to gauge her reaction to the dare.

"Fun. I have just the outfit for tonight." Mary's eyes sparkle as she claps her hands together in front of her chest.

"Okay then." Maddie eyes her sister with a knowing grin. She closes her eyes again and pulls another popsicle stick from the jar. "And tonight my dare is sing karaoke . . . in a lime-green tutu." Maddie's eyebrows hit her hairline, and her mouth opens slightly. And I can't hold back my grin.

"Ah, I was watching a lot of Sex and The City re-runs when I added that dare," I offered. Maddie looks at me with her mouth open. "You know, where she wears the pink tulle skirt and looks badass walking down the city blocks? That's what I was going for, but I thought lime-green would be fun."

"Lainey, we're three fair-skinned, freckled, redheads. Lime-green is not our color, babe," Maddie says as she looks at me, head tilted and eyebrows drawn together like I actually need a fashion intervention. Just because I like to wear old band tees doesn't mean I don't have a good sense of fashion. I just know what I like.

"Exactly," I say with a smirk.

Mary laughs as she gets up from my bed. "Ooh, you're good, girl. Nice subtle hit on all of us—I like it. Let's eat some dinner and then get ready. I'll check what the dining hall has on their menu for tonight." Mary heads to the kitchen where we have the month's dining hall menu tacked up on a corkboard.

"But . . . we don't even have a lime-green tutu—so, ha!" Maddie yells, thrusting a finger in the air.

"Except." I cross the room to my closet, open the closet door, and shift my clothes around so I can reach the three brightly-colored items in the back. Curling my fingers around the hangers, I wrangle the items out. "Ta-da!" I shimmy the hangers, causing the tulle skirts to swish around.

Maddie looks at me for a moment before she tips her head back and laughs. "Oh my god—Mary, come here and see what your crazy cousin did!"

I hear Mary's footsteps in the hallway, and she speaks before I can see her.

"Coming! Oh, and before I forget, tonight it's spaghetti bolognese"—Mary freezes in the doorway, her mouth falling open—"and what the hell are those?!"

"Why, our outfits for tonight, of course!" I answer cheerfully.

"But only Maddie has to wear the lime-green one!" Mary whines.

Maddie doubles over on my bed in laughter. "You put two more tutu dares in the jar, didn't you?"

I smooth the tulle down on the neon-orange skirt as a smirk tips up the corners of my mouth. "Sure did. And because we love you, we're all going to wear one tonight."

I untangle the lime-green tulle skirt and toss it to Maddie. I turn to Mary, who's still standing in the doorway, and hold out the remaining two tulle skirts. "Neon orange or hot pink?"

"I can't believe I'm going to wear a neon orange tulle skirt while dancing with a stranger tonight," Mary mock grumbles.

"Excellent choice, Mary. Might I suggest wearing a solid color to make the orange really pop?" I ask with a laugh. I unclip the neon-orange tulle skirt and toss it to her.

"We're going to look ridiculous at O'Malley's tonight." Maddie sighs dejectedly.

"Nah, we'll look amazing. They love us, and Jack would never let anyone say anything bad about us," I assure her. "Besides, we just graduated, let's celebrate!"

Jack is the owner of O'Malley's Irish Pub. I met him sort of randomly a couple of years ago. I was supposed to meet my then-boyfriend there to see a band, but he never showed up, and I ended up chatting with Jack for a while. A couple months later, I showed up with Mary and Maddie in tow for their open mic night and never looked back. Now, O'Malley's has become our go-to place for a night out.

I know they know our fake IDs are bullshit, but they never call us on it. We almost always order vodka cranberries, Long Island iced teas, and Baby Guinnesses—which does not actually have Guinness in it.

I still remember the look of disgust on Mary's face when she tipped the glass back and took a huge sip of what she thought was just a small-sized Guinness.

I thought for sure she was going to spew Kahlua and Bailey's all over the bar top that day. But by some miracle, she didn't. It took her like six months to even drink a latte again—something about the smell of coffee triggering her gag reflex.

"What are you laughing about over there?" Mary asks, eyes narrow and head tilted. "Because I draw the line at footwear, Lainey."

"Actually, I remembered the time we discovered what a Baby Guinness was." I smirk, quirking an eyebrow. "Do you remember that—"

Mary fake gags before I can finish my question. "Ugh. Yes.

Don't remind me, or I won't be able to look at a latte again for months," she whines.

I laugh. "Good times, good times. Now, shoo"—I flick my fingers in her direction—"and go change for dinner. We're celebrating tonight!"

"Yeah, yeah. I'm going," Mary mutters as she walks out of my room.

I hold up the neon-pink tulle skirt in front of me, twisting and turning it, and stare at my reflection in the mirror. The corners of my mouth curl into a mischievous smile.

Tonight is going to be unforgettable.

Pick up Wolf, the Brotherhood book 1, on Amazon today!
books2read.com/brotherhood1

ACKNOWLEDGMENTS

Thank you to my readers! Thank you for hanging in there with me on all those cliffs too, sending all of you air hugs for that!

To all the bookstagrammers and bloggers and readers that send me messages and create beautiful edits for my books—I'm still in awe. Thank you so, so much. On my most insecure days, I pull up your edits and kind words and never fails to reignite my spark.

Thank you to my husband who's always the first one to champion me. And I love that you're always shouting, "My wife's a romance author!" with pride to anyone you pass on the street. He literally told our new neighbors about my books ten minutes after we met! You're the best, and I love to so much.

To my tiny humans: I love you both more than all the stars in the sky. And you have to wait until you're older to read Mommy's books.

To my wonderful family who's encouraged and supported me— thank you, thank you! And thank you to each and every one of you who read my books. I'm looking at you, Grandma + Grandpa!

Thank you to the amazing babes on my ARC team! I'm so grateful to have you in my corner!

To my amazing beta readers! I'm so thankful for each of you. Your kindness and support means the world to me.

To Savy—I'd be lost without you, girl. One day, I'm going to hop on a plane and then tackle-hug you.

And finally, I want to thank each and every author who has been so kind and wonderful while I asked a million questions. There are far too many of you to thank, and for that alone, I'm forever grateful. There are a lot of wonderful people in this community, and I'm so glad to be apart of it.

READ MORE PENELOPE BLACK

The Brotherhood series

Wolf

Rush

Sully

Five Families

Gilded Princess

Twisted Queen

Vicious Reign

Standalone

When It Ends:

A Dark Apocalyptic Romance

King Sisters

The Wren

Coming this Summer